Book 13:
HELLION

M.M. Crumley

To Positivi-Kitty...
May his spirit of positivity grow infinitely strong...

Copyright © M.M. **Crumley 2023**

All rights reserved. Published by Lone Ghost Publishing LLC, associated logos are trademarks and/or registered trademarks of Lone Ghost Publishing LLC.

The moral right of the author has been asserted (vigorously).

No part or parts of this publication may be reproduced in whole or in part, stored in a retrieval systems, or transmitted in any form or by means, electronic, mechanical, photocopying, recording, or otherwise (including via carrier pigeon), without written permission of the author and publisher.

Author: **Crumley**, M.M.
Title: THE IMMORTAL DOC HOLLIDAY, HELLION
ISBN: 9798398254037
Target Audience: Adult
Also available in this series
THE IMMORTAL DOC HOLLIDAY: HIDDEN (Book 1)
THE IMMORTAL DOC HOLLIDAY: COUP D'ÉTAT (Book 2)
THE IMMORTAL DOC HOLLIDAY: RUTHLESS (Book 3)
THE IMMORTAL DOC HOLLIDAY: INSTINCT (Book 4)
THE IMMORTAL DOC HOLLIDAY: ROGUES (Book 5)
THE IMMORTAL DOC HOLLIDAY: EMPIRE (Book 6)
THE IMMORTAL DOC HOLLIDAY: OMENS (Book 7)
THE IMMORTAL DOC HOLLIDAY: CHASM (Book 8)
THE IMMORTAL DOC HOLLIDAY: FERAL (Book 9)
THE IMMORTAL DOC HOLLIDAY: OBLIVION (Book 10)
THE IMMORTAL DOC HOLLIDAY: RELENTLESS (Book 11)
THE IMMORTAL DOC HOLLIDAY: REQUIEM (Book 12)

Subjects:
Urban Fantasy/ Horror Comedy

This is a work of fiction, which means it's made up. Names, characters, peoples, locales, and incidents (stuff that happens in the story) are either gifts of the ether, products of the author's resplendent imagination or are used fictitiously, and any resemblance to actual persons, living or dead or dying, businesses or companies in operation or defunct, events, or locales is entirely coincidental.

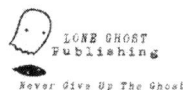

LONE GHOST
Publishing

Never Give Up The Ghost

Also by **M.M. Crumley**
Urban Fantasy

THE IMMORTAL DOC HOLLIDAY SERIES

BOOK 1: HIDDEN
BOOK 2: COUP D'ÉTAT
BOOK 3: RUTHLESS
BOOK 4: INSTINCT
BOOK 5: ROGUES
BOOK 6: EMPIRE
BOOK 7: OMENS
BOOK 8: CHASM
BOOK 9: FERAL
BOOK 10: OBLIVION
BOOK 11: RELENTLESS
BOOK 12: REQUIEM
BOOK 13: HELLION
BOOK 14: SHADOWS

THE LEGEND OF ANDREW RUFUS SERIES

BOOK 1: DARK AWAKENING
BOOK 2: BONE DEEP
BOOK 3: BLOOD STAINED
BOOK 4: BURIAL GROUND
BOOK 5: DEATH SONG
BOOK 6: FUNERAL MARCH
BOOK 7: WARPATH

THE HOUSE OF GRAVES SERIES

BOOK 1: THREE LITTLE GRAVES & THE BIG BAD WOLF
BOOK 2: OVER THE RIVER & THROUGH THE WOOD
BOOK 3: FIRE BURN & CAULDRON BUBBLE

Writing as **M.M. Boulder**
Psych Thrillers

THE LAST DOOR
MY BETTER HALF
THE HOUSE THAT JACK BUILT
MY ONE AND ONLY
WE ALL FALL DOWN

www.facebook.com/m.m.crumley
www.mmcrumley.com

Character List

Doc Holliday: our intrepid hero
Thomas Jury (witch): Doc's friend
Jervis (vampire): Doc's friend & Dulcis's manager
Señora Teodora / Tozi: the shaman who "turned" Doc

Abigail Jury (witch): Jury's mother, current head of the witches council
Ackley Underwood (witch): Abigail Jury's love interest
Adrian Gionta (witch): painter who trapped live people inside paintings
Ahanu/Grey Shaman (shaman): Meli's brother, Doc owed him a favor
Akashii: keepers of the memory
Alex Baudelaire (witch): Phillip Jury's son
Ana & Ina Zaitsev (vampires): sisters from Russia
Andrew Rufus (norm): Doc's friend from the past
Apollo (ghost): Tucker's sentient house
Ásleif (troll): Birger's wife
August Naese (witch): head of the Northwestern witches
Aylen/White Shaman (shaman): Meli's sister, also Pecos's wife
Babs Baker (witch): Baker children's aunt
Baker Children—Johnny, Jules, Addison (witches)
Bennie (Worm): Doc's previous go-to guy, Phillip Jury killed in book 8
Birger (troll): bridge troll, lives on the Baker estate
Bluegrass Goodhunt (shaman): Doc's friend, died facing Meli in book 6
Bosch (norm): previous head of the BCA, Doc killed in book 2
Boudica (witch hound)
Bree (banshee): Doc's adopted daughter
Della Harrow (witch): young girl, Doc killed her father, Abigail Jury adopted
Dr. Ursula Feyrer (witch): a reverse scryer who wrote a book about Doc
Dublin O'Connell (wolf shifter): Doc's friend, manager of Baker estate
Edgar Achaean (norm): the leader of the Acolytes, Doc killed in book 3
Eldwin (vampire): Jervis's brother, Jervis killed in book 7
Eli Gac (ghost): kidnapped Tucker in book 10, the ghost of General Custer
Elvira Naese (witch): August's wife, Doc released her from Blackwater

Emily (Myhanava): works for Dulcis
Erland (troll): Birger's son
Fiona (fairy): Rachelle's sister, Doc released her from a painting in book 10
Francisco (norm): Doc's real-life adopted brother
Frankie (norm) Baker children's babysitter
Isabel Naese (witch): August's daughter
Janey Falke (norm): Doc's friend from the past, also Andrew's wife
Lena Danser (norm): Doc's lady love who killed herself
Liadawn (unicorn): a woman Doc had an amorous moment with
Medusa (norm): Doc met in book 9 when he was in Bora Bora
Meli/Black Shaman (shaman): Andrew's nemesis
Nevin Tucker (ghost): Ghost Guy
Pecos Bill (norm): Andrew's friend from the past, Doc met in book 12
Phillip Jury (witch): Jury's father, Jury killed in book 8
Pino & his mother (norms): family Doc helped in the past
Rachelle Nesbit (fairy): head of the Cryptid Witch Academy
Rosa (?): Doc's plant-watering maid
Sami Caruso (norm): Jury's manager & Jervis's main squeeze
Solomon (norm): leader of an ancient order called the Sons of Solomon
Sons of Solomon: order of men who followed Solomon's orders
Sydney & Julian LaRoche (Roma): Doc's new go-to guys
Tetrarch Mitcham (Zeniu): previous tetrarch of the Hidden
Thaddeus or Thaddy Whythe: Doc's talking plant
The Memory: the mother's memory, another name is the Akashic record
Virgil Graves (norm): a private investigator who works within the Hidden
Winslow (norm): Jervis's assistant
Yiska (Akashii): Doc's guide to all things mystical

1

Doc Holliday grinned widely as he watched the Baker children stuff their faces full of food. He was certain Babs fed them, but they were eating as if they'd never eaten before.

"I uv ausage," Johnny managed to exclaim.

"Johnny!" Jules gasped. "Etiquette!"

"I only have to use etiquette when Auntie Babs is watching," Johnny said stubbornly. "Doc doesn't care. Do you, Doc?"

Doc took a large drink from his whiskey bottle. At seven o'clock in the morning.

"No," he said thoughtfully. "I don't think I do. At least not as it applies to table manners."

He was only lying a little. Would he prefer Johnny didn't talk with food in his mouth, yes. But why spoil the moment?

"See!" Johnny said triumphantly, sticking out his tongue at Jules.

Jules's eyes narrowed, and a pancake flew across the table and slapped Johnny square in the nose.

Johnny peeled the pancake from his face, and his eyes began to glow a strange shade of purple.

"Enough," Doc ordered. "Rosa works hard enough taking care of Thaddeus. She doesn't need to be peeling pancakes off the walls as well."

"Humph," Thaddeus grumbled. "As if I'm difficult."

"Of course not, old boy," Doc said soothingly. "But I have it on good authority that she dusts every single one of your leaves every single day."

"It's the closest I'll ever get to a massage," Thaddeus said mournfully.

"It's Frankie's birthday tomorrow!" Addison suddenly announced.

"Is it?" Doc asked in surprise.

Frankie turned bright red and nodded.

He'd known her birthday was coming, but he wasn't very good at keeping track of days.

"Sixteen?" he asked.

She shook her head and mumbled, "Seventeen."

"I missed one then," he said. "That means I owe you two birthday presents."

"You don't need to get me anything," Frankie stuttered.

"But I want to get you something," Doc said cheerfully. "What would you like?"

"She needs a car," Johnny said.

"A pretty green car," Jules added.

"With a sunroof," Addison put in.

"They're joking!" Frankie exclaimed, nearly knocking over her milk with an emphatic gesture.

"Do you have your license?" Doc asked.

"Not yet," she murmured.

"Are you planning to get it?"

"Sure," she said with a shrug.

He had the strange feeling she was lying; in fact, he knew

she was lying. Frankie was not an accomplished liar. But he couldn't think of a single reason why she'd lie about getting a driver's license.

"How did you get here?" he asked.

"The Flatiron Flyer," Frankie mumbled.

"Is that a bus?" Doc inquired.

"Yes."

He shuddered. "No. That just won't do. What kind of car do you want?"

"Green!" Johnny exclaimed.

"Sunroof!" Addison yelled.

"Shut up!" Frankie yelled back. "He's not buying me a car!"

"Why not?" Doc asked.

"Because... Because..." Her face paled, and she said in a wobbly tone, "Because that's what dads do, and you're not my dad."

Her words only hurt a little. He wasn't her dad, and he knew that. He was much better at occupying the fun uncle slot. But fun uncles didn't buy their nieces cars. Or maybe they did, but in Frankie's mind they didn't.

The room was silent now; and the Bakers were staring at Frankie, forks halfway to their mouths and eyes wide with concern and confusion.

Frankie swallowed awkwardly, said "I've gotta use the bathroom", and ran from the room.

"Interesting," Doc said once she was gone.

The children turned to look at him, eyes still wide.

"Will her father be buying her a car?" Doc asked.

The children shook their heads.

Very interesting, Doc thought, mind already evaluating Frankie's behavior and wondering how he could help her.

"I'm sorry," Jules said softly. "I didn't know that would upset her."

"It's hardly your fault," Doc replied. "We'll bring her around to our point of view."

"She doesn't even want a party," Addison said grumpily.

Doc could understand that. He'd flatly refused to celebrate a single birthday after his mother had died. There just hadn't seemed to be a point. He hadn't even acknowledged his birthday until Bree had come along.

Bree loved to celebrate birthdays and holidays and Wednesdays, anything that could be celebrated; but Doc had never been good at remembering days. When years passed by so quickly, little things like keeping tracks of dates on a calendar just stopped being important. Not that Doc had ever been good at it. When he was mortal, keeping track of the years had been no different than counting down to his death.

"I met a sprite yesterday," Addison said, interrupting Doc's melancholy thoughts.

"Is she pretty?" Doc asked.

Addison shook her head violently.

"She isn't?"

"She's a he," Addison said. "And he took the time to explain to me that HE is not pretty. He is handsome. At least he thinks he is; I still think he's pretty."

Doc swallowed a laugh and said, "Does he have a name?"

"Tricket."

"I look forward to meeting Tricket," Doc said solemnly. "Have you introduced yourself to the family of trolls?"

"Yes," Addison said, nodding her head. "Johnny made us. He said it was the polite thing to do. Ásleif made us tea and cakes. And she said there was so much unicorn breath in the cakes that there was hardly room for anything else!"

"Birger showed me his axe," Johnny said. "I couldn't even lift it without using magic."

Before Doc could reply, Jules said, "Did you know trolls have a written language?"

"They do?!" Thaddeus sputtered.

"Yes!" Jules exclaimed. "It's runic and so beautiful."

"Runic," Thaddeus murmured. "I'd quite like to see that."

"I'll copy out a sample and bring it next time," Jules promised. "Erland is teaching me to read it."

"What do you think of the trolls, Johnny?" Doc asked, trying to cut off Thaddeus's pontification before he could get started.

"You were right," Johnny said easily.

He grinned at Doc, grabbed the sausage off Frankie's plate, and continued eating.

Everyone was finished eating by the time Frankie returned. Her eyes were red-rimmed, and she was pale, but Doc didn't say anything as she sat back down; he just pretended that she'd been there the entire time.

When Doc had drained his entire bottle of whiskey, Jules said pointedly, "I need to speak with you in private."

A thrill ran through Doc at her words. This was why they were here. So Jules could tell him how to kill a spirit. Once he knew that, he would hunt down Eli Gac and finally end him.

"In private," Jules repeated, placing a lot of emphasis on the word.

Doc frowned. Maybe that's not why they were here.

Decision swiftly made, he stood and said, "You four keep Thaddeus company while Jules and I go for a walk."

"Four?" Thaddeus murmured. "If Jules is going how are there four?"

"I believe you're forgetting to count Boudica," Doc murmured. "Dangerous decision, old boy."

"The witch hound?" Thaddeus humphed. "Of course, I don't count it."

Doc cringed and slid his body between Thaddeus and Boudica. "He didn't mean it quite like that," he said calmly as he met Boudica's fierce blue eyes. "He doesn't like being called an it either, so I never do."

"What?" Thaddeus sputtered.

"I sometimes call him a plant though, and I like to remind him what dogs do to plants if they're so inclined."

"What are you talking about?!" Thaddeus demanded. "Oh," he said as he realized Doc's implication. "Quite right. I do believe I owe you an apology, Boudica. I'm not at my best in the morning," Thaddeus added, voice a tad quivery.

"I can certainly vouch for that," Doc said cheerfully.

Boudica sent Doc an image of Thaddeus spread out across the floor, leaves ripped to shreds.

"I'd rather you didn't," Doc said, sending back an image of what he imagined Thaddeus had looked like as a man.

Boudica sent back an image of the man falling off of Doc's balcony.

"He's still learning," Doc said. "Just pretend he's a child. You like to protect children, don't you?"

"A child!" Thaddeus grouched.

"Hush, old boy, I'm trying to save your life here, and I don't need your help."

"Save my..." Thaddeus trailed off and murmured, "I do sometimes feel as if I'm still learning, just like a child."

Doc swallowed a chuckle and said, "Give me your word you won't hurt Thaddeus."

Boudica growled softly but nodded her large black head.

"Very good," Doc said as he scratched behind her ears. "Thank you. Now play nice, children."

Jules followed him silently to the elevator, and when Doc pressed the hidden button, she gasped and said, "No! You never let anyone into the sub-subbasement!"

"You're not anyone," Doc said with a shrug. "And you've already been there in a way. Dr. Feyrer described it rather perfectly."

"Did she? I wasn't sure," Jules said, trying, but completely failing, to be nonchalant.

"She left out a few things, and she didn't really understand what it is," he added.

"It's your life," Jules said simply.

"Perhaps it would be better to say it's memorabilia from my life," Doc chuckled.

The elevator door slid open, and Doc walked down the short hallway to the metal door and keyed in the code. Jules was practically vibrating with excitement, but she was trying to hide it behind a very bland smile.

"After you," Doc said as he pushed open the door.

Jules stepped into the room and gasped.

"It's... I mean... I expected... But... Great Danu!" she finally managed.

"It's a little cluttered."

"It's magnificent," Jules breathed.

Doc sprawled out across the fainting couch and waited for Jules to come back to her senses. Bree's reaction had been completely different all those years ago. She'd taken one look at Doc's and Jervis's massive piles of possessions and said, "This room needs a good cleaning."

Jules on the other hand was reverently staring at the tapestries of Jervis.

"That's Jervis, isn't it?" she asked. "It doesn't look like him, but the eyes are exactly the same. It has to be him."

"It is," Doc replied.

Solomon was dead so Jervis was no longer in hiding. And since he was no longer in hiding, there was no point in keeping his age or identity a secret from Jules. Besides, Jules had read Dr. Feyrer's notes on Doc, and she now knew more about Jervis than anyone besides Doc and Bree.

"How old is he?" she asked as she ran a light finger over the intricate threads of the tapestry.

"A little over seven hundred. Give or take a few years."

"I've never known anyone that old," Jules murmured. "I can't imagine it. They say there are witches out there who are over a thousand years old, but that's just so long. What would you do in a thousand years?"

Doc could think of lots of things, but he was sure Jules wouldn't be that interested in his idea of a good time.

"I met Medusa," he said instead. "She's more than three thousand years old."

Jules whirled around to look at him, eyes wide with disbelief. "You're kidding!" she exclaimed.

"No. I met her when we were in Bora-Bora."

"And you didn't tell me?!"

"I just did."

"No, I mean then! Then!" Jules declared, stamping her foot irritably. "So many questions. I mean... Wow! What was she like?"

"Angry," Doc said. Very, very angry, he thought, remembering her furious eyes.

"You wanted to talk to me?" he prodded, trying to bring them both back to the point. "You said you know how to kill a spirit."

"Right," Jules murmured.

She headed towards him, but turned and feathered her hand over a table coated in green felt. "I imagine you played at this table when you were mortal," she said wistfully.

"I did," Doc said. "And again when I was immortal. I didn't have any money left when I died. The shaman who saved me gave me five dollars; and at that table, I turned it into a hundred. It was a good night," Doc said with satisfaction.

"You've had so many adventures," she sighed as she leaned down to inspect the steamer trunk Doc had taken to Europe the time he'd met Jervis.

"How does that happen, do you think?" she asked. "Why are some people destined to travel the world and meet amazing people and do amazing things while the rest of us sit at home and read books about amazing places?"

"I don't know," Doc admitted. "I didn't do much until after I died."

"I don't think that's true at all," Jules said. She carefully moved a white pawn two places forward before turning to face him. "Babs took us to Mrs. Jury's the other day, and I met Della."

"How is she getting on?" Doc asked.

"I only just met her that day," Jules shrugged. "But she seemed fine to me. She made us tea."

"She makes very good tea."

"She said my shadow is a dove," Jules added, tone a tad disgruntled.

"Doves are lovely," Doc stated.

Jules snorted and said, "Johnny won't tell me what she said his shadow is. Maybe it's some type of insect," she added hopefully.

"Are all the shadows Della sees animals?" Doc asked.

"I asked her that, and she said it just depends. I also asked her how she can tell if a shadow is good or bad, and she said it has to do with the eyes, but she couldn't really explain it. Sounds a bit like aura magic to me. Not that many people can see auras, so they can claim whatever they want to claim, can't they?"

"That's true," Doc agreed. "But I don't think Della's like that."

"No, probably not," Jules admitted. "She said your shadow is an ormr."

"Did she?" Doc replied, hating the tingle that feathered his skin at the reminder of Della's words about him.

"Yeah. And then she showed me her mom's journals and explained how ormrs defend the innocent and so on and so forth. She really likes ormrs."

Jules was studying him oddly now, like he was a butterfly pinned to a board.

"The thing is," she went on, "to me, your shadow looks just like you so I can't really know for sure whether or not there's a version of your shadow that's an ormr."

Doc raised an eyebrow and said, "Are you going somewhere with this?"

She cleared her throat awkwardly and said, "Do you think we could play gin?"

Doc was beginning to think that maybe, just maybe, Jules didn't want tell him something. But he understood about procrastination, so he stood, walked to the felt-covered table, pulled out a chair, and sat.

He shuffled his cards and dealt them each a hand. They played in silence for a long time, and Doc could see that Jules was trying to figure out what she wanted to say. Or at least how she wanted to say whatever it was she felt she needed to say.

"Gin," Doc said for the third time.

"The thing is..." Jules said as she pushed her cards towards him. "Have you ever heard of Yggdrasil?"

"The tree of life?" Doc asked.

Jules nodded and said, "In Norse mythology there's a dragon that lives in the roots of the tree. Now, there's the norm version of the myth, and there's the Hidden version of the myth. Norms always tend to paint dragons as bad and evil or wicked. In this case, the dragon is gnawing on the roots of the tree of life which will bring about the end of the world."

Jules was fiddling with the edge of the table as she spoke, and Doc could tell she was a little nervous.

"Regardless of whether or not Níðhöggr, that's the dragon," she added, "brings about the end of the world, the point is... Well, the point is that the stories say he torments the damned."

Jules cast him a quick glance before looking at the table once more. She cleared her throat and said, "The Hidden version of the story has a little more depth," she said quickly. "Níðhöggr actually consumes the souls of the damned which keeps them from poisoning the earth and Yggdrasil's roots."

An eerie feeling settled on Doc. He was beginning to understand where she was going with this, and he wished he could just walk away before she finished laying it all out.

"I don't exactly know how your thing works," she said slowly. "I have a suspicion it has something to do with your tattoo. Some of the symbols... Well, my point is... My point is..."

She trailed off and stared at him. Doc returned her gaze, not entirely sure what to say.

"When you kill someone," she said carefully, "what exactly happens?"

"Does this have anything to do with how to kill a spirit?" Doc asked irritably.

"Actually, it has everything to do with how to kill a spirit," she replied. "I'm not trying to pry, but it really does matter."

He thought about ending the conversation right there. He didn't particularly like to think about the process that occurred when he killed someone. He wasn't ashamed of it; he just didn't completely understand it, and he didn't like things he didn't understand.

But he trusted Jules and her ability to ferret out important information so he finally said, "When I kill a human, my body takes on their life force, or as I like to think of it, their remaining potential."

"Is that it?"

He sighed and said, "There is a slight possibility that their soul also enters me and stays... there."

"How slight?"

"Not very slight."

"So they do?"

"I'm relatively certain."

"That's good," she said. "Because you can't kill a spirit."

2

Doc stared at Jules for a full minute before saying, "I'm not sure I follow you. You said you'd figured out how to kill a spirit."

"I know what I said," she declared, tone exasperated. "I couldn't very well explain it to you over the phone, could I?"

"Explain what exactly?" Doc asked.

"A spirit is like water," Jules said, using her schoolmarm tone of voice. "It always exists even if its form has changed."

For a second Doc was a boy again, back in that tree, listening to Francisco explain how each spirit returned to the Great Spirit when it died and changed it just a little.

"Let's say that when my spirit is in my body it's water," Jules went on. "But when I die it becomes vapor. It's still there; it's still water; it's just different."

Her face creased in concentration, and she said, "Also keep in mind that you can't actually kill water."

"And by water, you mean spirit?"

"Of course."

She and Thaddeus belong together, Doc thought uncharitably.

"Even in its solid form, ice, if you stab it, it just breaks apart. It's not dead or finished. When it melts, it will all pool back together."

Doc resisted the urge to demand that she get to the point. The point he could actually understand.

"But you..." She stared at him, eyes wide with fascination. "You're a cup. Or a pitcher. Or an ocean! I don't know! There's no one like you so I can't say exactly what you are."

"A cup?"

"Yes!" she said excitedly. "The water goes inside you."

"We're still talking about spirit, right?"

"Yes! I didn't get it until I talked to Della, and she told me about your shadow. And then I started thinking about Yggdrasil, and I realized that you're Níðhöggr, the dragon in its roots. In Norse mythology, Hidden version of course, the earth births the vessel and the tree gives it spirit. The vessel goes back to the earth and feeds it. The spirit goes back to the tree and feeds it. BUT if too many people are evil or corrupt, the tree will die. Níðhöggr keeps that from happening. He eats the souls of the wicked to protect the tree! That's you!"

Doc opened his mouth to argue or say anything, but he simply didn't know what to say. He did have souls inside him. And they were all corrupt souls. And he was keeping them from the mother, keeping them from tainting her already weary soul. So maybe Jules wasn't wrong. Maybe he was Níðhöggr. Or a Níðhöggr. He surely wasn't the single dragon that the kept the tree of life in place.

After all, it wasn't as if Tozi had given him some sort of instruction manual for his new life. The entirety of her instructions had been, "Kill people to continue living." She hadn't even told him to kill evil people; he just did.

But they weren't talking about him. They were talking about Gac. At least, Doc would prefer it if they were talking about Gac.

"Can we circle back around to how this helps me with Gac?" he asked.

"Sorry!" Jules exclaimed, blushing slightly. "I'm just really excited. You're like a mythical being."

"I'm just Doc," he said, being careful not to sigh. "I'm the same person I was when you weren't that impressed by me."

"You're not that impressive," she said haughtily.

"Good. Let's keep it that way. Now about Gac?"

"Right! There's an old story from the Celts. There was a witch named Cathassach, and somehow his nature became revealed when they were fighting the Romans. He and his entire family were captured, and the soldiers were taking them to Rome to the emperor. It doesn't say how they were captured, which is weird because it shouldn't have been that easy to take a family of witches—"

Doc cleared his throat.

"Sorry," Jules said sheepishly. "So they were on the way Rome, but Cathassach knew it would spell disaster for their people if the emperor discovered all their secrets, so he killed his entire family one night, and then himself."

"It would have been better to fight," Doc stated.

"That's what I thought," she agreed. "I suspect that something was keeping him from fighting, but that's not the point."

"There's a point?" Doc drawled.

Jules blushed again and said, "I'm sorry! I'm getting there. Cathassach's youngest daughter, Neassa, didn't die as her father thought. So she lay there surrounded by the blood and bodies of her family, far from her homeland, and she cast a spell to take the spirits of her family inside herself."

Jules paused here, and Doc gestured impatiently for her to continue.

"The rest of its not that important," she muttered. "Neassa managed to escape, get all the way home, and then she released the souls. But we're not really interested in that part. We're interested in the spell she cast."

"Both spells actually," Doc said.

"Both?"

"The one for releasing as well."

"Oh... Well, the thing is," Jules said, suddenly very interested in the table.

"Yes?"

"By all accounts, she wasn't a witch. Which is weird too. I've never heard of a witch having a norm child."

"Bosch's mother was a witch," Doc interjected. "And he was a norm."

"Really?" Jules asked with surprise. "I didn't know that. How interesting."

"It's been argued that witches are just norms with the ability to affect the elements," Doc added.

"It has?!" Jules gasped. "By whom?"

"August Naese."

"The leader of the Northwestern witches?"

"Yes."

"Hum," she murmured, mind obviously spinning. "But Neassa had to be something, don't you think?" she insisted. "Otherwise, how could she have done it?"

"A shaman?" Doc suggested.

"I don't know."

She didn't go on, so Doc said, "What do you know?"

"I know you can't kill a spirit," she said feebly. "But you can take it inside yourself. You already do that. In your current state you have to use the vessel, the cup, the body of the other person, as a sort of conduit to move their soul into you. Killing a person closes the circuit, if you will. But the story seems to suggest that it's possible to do it without the other person being alive. Like a vacuum. A soul vacuum!" she said triumphantly.

"Yes, but do you know how?"

Her face fell, and she mumbled, "No. I haven't figured that bit out yet."

"I see," Doc said, disappointment filling him.

"But I will figure it out!" Jules insisted. "Rumor has it there's a copy of Neassa's journal out there. I just have to find it."

"I'm sure that will be an easy task," Doc said with a short laugh.

"It's not in the library index," Jules admitted. "But I'm going to find it."

He grinned at her, both amused and impressed by her tenacity, and said, "Shall we go back up to the others?"

She cast a longing glance around the basement and said sadly, "If we must."

"Who knows what Johnny and Addison might get up to without your civilizing influence," Doc murmured.

"You're right," Jules said worriedly. "We'd better go."

They left the room, and it wasn't until they were inside the elevator that Jules said, "Thank you. Thank you for trusting me with... so much. You're... You're... I'm really glad we met you," Jules whispered. "It was definitely the luckiest moment of my life."

Doc wrapped his arm around Jules's shoulders and pulled her in for a hug. "Easily in the top ten for me," he said.

"That high?" Jules asked as she hugged him back.

"Absolutely."

"Cool."

They didn't say anything more as the elevator moved swiftly upwards. When the doors slid open on Doc's floor, he tightened his hug for a moment and said softly, "I love you, Jules; I love all of you, and I'm very sorry I couldn't keep you."

The words were hard for him to say, but he'd never told Bree often enough, and he didn't want to make the same mistake with the Bakers.

"You did keep us," Jules said as she pulled away from him. "I'm here, right? And we woke you up at six o'clock in the morning. You didn't get rid of us," she said, grinning brightly. "You just gave us a permanent home. A home we love. Although not as much as we love you," she added.

He had a feeling it was just as difficult for Jules to say as it was for him.

"Good," Doc said firmly. He raised an eyebrow and added, "My suite is soundproofed, you know; and I can still hear Addison screaming. What do you think she's done?"

Jules tilted her head to listen, then said hopefully, "Maybe we should go back downstairs?"

"And leave poor Frankie alone?" Doc chuckled. "I don't think so."

"You're right," Jules sighed.

They smiled at each other before walking quickly down the hallway. Doc opened the door and peeked inside. Addison was sitting on the floor, surrounded by buttons, and she was screaming at the top of her lungs. Doc could barely hear

Thaddeus reprimanding her, and Johnny, Frankie, and Boudica were nowhere to be seen.

"Hush!" Doc commanded.

Addison's mouth snapped closed, and she opened her wet eyes and stared at him.

"Are you injured?" Doc asked as he knelt beside her.

"No," Addison blubbered.

"Then there is absolutely no call to make such a commotion," Doc said sternly.

"But—"

"No buts," he interrupted. "Dry your tears and clean up your mess."

Addison's gaze turned a little mutinous, and Doc raised one eyebrow. She didn't say anything, just started picking up the buttons and putting them back into the bowl.

Doc stood and looked around his suite, sighing when he saw Frankie and Johnny peeking out of the kitchen.

"Why are you hiding?" Doc asked.

"We weren't hiding," Johnny insisted. "We were... um... looking for some earplugs?"

"That was nothing," Doc said. "You should have heard it when Bree screamed. My eardrums have permanent damage."

Frankie didn't laugh. In fact, she wouldn't even look at him. She kept her eyes on the floor as she walked across the room and pulled Addison to her feet.

"We'd better go," Frankie mumbled. "Babs will worry."

Amidst much protest, she dragged Addison towards the door. Johnny and Jules looked at Doc and made identical shrugs before following after her.

"I think you're forgetting something," Doc said sternly.

Addison yanked her hand free and ran back to Doc. When she reached him, she threw her arms around him.

"That's better," Doc chuckled.

She released him and reached up to grab his face. Once his eyes were level with hers, she said solemnly "love you; see you soon" and kissed him on the forehead.

"I love you too, little unicorn."

Her eyes brightened, and she whispered, "Della said my shadow is a unicorn."

"A unicorn!" Jules exclaimed. "How come you get a unicorn?"

Addison just shrugged.

Jules and Johnny hugged Doc before they started in arguing about shadow magic.

"Della's just a child," Johnny said dismissively. "Maybe she does see something, but she surely doesn't know what anything means."

"You were just a child ten minutes ago," Jules retorted. "And I still took you seriously."

Doc laughed as the door closed tightly behind them.

"I need a little something," Thaddeus spoke up. "My ears are feeling... stressed. Thank goodness you arrived when you did. I was actually making an attempt to wiggle my pot off the table."

"Suicide, old boy?" Doc drawled. "That's so unlike you. Is that what happened to your last pot?"

"I said I don't want to talk about that," Thaddeus grumbled. "And you weren't here; it went on for hours."

"I was only gone twenty minutes," Doc laughed as he poured most of a bottle of brandy into Thaddeus's pot.

Doc's earlier excitement had drained away, leaving him feeling slightly weary. He still didn't know how to kill Gac; and according to Jules, the only way he could get Gac off the board was to absorb him. Or contain him, like Jury and Bree had contained the others spirits inside the rock. The rock Gac had somehow managed to escape from.

Doc removed the slightly pulsing rock from his safe and stared at it. How could such a small thing contain all those spirits? He rubbed his hand over his chest, wondering the same thing.

He had never spent too much time thinking about what he was. What he was had never really mattered, but Jules's words had left him wondering if he'd just stepped into some kind of archetypal slot. He wasn't Níðhöggr. He didn't live at the base of the world tree. But maybe he did carry out Níðhöggr's task. Maybe that was his purpose. Maybe that was why Tozi had made him.

Doc frowned at the thought. He was who he was, and it didn't matter what he was. It didn't matter if he did fill an archetypal slot. It didn't control him. The role cast upon him didn't make him love the Bakers, it didn't make him worry about Tucker, it didn't make him friends with Jury.

And since it didn't control him, he was going to do something that had nothing to do with consuming the souls of the corrupt.

He put the stone back into his safe and closed the safe door. Once it was locked, he pulled out his phone and called Jervis.

When Jervis answered, Doc said, "I'm wondering about Frankie."

"I'll be right up," Jervis replied.

"Interesting," Doc murmured to himself. Jervis clearly had something to say about Frankie, which wasn't entirely unsurprising.

Doc retrieved a bottle of whiskey and Jervis's cordial from the kitchen, then he sat on the couch to wait.

A few seconds later, Jervis opened the door and swiftly crossed the room. He handed Doc a folded piece of paper before sitting down across from him and pouring himself a cup of cordial.

Doc unfolded the paper, frowning when he saw the photograph of a younger Frankie staring out at him. The paper read, "Missing, help bring me home." It identified Frankie as one Francesca Falon Foxall, and said she'd been missing for over three years now.

"When did you find this?" Doc asked.

"The day they first came to visit you."

"You've had it this whole time?"

"That's what I said."

"And you didn't think to give it to me?"

"You clearly weren't interfering," Jervis said dryly. "Now you are."

"Remind me to redact your raise."

"You haven't given me one today," Jervis pointed out.

"Give yourself a raise," Doc ordered. "And then take it away."

"Done, sir."

Doc rolled his eyes, but continued to study the missing poster. "She's clearly not missing," he finally said.

"Clearly."

"What else did you find?"

"There wasn't much actually."

Doc looked up in surprise. "What do you mean there wasn't much?"

"Whoever Frankie is, she's not a regular part of the system."

"What does that mean?"

"There are several Foxall families on record," Jervis replied. "But there's no record of a Francesca Falon Foxall."

Very interesting.

"However," Jervis said.

Doc grinned; he loved it when Jervis said "however".

"There is a number on the poster."

"Wouldn't there always be a number?"

"Yes, but this is not the normal number. If I had to guess, I'd say someone hacked the system to put up the poster, and the number obviously connects to whoever is looking for Frankie."

"Did you run the number?"

"I'm insulted."

"Well?"

"Well nothing. It's a burner."

What a mystery this was turning out to be. A missing girl who wasn't really missing, and the people looking for her were clearly not normal people.

"I think I'll give it a call," Doc said.

"You don't want to sit on it overnight?" Jervis inquired.

"Never been my style."

"You realize that once you open this particular can of worms, there'll be worms everywhere, and you'll have no hope of putting them back."

"But," Doc said cheerfully, "they'll be on the sidewalk, which will make them easier to step on."

"Perhaps."

"Stop being a spoilsport," Doc chided. "Frankie's obviously hurting, and I want to know why."

He'd never excelled at watching people he loved suffer. He hadn't been able to help his mother, so he'd read to her and brought her flowers and told her all kinds of stories. But he hadn't actually been able to take away her suffering. He hadn't been able to do anything for Andrew when Doyle and

Janey and Bill had died. Not a damn thing. But this Frankie situation was something he could fix. Maybe. He refused to consider that he might just be making it worse.

After Jervis had left, Doc called the number on Frankie's missing poster, and he was taken slightly aback by the quavery voice that answered the phone.

"Hello? Who is this?"

Doc was suddenly not sure how to play his hand so he decided for caution. "This is Marcus Nettle, ma'am. I saw a poster of a young missing girl named Francesca."

"Oh! Do you have information about my Franny? Please tell me you do!"

Doc's eyes narrowed. He didn't know much about what was going on, but he did know that Frankie would absolutely loathe being called Franny.

"Maybe, ma'am. I'm not sure. Would it be possible to meet in person?"

"Is that really necessary?" the old woman asked. "If you have information that will help me bring Franny home, you should just tell me."

There was a thread of steel to her tone now, and Doc grinned. He loved it when they put up a fight.

"I'd really feel more comfortable face to face," Doc insisted. "To be honest, I'm not even sure it's the same girl."

There was a long pause. Finally the old woman said, "I'm currently in Wales. I imagine that's a little outside of your range, isn't it?"

"Not at all," Doc said smoothly. "In fact, I could be there tomorrow."

"Isn't that convenient," the woman muttered.

"I've business in Ireland; Wales isn't even out of my way. Where should I meet you?"

She rather reluctantly gave him an address, to which he replied. "Excellent, and may I ask whom I'm speaking to?"

"Mrs. Foxall," she said irritably. "Franny's grandmother."

"So nice to talk to you, Mrs. Foxall," Doc drawled. "I certainly hope I have some good news for you tomorrow."

He disconnected and called Jervis.

"I guess I'm going to Wales," Doc said when Jervis answered.

"Indeed."

"I'll stop by Bree's on the way home."

"Excellent idea."

"Would you like to come?" Doc asked on a whim.

"I do believe I would."

"Really?"

"Certainly. It will give Winslow the opportunity to prove that he's taken my lessons to heart."

"Ah."

"What's that mean?"

"Nothing," Doc said, swallowing his chuckle.

"It meant something."

"Does he know you're testing him?"

"He should. Assuming he has a mind between those large ears of his."

"I'll meet you at the airport in an hour," Doc said before disconnecting and giving into his laughter.

"What's so funny?" Thaddeus grumped.

"It's an inside joke," Doc chuckled.

"It's always an inside joke," Thaddeus murmured. "Just once, I'd like to be on the inside."

"Maybe someday, old boy."

There was a soft knock on the door, and Doc called out, "Come in, Rosa!"

The door inched open, and Rosa's round face peeked inside.

"Yes, I'm here," Doc said with a chuckle. "But I'm leaving, and I'm sure Thaddeus would appreciate your company."

Rosa stepped slowly into the room, eyes cautious.

"What have I done to make you fear me?" Doc asked softly. "It's been eighteen years now; and, as far as I know, I haven't done anything to cause you distress."

Thaddeus made a strange noise, but didn't say anything.

"You're the souleater," Rosa murmured.

"We went over this," Doc replied with a sigh. "Evil souls."

"Yes," she murmured, eyes a little frightened now.

"I see," Doc drawled.

Thaddeus made another noise, but this time it was a sound of distress, and Doc heard him whisper, "Please don't kill her; I've grown rather attached."

"Whatever it is you've done or think you've done," Doc said firmly, "I can guarantee you that you wouldn't be inside this room if you were worthy of death. Jervis is very thorough."

Rosa's face was white now, and Doc could hear her heartbeat from across the room.

"You can't know that," she whispered.

"I can. Now, Thaddeus was complaining about his pot again. Do you think you could paint some butterflies on it or something?"

"Butterflies?!" Thaddeus sputtered. "Do I look like a man who enjoys butterflies?"

"Skulls?" Doc offered.

"Absolutely not!"

"Cages?"

"If I had my hands, you reprobate, I'd wring your neck!"

"But you don't," Doc laughed. "Kittens it is."

"I do not want a kitten on my pot!" Thaddeus screamed. "Kittens are repulsive!"

"He doesn't mean that," Doc drawled as he lifted Rosa's hand and kissed her fingers lightly. "You're invaluable to me, Rosa. If it weren't for you, I'd have to dust every single one of Thaddeus's leaves, and I just don't have the patience for that."

She stared at him in confusion for a moment before saying softly, "Don't you even want to know?"

"Nope."

"But—"

"I trust you," Doc interrupted with a wide smile. And he did. With his room and with Thaddeus. Not with his secrets or his thoughts, but he trusted very few people with those.

"See you later, old boy," Doc said, and then he walked out the door. He hadn't packed a bag, but Jervis kept a variety of clothes in the plane, so Doc wasn't worried about it.

As he rode the elevator up towards the parking garage, he tapped his fingers on his thigh thoughtfully. He was getting a tad sidetracked, but it wasn't as if he knew where Gac was; and even if he did, he didn't know how to kill him. Besides, he really did need to go see Bree. After all, he'd promised her, and he always honored his promises.

3

"This is fun," Doc said sometime later as the plane lifted off the runway. "We haven't done anything together since... I can't actually remember. Maybe the mid-nineties."

"It hasn't been that long," Jervis retorted.

"I think it has been," Doc insisted.

"We just fought Gac last week."

"That's not the same," Doc shrugged.

"What about the Solomon thing?"

"Definitely not the same."

"How are you measuring?" Jervis demanded dryly.

"With a stick and a bottle of whiskey," Doc chuckled.

"That's your problem right there," Jervis said, face entirely serious. "You have to use wine to measure. Everyone knows that."

He handed Doc a bottle of whiskey and opened a bottle of cordial for himself before saying, "Gin?"

"Let's shake things up," Doc replied. "Canasta."

"Too many rules," Jervis countered. "Cribbage?"

"Perfect," Doc said as he began to shuffle.

"It's hard to believe you still have these," Jervis said as he looked at his cards.

"Jury put a protection spell on them."

"Did he?"

"I didn't know," Doc said. He put two cards into the crib and added, "He just told me a while ago."

"Jury can be quite thoughtful when he wants to be," Jervis stated.

Doc snorted and said, "Even if he doesn't want to be."

"He's very stubborn like that," Jervis agreed.

Doc played a ten and said, "Twenty-nine."

"Go," Jervis replied.

"Go," Doc said.

Jervis counted his cards, then Doc counted his cards.

"I won that round," Doc said easily.

"As if I expected anything different," Jervis said flatly.

Doc handed Jervis the cards; and as Jervis shuffled, Doc said, "Do you remember when we went on our first flight with Howard Hughes?"

"It was a wretched experience," Jervis declared.

"No worse than being stuck on a ship for days on end. Howard got us from New York to Los Angeles in under a day."

"A very long day."

"He was so excited when he made that movie about me," Doc reminisced.

"I don't know why," Jervis snorted. "It was ridiculous."

"It was funny. You're just upset that no one's ever made a movie about you."

"Hardly. I would hate to watch a movie about myself. And if someone ever did make a movie about me, I certainly wouldn't make you watch it a half dozen times," Jervis said pointedly.

Doc laughed softly and said, "It does get boring after a while, doesn't it? It's funny how people think they know you just because they read an article about you or heard about a poker game you once played."

"As if anyone could truly understand the depths of Dr. John Henry Holliday," Jervis said, grinning slightly.

"You forgot a few of my titles," Doc laughed, playing another card.

"Hardly. I just think your ego is quite big enough without them."

They played in silence for a while, then Jervis cleared his throat and said, "I have a request."

Doc froze, Jervis's tone of voice immediately putting him on guard. "Yes?" he said carefully.

"It's nothing really," Jervis said awkwardly. "If you feel you have to say no, I completely understand."

"I haven't even heard the request yet," Doc said.

"It's not life or death," Jervis insisted. "So you shouldn't feel that you don't have a choice."

"Would you just spit it out already?" Doc growled, mind racing to figure out what the hell Jervis could possibly want.

"Sami would like you and Jury to, um, well, to come to dinner."

"What?" Doc replied automatically, mind seemingly incapable of processing Jervis's words.

"Come to dinner," Jervis repeated. "In a few days, when we're home, I mean. You and Jury."

Doc swallowed the laugh that tried to bubble up and said solemnly, "Is it formal wear?"

"Would you dress differently if it was?" Jervis snapped.

"Of course not. I was just checking. In your suite or her apartment?"

"My suite is her apartment," Jervis said stiffly.

That was news to Doc. Not bad news. Just news. He was happy for Jervis. He just wished that Sami had had the decency to be born a vampire. But that wasn't an issue today. Today Sami and Jervis were happy. Sami was anyway; Jervis was choking on his own words.

"We'll be there," Doc promised. "Just be sure to tell me when."

"I... I..." Jervis played a card before finally saying, "Thank you."

"Anything for you," Doc said solemnly. He was having some difficulty keeping his laughter from exploding, but for Jervis he was sure he could manage.

"She would... She apparently wants to do things that couples do," Jervis said, voice a little strained. "We went to the theater the other day."

"That's nice," Doc said. "And it's good for you."

"I haven't done anything like that... Ever," Jervis said. "Except for the few times I went out with you or Bree, I just... I haven't."

He sighed heavily and said, "I'm not entirely sure that I've moved with the times. There's still a part of me that thinks everything should be the same as it was four hundred years ago; and instead of going out, I expect a traveling minstrel to wander up to the door." He paused before saying softly, "I really would prefer that."

"There are a lot of things I would prefer," Doc agreed. "The trick is not to think about them. You have to enjoy today for today. And you have to know that all the people you love today wouldn't be here if it was a hundred years ago."

"You would be here," Jervis said stubbornly.

"Yes, but not Bree or Aine or Sami or the Bakers."

"I'm not that attached to the Bakers."

"Did you know that when you lie your left eyelid closes just a bit?"

"Who's lying?" Jervis retorted.

"You," Doc laughed.

"Hardly."

"You never want to leave Dulcis."

"I want to see the Banshee Palatium."

"Bree sent us a video tour just yesterday."

"You really can't tell anything from those videos," Jervis shrugged. "Too blurry. I won that round," he added.

Doc took the cards and dealt out another round. He really did miss going out with Jervis. When they'd lost track of the Sons of Solomon over fifty years ago, Jervis had started staying close to Dulcis. It was nice knowing he would always be there when Doc returned, but Doc was looking forward to unraveling Frankie's mystery with Jervis at his side.

"Jules tricked me," Doc said as he put two cards into the new crib.

"Really?"

"She told me she knew how to kill a spirit."

"And?"

"She doesn't. Or she does. There's apparently no way to kill a spirit."

"I suppose that makes sense."

"I suppose," Doc sighed. "Gac escaped the rock. I saw him in the dreaming last night."

"I see."

"And Jules said when I find him that I have to suck him into me like a vacuum. She's looking for the spell to do it."

"Hum," Jervis murmured.

Rather noncommittally in Doc's opinion. He studied Jervis through narrowed eyes, then said, "Tell me about the ormr."

"What ormr?"

"The ormr you knew about since childhood."

"Nothing much to say."

"I'll call Sami and tell her how much you enjoy abusing me when we're in the sub-subbasement," Doc threatened.

"I don't think she'll mind."

"I'll tell her about your list."

"You wouldn't dare," Jervis growled.

"I would. You're clearly hiding something from me, and I want to know what it is."

Jervis's nostrils flared, and he said, "The list is inside the brotherhood vault."

"Do they taste different?" Doc asked slyly.

"Like wealth and privilege," Jervis murmured.

Doc grinned, amused at Jervis's expression. Jervis had long since made a hobby of sneaking into the homes of people in power, royals, presidents, dictators, and taking just a little nip. He had tasted quite a few bloodlines over the years, but that was hardly the point. The point was that Jervis was avoiding something, something to do with Doc.

"Tell me about the ormr," Doc said once more.

"I'd rather not."

"Jules already told me about her version of the ormr," Doc said.

"How interesting. What did she have to say?"

"Tell me your version first."

"Another round?"

"Why are you hedging?" Doc demanded.

"Because I really don't think you'll like what I have to say."

"When has that ever stopped you?"

"You'd be surprised," Jervis grumbled. He stared at Doc for a long minute before finally saying, "My family has long considered the world tree as a truth. I would not go so far as to say we worshiped it, but we always offered up a gift to the world tree in the spring when the oak trees began to bud."

Jervis had slipped into German, as he often did when he was talking about his past.

"We honored it, and we honored the ormr that lay in its roots."

A chill ran down Doc's spine, and he began to wish he hadn't started this particular conversation. But he had, so he waited silently for Jervis to continue.

"There is, or was, a code that our people lived by," Jervis went on. "We observed the natural laws. Not laws that men put in place, not morals that religion pushed onto people, but the bone-deep truths. We honored the earth, and we honored all of our siblings. If our people needed meat, we hunted it, but we used what we took and we thanked the spirit of the creature we took from. We did not ever kill for the pleasure of it; we killed out of necessity."

Jervis paused here, eyes distant. "I suppose all the signs were there with Eldwin. He skirted the edge of the natural laws many times, but I could never see the truth of him. He was my brother, and I... loved him."

He shrugged and said, "That's not what you asked though, is it?"

"I'm happy to talk about your family," Doc said truthfully.

"I had a beautiful family," Jervis said with a sad smile.

"Tell me about them."

"My daughter's name was Hemma. She liked to watch the sunrise, and she couldn't bear to see any type of creature in pain. She was a great healer. My son was named Gervasius, after me," Jervis said softly. "He was an excellent huntsman. He was even faster than I am. Not a day goes by that I do not think of them, that I do not miss them. It's been over two hundred years, and I swear the pain has barely lessened."

He stared bleakly out the window for a moment, then said, "I must have been out of my mind to even entertain the idea of being with Sami. I don't know that I can bear any more pain."

"I think it's probably a little late for regrets," Doc said gently. "And even though it hurts, I wouldn't give away my time with Lena for anything. Or Andrew. Or Bree."

"I know," Jervis said. "It was very cruel of our mother to make us so long-lived. Very cruel indeed."

Doc couldn't argue with that.

For a long while, neither of them said anything; and Doc shuffled his cards without looking, thinking of the cruel nature of a long life.

After a while he said, "Don't think I've forgotten how this conversation started."

"I've never known you to forget anything," Jervis sighed. "Where was I?"

"You said your people lived by a code."

"Ah." Jervis nodded and said, "Those who broke the code were punished. Not in their mortal form, however. Their spirit was punished." He paused here, and Doc dealt out the cards while he waited for him to continue.

"The dragon, the ormr, consumes the souls of the wicked," Jervis finally said. "While other spirits continue on, the spirits of the wicked cease to be. I confess that when you first told me about Señora Teodora and the terms of your long life, I was reminded of the dragon."

"Why would I not like that?" Doc asked irritably.

"Because you despise it when roles are cast upon you. You believed that Señora Teodora made you for a specific purpose, to save her granddaughter. That was not a role; it was a mission. But if in fact, Señora Teodora had something different, something greater, in mind, it becomes a mantle."

Doc shuffled his cards one handed, moving all the aces to the top, while he considered Jervis's words.

"What exactly are you saying?" he eventually asked.

"Why are we on this plane headed towards Wales?" Jervis replied.

"Because Frankie needs us."

"Did she say she needed us?"

"It was implied."

"And when did you make this decision to interfere in Frankie's life?" Jervis asked. "Was it after Jules told you about her version of the ormr?"

"I don't see the relation," Doc muttered.

"I think that you do."

"Let's pretend that I do," Doc said. "What does it matter? Even if Señora Teodora did make me for a greater purpose, I'm still my own person; I'm still doing what I want to do. No one is making me do anything, certainly not a goddamn spell that's carved into my chest."

"I never said that it was," Jervis remarked.

"You implied it."

"I didn't. You are so far beyond compulsion that it's a ridiculous concept."

"Then what are you saying?"

Jervis shrugged and said, "If I cast you into the role of the jester, you would not perform, even if I dressed you in bangles and curly toes. Perhaps you were cast into the role of a soul-devouring dragon, but you do it because you want to, not because you have to or because someone else wants you to. Señora Teodora gave you the means to devour souls, but she didn't force you to do it. You might have lived out a normal life and died happily years ago. You are the one who chooses to continue."

Doc wished he could be certain that was true. The few times he'd gone without killing someone for a while had ended with him going rather feral, and it was not a sensation he had enjoyed. But he did enjoy the kill. He always had. There was something quite satisfying about it. He had never minded before, but what if he wasn't killing to satisfy his own desire? What if he was killing to satisfy someone else's desire?

"I can see you doing it right now," Jervis sighed.

"Doing what?"

"Evaluating your actions and trying to decide if you're being used as a puppet."

"Am I?"

"Goddamn it, Hans! This is why I didn't say anything. You are a good man, and you do good things. You restore the natural order. You balance out the scales. And who cares if that's exactly what someone wanted you to do. It's not a bad role to have."

"I suppose," Doc admitted reluctantly.

"Are you just saying that to get me to leave you alone?" Jervis demanded.

"Would I do that?"

"Yes!"

Doc grinned and said, "I'm not."

"Fine. I'm going to sleep now."

Doc blinked twice before saying, "What?"

"I said I'm going to sleep."

"I heard you; I just don't believe you. In all the years I've known you I can't remember you ever going to sleep."

"I do sleep," Jervis snorted. "And between Dulcis and Sami I haven't gotten any sleep at all lately. I almost took a bite out of Winslow just yesterday."

"Yuck," Doc muttered. "I bet even his blood is cheerful."

Jervis actually cringed before saying, "Wake me when we get there."

"I bet you five dollars that you wake me."

"What kind of fool do you take me for?" Jervis retorted.

"So no bet?"

"No."

Jervis glared at him for a second, then his face softened slightly and he said, "I enjoyed talking about them. Thank you for listening."

"Anytime," Doc said.

Jervis nodded, then tilted back his chair and closed his eyes.

Doc watched him for a while, mind turning over everything Jules and Jervis had said. He was annoyed at Tozi, but he wasn't entirely sure why. She hadn't exactly lied to him about his immortality. She'd told him the terms of his gift, and he'd heard her words as she had imbued him with it. Nothing had changed. And Jervis was right. Restoring the natural balance of things wasn't a bad role to have.

But still. It was like realizing that you were only sitting at the high-roller's table because someone wanted you there, not because you really deserved to be there. It was like finding out that your lover was thinking of someone else while she murmured your name. It was like finally realizing that you were a pawn on the chessboard and someone else was making all your moves. And he didn't like it. Not one little bit.

He tapped his fingers irritably. Maybe if he went to sleep he would dream of Tozi; and if he did, he wouldn't get distracted by her lovely eyes and hair. Instead he would hold firm and demand answers.

But she must have known he was looking for her because the second he fell asleep, he opened his eyes to his empty throne room.

He swung his feet up onto his bone footstool and stared out at the barren landscape beyond his throne room, wondering if Gac was out there watching him. Fury filled Doc at the thought. This was his place, his oasis, his sanctorium. Gac was not allowed here. He was not allowed to interfere with Doc's ancestors, with Doc's people.

The anger within him grew even more as he imagined Gac perching on the stones outside, peering in while Doc was talking to Andrew or Francisco.

A rumble passed through the room, and Doc's throne shook slightly, but Doc ignored it. He was too caught up in his anger to think about anything else. The mere idea of Gac playing the watcher while Doc was unaware of it filled him with absolute fury.

The vibration suddenly increased, finally pulling Doc from his thoughts; and as he visually searched for the source, the edges of the onyx floor began to extend upwards. All around the room, the shining black rock crept up, slowly shifting as it went into a sheet of opaque white stone until Doc's throne room was completely surrounded by rock.

"Hell and damnation," Doc breathed.

Had he done that? He must have. Who else could have done it? He'd been thinking about Gac peering in, and now

Gac couldn't. But he hadn't put forth a conscious thought on keeping Gac out. It was almost as if... He really didn't want to think it, but it was too late. The thought had already taken root. It was almost as if the throne room was him, or an extension of him. It had read his desire to be shielded from Gac and had raised the walls to fulfill it.

Doc suddenly wanted to know exactly where the throne room had come from and when it had come. But he couldn't remember a time without it. It had always been here, and it had long ago ceased to shock him, but he could still see the look on Bluegrass's face the first time she'd seen it. A look of absolute horror.

"You've been redecorating," a soft voice suddenly said.

"Bluegrass," Doc murmured, trying to be surprised that Bluegrass was suddenly standing in front of him, but knowing deep down he'd called her to him.

"Didn't like the view?" she asked, green eyes twinkling with humor.

Doc really couldn't say.

"I miss you," he said instead.

"I'm right here."

"Yes, but I miss you in your house. I miss your clutter and your tea."

She sat on the footstool and studied him carefully. "Something is bothering you."

"Nothing more than usual."

"I think it is more than usual. You have that same hunted look you had once before. Has Meli returned?"

"Andrew killed Meli," Doc said. "She's gone."

"Then what is it?"

Doc sighed and said, "I made an enemy."

"Is that unusual?"

"Not really."

Doc closed his eyes for a second and thought of Bluegrass's healing tea, then he held out a hand and closed his fingers around the slender stem that suddenly appeared. He sniffed it before handing it to Bluegrass, then took another goblet of tea from the air.

"This is very nearly perfect," Bluegrass murmured after she'd taken a sip.

"What did I forget?"

"The St. Johns," she chuckled. "Now tell me why you built a wall."

"I'd rather talk about you."

"I visited with Cleopatra the other day," she said.

"Is she as beautiful as they say?"

"Probably more so," Bluegrass admitted.

"How does it work?" Doc asked. "Could you warn her?"

"This sounds silly, even to me," Bluegrass said. "I've always hypothesized that the dreaming has a filter of sorts. I can't say anything to anyone to change things. There are constraints in place. Constraints that keep dream walkers from unraveling all of time."

"I suppose that's a good thing," Doc said.

"A very good thing. I've never tried to interfere in the dreaming. I've always know that the consequences would be far too vast, but I'm certain not everyone has my same principles."

"Where are the incubi within the dreaming?" he asked.

She blushed and said, "As I told you once before, there are layers. The incubi exist in a deeper layer."

"I see," Doc murmured. He didn't really though. Layers of existence all on top of each other reminded him of the Hidden, and he'd never been able to wrap his mind around the idea that two separate buildings could exist in exactly the same space. But he supposed that was the point. It wasn't exactly the same space.

"Now about this enemy you've made?" Bluegrass prodded gently.

"He's learned to find me in the dreaming," Doc said. "He can't enter my throne room, but he scuttles around outside of it."

"That explains the wall."

"I just didn't want him looking in and stealing my moments. Like this one, with you."

"I understand," she said.

"I sent Apollo and Tucker into the dreaming once to look for him, but they couldn't find anything."

"Why Tucker?"

"Because my enemy is a ghost."

"Oh," she said.

"I can't find him," Doc admitted. "And even if I could, I apparently can't kill him. I can only take him inside me, which I haven't figured out how to do yet."

She grinned widely, the skin around her eyes crinkling with humor.

"What?" Doc asked.

"So business as usual?" she chuckled.

"Yes," Doc sighed. "Business as usual."

She laughed, and he laughed with her because he liked watching her laugh.

"I'll see if I can find him," Bluegrass said after her levity had died down.

"But you don't know him."

She shrugged and said, "The dreaming is easy to navigate, at least for me. Tell me more about him."

"His name is Eli Gac," Doc said. "But his soul belongs to General Custer, a man from the 1800s."

"I once heard a fascinating story about him," Bluegrass said, leaning forward with interest. "I heard he lived on in a different body."

"He did, does," Doc confirmed. "Except he steals them. That's how we met."

"He wanted your body," she surmised.

"Exactly. His spirit is quite damaged now," Doc added. "I didn't realize that torture in the dreaming would... stick."

"Oh."

"I wouldn't have done it if I'd known," Doc went on. "I was trying to kill him."

"You can't kill spirit," Bluegrass said.

"I know that. NOW."

She chuckled once more before saying, "And he's been here?"

"Not inside the throne room," Doc said. "He can't enter the throne room. Just outside."

"I will look for him," Bluegrass promised. "How is Apollo doing?"

"Haven't you seen him?" Doc asked.

"Once or twice, but he always puts on such a brave face."

Doc snorted and said, "He and Tucker seem to get along. When they aren't fighting."

"Apollo loves to fight," Bluegrass said with a laugh. "He was a master of rhetoric. Which basically means that he argued professionally."

Doc laughed with her, but suddenly jerked awake when someone touched his arm.

"I hate it when you do that!" Doc snapped.

"Do what?" Jervis replied.

"Sneak up on me."

"I didn't."

"You always do. You can't help it. It's your nature."

"I apologize for being a vampire," Jervis said dryly.

"You should," Doc grumbled. "Are we there?"

"We're there."

"Good. I'm ready to kill someone."

"What makes you think you'll be able to kill anyone?" Jervis asked.

"The old woman called Frankie Franny," Doc replied.

"Ah," Jervis said. "In that case I do believe this is going to be a most fruitful adventure."

4

"I'll stay outside and watch the perimeter," Jervis said the next morning.

They were standing on a ridge looking down at a small cottage. At a glance it all looked completely innocuous. The cottage was fairly tiny, not large enough to house an ambush; there was only one outbuilding, also not very large; and there wasn't much in the way of hedges or growth. But over the years, Doc and Jervis had learned to expect the worst of everything or, at the very least, the completely unexpected.

"I'll go in and talk to Granny," Doc murmured.

"My, what big teeth you have, Granny," Jervis said, tone completely serious.

"The better to eat you with, my dear," Doc replied.

"I prefer the version with the evil huntsman and the daring, brave wolf," Jervis remarked.

"So does Dublin," Doc chuckled. "I suppose there's no point in procrastinating."

He stood and followed the rocky path down through the verdant growth; and before long, he was knocking at the front door. In a matter of seconds, a stooped old woman with half-moon glasses opened the door and gazed up at him.

"You'd be Marcus Nettle?" she asked in a wobbly tone.

Doc knew instantly that it wasn't the same woman he'd talked to on the phone yesterday, but he just smiled and said, "Certainly. It's so nice to meet you in person, Mrs. Foxall."

"Do come in," she said with a shaky wave.

Doc followed the fake Mrs. Foxall into a small sitting room and sat on the dainty little settee that she gestured towards. She sat in the rocking chair across from him and picked up a pile of yarn. "You don't mind if I knit while we talk, do you? It helps calm my nerves. I'm making a scarf for my dear Franny. Yellow's her favorite color."

Doc had never seen Frankie wear yellow. Not once.

"Do you know where Franny is?" she asked as her knitting needles began to click softly.

"Do you have another photograph of her?" Doc asked instead of answering her question.

"Of course," Mrs. Foxall murmured.

She lowered her knitting pile, picked up a folder off the side table, and handed it to him. Doc opened it without a word and studied the photographs inside.

It was definitely Frankie. The girl in the photographs had Frankie's same awkward smile and her same guarded eyes.

"This is her," Doc said, watching the woman's face.

Her eyes brightened, and she leaned forward. "Are you certain?" she asked, pretend age completely forgotten.

"Yes."

"Where is she?"

"Why do you want her?"

"I'm her grandmother!" the woman exclaimed.

"No, you're not."

Her eyes narrowed, and she murmured, "That was a very foolish thing to say."

"Was it?"

"Quite. Here I thought we could have a nice sociable conversation, and you went and ruined it."

"So what now?" Doc asked.

"I tie you to the chair and ask you where Francesca is; and if you don't tell me, I'll poke holes in your pretty face until you do," she said as she brandished one of the steel knitting needles.

"You think my face is pretty," Doc said with a grin. "Why do you want Francesca?"

"You're redundant," the woman said as she leaped with lithe quickness from her chair. She landed right in front of Doc and stabbed downward with her knitting needle towards his hand.

Doc yanked back his hand and kicked out with his feet, throwing her across the room into a side table covered with trinkets. Ceramic figurines crashed onto the floor around her, and she brushed them away from her and stood with a snarl.

She pulled the mobcap from her head, revealing a short blonde bob and said, "I see you're going to be difficult. One hundred thousand dollars, you tell me where the girl is, and I'll let you leave here in one piece."

"You tell me why you want her, and I'll let you die in one piece," Doc counteroffered.

"Why do you care?" she spat.

"Frankie belongs with me now," Doc said firmly.

The woman turned pale, and she chewed her bottom lip nervously. "Did she tell you?" she asked.

"Let's just assume she did," Doc said, knowing full well that whatever it was, Frankie had not told him.

The woman didn't seem to know what to do next. It was almost as if she'd been given very specific orders, and the orders hadn't covered this particular contingency. But after a few seconds, she seemed to make up her mind.

She tightened her grip on the knitting needle; and with her other hand, she reached into her formless dress and pulled out a gun.

"Sit down," she ordered.

"No," Doc drawled.

"Do you see I'm holding a gun?" she spat.

"Guns just aren't that frightening to me," Doc said as he took a step towards her.

"Stop right there!"

"Or what? You'll shoot me? You need me alive," Doc shrugged. "I, on the other hand, could go either way. I suggest a wager. I bet you ten dollars you end up in the chair."

The woman's eyes were panicked now, and she looked rather desperately towards the door.

"I brought backup," Doc said cheerfully.

He was just a few steps away now; and when she looked back at him, her eyes widened and her finger moved on the trigger. He could have probably dodged the impact, but he didn't. He just stood there, and let the bullet tear through his arm. He glanced down at the small patch of blood, back at her, grinned, and said, "Ouch."

She threw the gun at him and raced towards the door. He dashed after her, grabbing the back of her dress and yanking her backwards. She fell into him, then twisted around and jabbed towards his face with the knitting needle. Doc blocked her attack and ripped the needle from her hand. She yanked another needle from her dress and stabbed him in the stomach.

"Not trying very hard to keep me alive," Doc pointed out as he pinned her empty hand to the floor. "Don't you think Mrs. Foxall will have a problem with that?"

"Mrs. Foxall isn't here," she muttered as she desperately fought against his hold.

"That's what I always say, but no one ever listens."

She was so quick that she actually managed to stab him several more times with the second knitting needle before he was able to catch her hand. As soon as his fingers wrapped around hers, he squeezed tightly, crushing her bones. With a shriek of pain, she dropped the knitting needle, and he loosened his hold.

"Now about that chair," Doc said conversationally as he pulled her to her feet and pushed her slowly towards it. He shoved her into it, not terribly surprised when she immediately tried to leap back out. He pushed her back; and when she was sitting once more, he grabbed her hand and shoved the knitting needle he was still holding through it, pinning her hand to the chair arm.

"Stay," he ordered, ignoring her gasp of pain.

He heard her shoe scrape as he bent to snatch the yarn off the floor, but he was still surprised when he felt the needle pierce the side of his neck. He spun around quickly, grabbed her once more, shoved her back into the chair, and tied her to it with the yarn he'd just retrieved. Then he pulled the needle from his neck and thoughtfully studied the bloodied length of it.

"I admire your tenacity," he said softly. "I still have to kill you, but how I kill you is up to you."

"Who are you?" she demanded.

"Frankie's guardian."

"I don't understand."

"You don't need to understand. Tell me why you're looking for her."

"So she hasn't told you."

"I asked you a question," Doc said.

He balanced the knitting needle on his finger before tossing it into the air, catching it, and driving it through her thigh. She yelped in pain, but managed to control herself enough to snarl at him.

"We should experiment," Doc said as he drew his knife. "I'll stab my knife through the other thigh, and you can tell me which one hurts worse. Or you can just tell me what I want to know, and I'll kill you as painlessly as possible."

He hadn't bothered to tie up her legs, and she kicked at him as he stepped towards her.

"You're just postponing the inevitable," Doc sighed.

She growled fiercely and kicked at his knee. Doc merely stepped to the side of her and drove the knife through her thigh. This time she screamed in agony, but only for a second.

"I have to say, I'm thoroughly impressed with your pain tolerance," Doc said.

Her eyes were already a little glazed with shock though, and he knew she wouldn't last long. At least, he hoped she wouldn't. Torturing women had never been his forte.

"How are you related to Frankie?" Doc asked.

It was a guess based on the shape of the woman's nose. It didn't particularly matter how she was related, but he thought if he asked her a simple question, she might answer it, and then it would be easier for her to answer his other questions.

She just glared at him, so he said softly, "Remember what you said? Mrs. Foxall isn't here, but I am. And I have all the time in the world to pry the answers from your uncooperative lips."

"I'm her aunt," she whimpered.

"You clearly don't know her though," Doc said critically. "She'd hate being called Franny. Is Mrs. Foxall your mother?"

She considered lying to him; he could see it in her very frightened eyes, but she eventually said, "Yes."

"It's so much easier just to answer my questions, isn't it?" Doc asked. "Now tell me why your mother is looking for Frankie."

Her lips pursed together, and her eyes grew stubborn, so he wiggled the knitting needle back and forth before ripping it from her leg. She gasped, but still didn't speak.

He wrapped his fingers around the knife in her thigh and began to wiggle it back and forth.

"I have a suspicion that the knife hurts worse," he said confidentially. "Am I right?" He tore it free, and blood spurted onto her leg. She managed to swallow her scream but started crying softly; and he said, "It doesn't have to be this way. Just answer my question."

She whimpered for a second, but finally lifted her face and said, "I... Francesca's father told her—"

A bullet suddenly tore through the woman's forehead, and she stared at Doc with wide eyes before her head dropped forward.

"Jervis," Doc murmured as he quickly ran from the cottage out into the yard.

Before he'd taken two steps, Jervis tackled him, and together they rolled behind the small shed.

"Can of worms," Jervis said softly.

"I only had one. If you don't count the shooter," Doc said. "How many did you have?"

"Eight. I don't imagine you're in any danger," Jervis added. "After all, you're the only one who knows where Frankie is."

"I'm afraid we're going to have to reschedule with Bree," Doc sighed.

"She'd expect nothing less," Jervis replied.

That was certainly true. Bree had learned a long time ago that things tended to come up. Things like hunting down Frankie's murderous family.

"Shall we kill the shooter?" Jervis asked.

"I didn't get any answers from the woman," Doc admitted. "Do we let them follow us or try to follow them?"

"I think following them is out of the question," Jervis replied. "It's difficult to get behind someone when they're already watching you."

"True. I'll go distract him, and you can grab him. Maybe we can squeeze an answer or two out of him."

Doc stood and walked back out in front of the little cottage. "Are you still here?" he shouted. "I want to talk to Mrs. Foxall. The REAL Mrs. Foxall!"

There was no response; and after a few moments, Jervis reappeared and said, "There's no one out there."

"I'd imagine they put a tracker on the car," Doc said thoughtfully.

His phone rang, and he pulled it out.

"Or not," he said as he showed Jervis the screen.

"Mrs. Foxall?" Jervis asked.

"Mrs. Foxall."

Doc hit the ignore button, and they started walking back towards the car.

Mrs. Foxall called three more times during their quick trek, but Doc still didn't bother to answer. Instead he and

Jervis thoroughly inspected the car. They didn't find any obvious trackers, not to say that there weren't any, but Doc didn't really care one way or the other about trackers. He was more concerned with explosives. After all, it was rather difficult to heal when your body was in a hundred different pieces.

Inspection complete, they got into the car and waited; and this time when the phone rang, Doc answered it.

"Mrs. Foxall."

"Mr. Nettle."

"I was disappointed not to meet you," Doc drawled.

"I was disappointed to have to kill my daughter."

"You didn't have to kill her," Doc replied, working hard to keep his disgust from his voice.

"She was going to betray me; and in my family, betrayal equals death. What is it you want, Mr. Nettle?"

"I want to know why you want Frankie."

"Ghastly name," she muttered. "I cannot imagine what possessed Wesley to call her that. Francesca is a perfectly respectable name."

Doc didn't respond. Every word he said at this point might reveal more of his hand than he wanted.

"Where is the girl?" Mrs. Foxall demanded.

Doc still didn't respond.

"How much do you want?"

"Frankie's freedom."

"That's not possible; she belongs with her family."

Doc wanted to retort that she was with her family, but he didn't. He didn't say a word. He wasn't used to negotiating over the phone. He could tell certain things from Mrs. Foxall's tone, but without seeing her face, he was basically playing blind.

"I'll pay you a million dollars for her location," she said.

Which meant she'd actually pay ten times as much, and it also meant that whatever Frankie knew was worth a hundred times that.

When Doc didn't respond, Mrs. Foxall said, "You're making a very big mistake, Mr. Nettle."

"Maybe," Doc said.

"I will have her."

"You won't," he stated.

"She's not worth your life," she said sternly. "Three million, her location, and you get to live."

"Only if you'll meet me personally for the exchange," Doc said.

"I find I don't entirely trust you," she replied.

"Then I'm afraid we don't have a deal."

"Five million."

"No."

"In that case, I'll have the information tortured out of you."

"You can certainly try," Doc chuckled.

He disconnected before she could respond and put his phone in the car's console.

"This should be fun," he said.

Jervis shrugged. "It's always the same old same old. She'll send ten men after us, and we'll kill them. Then she'll send twenty men after us, and we'll kill them too. Then she'll call and offer you eight million, but you'll say no. Then she'll send thirty men after us—"

"And we'll kill them," Doc broke in. "But isn't it fun?"

"It would be more fun if she'd start with a hundred men."

"It would," Doc replied with a grin. "How many goons do you think five million dollars can hire?"

"A fair amount."

"Whatever Frankie knows..." Doc trailed off.

"It's worth billions," Jervis supplied. "Or at least Mrs. Foxall thinks it's worth billions."

"We should bet on it," Doc said. "I'm going to guess that Frankie was born into a crime syndicate. Later in life, her father regretted his actions, stole a large portion of money from the syndicate, and paid for it with his life. And Frankie's the only person who knows where the money is."

Doc paused to think before saying, "Check that, I think he stole the money, but actually died from some sort of illness." He hadn't forgotten Frankie's anguished expression when he'd told her about healers back in Bora Bora.

"How much are we betting?" Jervis inquired.

"Two hours with Thaddeus?"

"For me if I lose," Jervis agreed. "For you, two hours with Winslow."

Doc cringed. He'd rather spend a hundred hours with Thaddeus. He was used to his gloomy moods. Winslow was just too goddamn cheerful.

"Deal," Doc said, hoping he didn't regret it. "Two awake hours."

"Agreed," Jervis said.

"What's your bet?"

"I'm going to say it's actually a family of scientists, and Frankie's father was working on the development of something new. At some point he realized the awful ramifications of his invention and went underground, taking the invention and Frankie with him. At which point he died, from sickness as you say, and Frankie continued running on her own."

"That's a fascinating suggestion," Doc said. "But for my own sake, I hope you're wrong."

"We'll never know if you don't get a move on," Jervis retorted.

"I'm going," Doc laughed.

He shifted the car into gear and headed back towards Cardiff, eyes scanning the hills as he drove. He knew they'd never make it all the way to the airport. On that, he and Jervis could agree.

5

Doc and Jervis were just outside of Cardiff when a black van pulled out onto the road in front of them.

"Waited longer than I thought they would," Doc observed as a second van pulled in behind them.

"This is exactly where I would have done it," Jervis replied.

"Really? Why?"

"I just said that," Jervis said, tone slightly amused. "I would have waited until the airport."

"Me too," Doc agreed.

He watched the van in his rearview mirror, waiting for them to make their move. At exactly the same time the van in front of them slowed down and the van behind them sped up. Doc considered letting them have it, but he didn't want to give in too easily so he maneuvered his car into the other lane.

"Why are you dragging it out?" Jervis demanded. "If you give them an easy win, their sense of confidence will be inflated, and they'll be that much easier to defeat."

"It's not in my nature," Doc replied.

The second van rammed into Doc's rear fender, pushing Doc's car back towards the other lane. Doc pressed the gas pedal all the way to the floor and zoomed up past the first van.

"You're being ridiculous," Jervis muttered.

Doc rolled his eyes, but he mostly ignored Jervis as he cut in front of the first van and slammed on his brakes. The van collided into the back of Doc's car, but Doc had already let off the brakes and now he let the momentum carry him forward, quickly changing lanes so he didn't crash into the car in front of him.

"If you drag this on too long, someone else might get hurt," Jervis pointed out.

Doc glanced over at the car he was passing and grimaced when he saw a little boy staring out the window at them.

"Fine," Doc said. "I'll let them run us off the road."

"That would be preferable."

Doc waved at the boy, then sped up until he was far in front of the boy's car. He could see the vans trailing behind in the rearview, and he slowed down a little so they could catch up. They were approaching an exit now, and Doc shifted lanes until he was in the exit lane. The vans followed him as he drove down the exit and merged onto a side road.

As soon as they were all three on the side road, one of the vans sped past Doc's car and moved in front of it before slowing down once more.

"You need three vehicles to make this trick work," Doc sighed just before impact. "It's just sloppy. I hate to give it to them."

"For Frankie," Jervis replied.

Doc barely heard him over the sound of metal crumpling.

The airbag burst from the steering wheel, but instead of crushing Doc, it popped on the tip of his extended knife.

"I hate those things," he muttered. "They always get in the way."

The other van crashed into the backend of Doc's car, shaking it violently.

"Horrors," Doc gasped with pretend surprise. "I did not see that coming."

"Be quiet," Jervis said, flicking Doc's arm with his finger.

Doc swallowed a laugh, and they both slumped forward and pretended to be unconscious.

Nothing happened for a long while. Mostly because the car doors had bent, and the goons couldn't figure out how to get in. Doc was beginning to think he and Jervis would just have to free themselves when someone finally broke the driver's side window and started trying to tug Doc through it.

He waited until he was lying fully on the ground and surrounded by crouching goons before opening his eyes and saying, "Tricked you."

Doc grabbed the nearest man's neck and ripped it out before rolling to his feet and throwing a knife at another man.

There were only ten of them, just as Jervis had predicted; and by the time Doc was killing his fourth man, Jervis had already killed the rest.

Doc stretched lazily, enjoying the heat that was coursing from his tattoo out into his body, and said, "Next time, try to leave me some."

"I did," Jervis replied.

"So you did," Doc chuckled.

He walked back to his ruined car and reached in to retrieve his phone from the console. Then he walked up to the first van and looked inside.

"They left the keys in it," he said as he climbed into the driver's seat. "Wasn't that thoughtful?"

"Very."

Doc started the van and headed back towards the highway.

"Can that car be traced to us?" he asked.

"Of course not," Jervis snorted.

"Excellent."

Doc picked up his phone and called Mrs. Foxall.

"I do hope that wasn't your best effort," Doc said when she answered. "And I also hope that your men didn't have anything on them that would connect them to you. That might cause you some trouble when the local police show up to process the scene."

"What do you mean?" she asked carefully.

"Two vans, ten men, all dead."

With that, Doc disconnected.

"I bet we make it all the way to the States this time," he said.

"Given that we're only twenty minutes away from the airport, I'm not going to take that bet," Jervis replied.

Doc laughed softly and said, "Thanks for coming. I know how much you hate to leave Dulcis."

"Yes, but I find that I miss doing things with you."

Doc cast him a wide grin and said, "You've obviously forgotten about the incident in Arkansas."

"I haven't."

"You said you'd never go anywhere with me ever again."

"And I didn't," Jervis replied. "Not for ten years. That's equivalent to one never."

"You're making that up," Doc laughed.

"I'm not," Jervis insisted. "In my family, never is ten years, never ever is twenty, a lifetime is thirty, forever is fifty, and an eternity is a hundred. So if I said I'll hate you for all eternity, I really only mean a hundred years."

"But what if you really mean you'll hate me for all eternity?" Doc asked.

"I'd just repeat myself in a hundred years," Jervis shrugged.

"I'm not sure how I feel about that."

"You have to make allowances for life expectancy," Jervis said. "Forever to a vampire is a very, very, very long time. And in most cases, a hundred years is far too long to hold a grudge."

"If I had a grudge large enough to hold for a hundred years, I'd just kill whoever it was," Doc said matter-of-factly.

"Exactly," Jervis replied. "There is one exception," he said softly. "When we say we'll stay by someone's side forever, we mean it in the truest sense."

"That's good," Doc said, unable to entirely cover up his relief. "Because you've been with me for more than two forevers already."

"You have to stop worrying, Hans."

"I don't know that I can," Doc sighed. "People leave me. They always have."

"Not by choice."

"Some by choice," Doc retorted, thinking of Lena and Andrew.

"But not I," Jervis said firmly. "All the hellions in all the world could not pull me from your side."

Doc nodded, but as much as Jervis assured him and as much as Doc was convinced that Jervis would never leave him, he still worried.

"Luck hates a worrier," he muttered. "I'm glad you came," he added. "I've missed you as well."

He parked beside the plane and studied it for a moment before saying, "Do you think they managed to get anyone on the plane?"

"I don't get the impression this is their specialty," Jervis replied.

"Damn," Doc said. "That probably means the crime syndicate is out."

"Perhaps," Jervis agreed.

"Is there a time of day that Winslow is less cheerful?"

"No," Jervis said disdainfully.

"Whatever possessed you to hire him in the first place?"

"He passed the application process. All seven tiers."

"What does that mean?"

"Applicants have to pass at least two of the tiers to even be considered for hiring. These are mostly just simple questions that test their level of cognition and so on. If they pass five of the tiers, which cleverly encompass some of the morality issues that might occasionally arise in our employ, they might be considered for the special teams. I have never had anyone pass all seven tiers."

"Do you think I could pass it?" Doc asked.

"Easily. You and I have lived a long time, and our thinking and actions reflect that."

"But Winslow passed all seven?"

"Yes."

"Interesting. Too bad he had the impudence to be born a norm," Doc said. "A cheerful norm at that."

"It's the popular disease this season," Jervis replied. "Are you sitting here because you want them to catch up with us?"

"I never say no to an inflight meal," Doc drawled. "Besides, you said I had to take it easy on them since they're clearly not very good at their jobs."

"Not this easy."

"Let's go then," Doc said cheerfully.

They both exited the van and headed towards the plane. Once they were on board, Jervis checked in with the pilot, and Doc did a quick sweep of the plane, but no one was hiding in any of the dark corners and nothing seemed out of place.

"Where are we going?" Doc asked when Jervis returned.

"North Carolina."

"That'll be fun."

Doc shuffled his cards and dealt out two hands of gin. Jervis sat and picked up his cards.

"Have you always had an application test?" Doc asked as he drew a card.

"Since 1927," Jervis replied. "You remember Henry Birchman."

Doc cringed and said, "Unfortunately. I should have Fernsby delete that portion of my memory."

"If only," Jervis sighed. "I designed the application test after Henry's time at Dulcis."

"You did a fine job," Doc praised. "We've never once had another Henry."

"No, just Pierre."

"That was hardly your fault," Doc argued. "He worked for us over nine years before he turned on us."

"I never did like him," Jervis admitted. "I should have trusted my instincts."

"A test can never trump instincts," Doc agreed. "I didn't like him either; but when food has lost all meaning, he could at least cook up something that tasted good."

"That's exactly why I put up with him; his cooking was unrivaled."

"Gin," Doc said.

He took the cards and shuffled again.

Jervis's phone rang, and he pulled it out and frowned at it. "It's Winslow," he said as he stood and strode to the other side of the plane.

Doc watched him with a slight grin, feeling very glad that Jervis wasn't employing fake forevers on him.

The curved wall of the airplane faded, and Doc drifted into a memory. He was sitting on one side of a small fire, and Jervis was sitting on the other. They hadn't said a word in a while now, but Doc didn't mind. He was too fascinated by the prospect of another person who could potentially live as long as he could. A person who had already lived Doc's life nearly twelve times over.

"What's it like to live so long?" Doc asked in French.

"What's it like to talk so much?" Jervis replied in German.

"I hardly talk at all," Doc snorted. "You should meet Andrew. He loves to talk."

"I'd rather not."

Jervis hadn't yet asked Doc's name, so Doc said, "I'm Doc, by the way."

Jervis looked up from the fire, silvery eyes glinting. "Doc?"

"Doc."

"That's your given name?"

"No."

"What is your given name?"

"John, but I rarely answer to it."

"I absolutely refuse to call you Doc," Jervis said.

Doc grinned slightly and said, "It's my name."

"It's a pet name, and you are not a pet. Can we settle on Hans?"

"Sure," Doc shrugged.

It was really all the same to him. He just didn't like answering to John because it reminded him of his mother. And also when people were spreading tales of intrigue about him, John Holliday sounded rather quiet and plain but Doc Holliday sounded exciting and robust.

"What city are you traveling to?" Jervis asked.

"Any city," Doc replied.

"You're trying to lose yourself," Jervis stated.

"A bit, but for some reason, it's terribly hard to do."

"I know," Jervis said, tone unbelievably sad.

Doc blinked and refocused on the present and the present-Jervis sitting across from him.

"Crisis handled?" Doc asked.

"Maybe," Jervis sighed. "What were you thinking about?"

"You refusing to call me Doc."

"That's a decision I certainly do not regret," Jervis said, lips curling upwards.

"No one else has a problem with my name," Doc pointed out.

"It's not a name; it's a title."

"You've no imagination."

"Gin."

"Damn," Doc muttered. "You distracted me."

Jervis grinned fully and said, "I did."

They played several more rounds before Jervis said, "I'd better get in another nap before we land. Once I return to Dulcis, I won't have a moment's rest."

"It's only been a day. I don't think Sami has missed you that much," Doc chuckled.

"Winslow hired another chef."

"So now we have two?"

"Three. For some reason he thinks we should have a more diverse menu."

Doc rolled his eyes and said, "It's not about quantity."

"I know."

"It's about quality. Six dishes done well."

"I know."

"He really passed the test?"

"Yes," Jervis said as he adjusted his seat and closed his eyes. "He really did."

For a moment, Doc imagined the Dulcis menu with folds instead of just being a single sheet, and he shuddered. He always chose quality over quantity. He always chose quality over cost. That's what made Dulcis so special. Not a single corner had been cut. The quality of the sheets was exactly the same as it had been a hundred years ago. So what if they'd had to create their own linens business to make the sheets. It was worth it.

Doc tapped his fingers on the table, mind drifting from Dulcis to Frankie. Francesca Falon Foxall was keeping a lot of secrets, and it annoyed him. Not that she was keeping them, but that she hadn't even considered that he might be able to help her. Living on the run, always looking over your shoulder, always worrying that one day they'd catch up to you was no way to live at all. Doc knew because Jervis had lived like that for nearly two hundred years.

If Solomon had found Jervis at Dulcis, they would have lost Dulcis and Denver. They would have lost everything they had worked to build. But Lady Luck had been with them. Or maybe Dulcis had a personality of its own, and it had shielded Jervis. After all, Jervis had saved it.

Doc smiled as he remembered the first time he'd seen the building that would one day become Dulcis.

He hadn't thought much of it at first glance, and his opinion hadn't improved as he and Jervis had walked up the very worn stairs of Holderman Luxury Suites.

"You want to buy this?" Doc said with a gesture at a torn strip of wallpaper. "Wouldn't it be easier to tear it down and build a new one?"

"Absolutely not," Jervis insisted. "This building has character. It has soul. A new building is empty, void. This is the one I want."

"Do I have enough funds?" Doc asked.

"Barely. We'll need more for the restoration," Jervis said, handing Doc a hundred dollar bill. "This is all that's left."

Doc took the bill and grinned widely. "I'll go make some magic happen."

He had too. He'd made lots of magic happen. So much magic, in fact, that Jervis had been able to hire three crews to work on the hotel.

And it was because of one of those dark gambling tables in some smoky backroom that Doc had met Lena. He grinned at the mere thought of her and allowed himself to drift into a different memory.

"Call," he said as he tossed a five dollar bill onto the pile of money.

His opponent had a pretty good hand; Doc could just tell from the way he was sitting. But Doc had luck on his side, and a straight flush, so he was willing to bet that he was going to win.

The man laid his cards onto the table and sat back, face satisfied. Doc flipped over his hand without looking at it and kept his eyes on his opponent. The color left the man's face, and his eyes narrowed, but he didn't argue, just said, "You win."

"I know," Doc drawled. "I'm done for the night," he added as he pulled the pile of money towards him.

"Good to know when to walk away," the man agreed.

"Did you walk away soon enough?" Doc asked.

"Sure."

He hadn't, but that was hardly Doc's problem. He never bet when he couldn't afford to lose.

"My sister sings here," the man went on. "She says you never lose."

"That's hardly true," Doc shrugged.

"She says you're the luckiest player she's ever seen."

"Now that is true," Doc chuckled.

He carefully tucked the money into his coat pocket before giving the man his full attention.

"Are you going somewhere with this?" Doc asked.

A conversation like this usually ended with someone accusing him of cheating, but he didn't think that's where this particular conversation was going.

"How lucky are you?" the man asked.

"Incredibly lucky."

"Name a card."

Doc raised an eyebrow, but decided to play along. "The four of spades."

The man drew a card from the deck and revealed it. It was a four of spades.

"Name another one."

"The queen of clubs."

The man drew another card. It was the queen of clubs.

"Another."

"How long are we going to do this?" Doc drawled.

"Just once more," the man insisted.

"The jack of diamonds."

The man threw a card onto the table, and Doc didn't even need to look to know it was the jack of diamonds.

"If I was as lucky as you are, I'd never quit playing," the man said.

"You have to know when to walk away," Doc replied easily.

"Come to dinner with me," he insisted. "My sister wants to meet you."

"I'm not the marrying kind," Doc said firmly.

"Neither is she."

"I know when to walk away," Doc repeated as he stood.

"She walks every day in City Park," the man said. "Around lunchtime. She takes a book and sits at the feet of Burns and reads. Her name's Lena."

Doc paused and turned to study the man. "Why do you care?" he demanded, curiosity fully roused by the man's insistence.

"Her eyes light up when she talks about you." He smiled sadly and added, "I miss seeing her eyes light up."

"I understand," Doc said softly, "but I can't help you."

"Just think about it," the man urged.

For days, Doc ignored the man's plea. He didn't do things because other people wanted him to. Not ever. But his curiosity finally overrode his common sense; and one fine afternoon, he went walking in City Park near Burns' statue.

And there she was. Lena.

He recognized her instantly. She sang beautiful French songs, which were made even more beautiful by her sensuous tones. Doc had watched her surreptitiously several times. In fact, he watched her so much that he had actually lost once.

She looked up from her book and met his eyes, almost as if she'd been expecting him.

"What are you reading?" he asked as he sat beside her.

"Burns," she replied. "It would be rude to read anything else while sitting at his feet."

"Which one is your favorite?"

"*Epigram on Miss Davies*," she replied, grey eyes twinkling.

Doc swallowed a snort and said, "Interesting choice."

She shrugged one delicate shoulder and said, "Which one is your favorite?"

"*Address to a Haggis*."

She burst out laughing, and he joined her. They laughed loudly for several minutes, but once she'd regained control of herself, she held out her hand and said, "I'm Lena Danser."

"Doc Holliday," he replied.

And with those words, his life was changed forever.

6

"We're here," Jervis said, breaking into Doc's fond memories of Lena.

Doc glanced out the window and said, "What do you suggest we do now?"

"Go to a hotel?" Jervis offered.

"You know how I feel about other people's hotels," Doc muttered.

"And you know how I feel about other people's hotels," Jervis retorted.

"Exactly. You don't think they're already out there waiting for us?"

"One can hope."

"Fine," Doc sighed. "But it can't be one of the hotel chains. Remember when Motel 6 started popping up all over the country?"

"They wanted people to travel," Jervis said pragmatically. "So they needed to provide them places to stay."

"I don't care," Doc shuddered. "They had televisions in every room."

"That's considered standard now," Jervis stated.

"We don't do that, do we?" Doc demanded.

"Hardly. People don't stay at Dulcis to watch television."

"You had me worried there. If we dally long enough, maybe we won't have to leave the airport," Doc added hopefully. "I bet she sends eighteen men this time."

"Twenty-one," Jervis countered.

"For two measly men?" Doc laughed.

"Fifteen more minutes with Winslow," Jervis said.

"Deal."

Doc finally stood and headed towards the exit. They made it all the way to the town car Jervis had rented before three vans drove out onto the airfield and surrounded them.

Doc leaned against the rented town car and waited for them to exit the vans, but they didn't. Instead one of the doors slid open, and a man yelled, "Get in the van!"

"What's my motivation?" Doc asked.

"We'll shoot you!"

"You can't shoot me," Doc replied. "You need me."

A gun fired, and Doc saw Jervis's shoulder twitch.

"That was very foolish," Doc said as he hurled a knife into the van.

Heat rushed into Doc's tattoo, but he blocked the sensation and focused on the men who were leaping out of the van. He threw knife after knife with perfect precision until all of them were dead, and he was just turning to check the other vans, when the first van started to back away.

"I don't think so," Doc snarled.

He dashed in front of it and hurled a knife as hard as he could towards the driver. The knife crashed through the van's windshield and into the driver's head, completely obliterating the man's face.

He turned around, knife in hand, but there was no one left to kill; Jervis had already finished the rest of them. Doc put away his knife with a sigh and waited for Jervis to step out of the third van.

"You killed nine," Jervis remarked as he wiped away a bit of blood that had splattered on his chin. "I killed twelve."

"And that's... damn," Doc muttered. "Exactly twenty-one. Are you positive?"

"Yes. That's fifteen minutes for you."

"Yes, I know," Doc grumbled.

He pulled out his phone and called Mrs. Foxall.

"You're going to have to try harder than that," he said when she answered.

"Whatever do you mean?"

"Twenty-one goons, three vans, all dead," he stated. "It grows wearisome," he added.

"Eight million dollars," she offered.

Doc covered the microphone and said, "You called it."

"Eight million?"

"Eight million." He uncovered the phone and said, "Only if you give me the money in person."

"Why would I do that?"

"Why wouldn't you do that?"

"Ten million."

"No."

"You are making your life very difficult, Mr. Nettle."

"No," Doc laughed. "You're making your life difficult."

He hung up, pulled the sim card from his phone, and destroyed both it and the phone.

"Next time, let's keep one alive," Doc said as he returned to the plane.

"Only if I get to torture him," Jervis replied.

Doc cringed and said, "I'd rather you didn't."

"It's much more expedient."

"Fine," Doc muttered. "You can do it. I'm betting it'll only take five minutes before he breaks and tells us everything about everything."

"Three," Jervis countered.

"Deal."

When they landed in Wisconsin, they made it all the way to their room at the Charmant Hotel in La Crosse. Doc was eating the pillow truffle when someone knocked on the door.

"Seems a shame to ruin this room," he said thoughtfully.

"Shall we jump off the balcony?" Jervis asked.

Doc opened the sliding door and walked out onto the deck, feeling pleased when he saw that it was already late evening and there weren't any pedestrians out and about. He'd much rather fight outside than get blood all over the clean white bedspread.

"Good idea," he said as he grabbed the deck railing. He looked back at Jervis and said, "I'm having the best time."

"Me too," Jervis said with a grin. "Come in!" he called over his shoulder, and then he ran out onto the deck and leapt over the railing.

"We're going down," Doc said cheerfully when the first goon poked his head inside the room.

Doc waved and then jumped over the railing, laughing when he heard the man cursing violently from the room above him.

There was a park bench on a nearby patch of grass, and Doc joined Jervis there.

"I think it'll take them at least a full minute to figure out what happened," Doc said.

"Thirty seconds," Jervis countered.

Doc checked his watch. "Are we counting from when we jumped?" he asked.

The goon from the room was out on the deck now, glancing around frantically. When he saw Doc and Jervis on the bench, he turned with a yell and ran back inside.

It was another minute before a handful of men poured out onto the street from the side door of the hotel.

"I don't think either one of us won that bet," Doc said. "It was a hard one to gauge. There're only fifteen of them," he added with disappointment.

"Give it a minute," Jervis advised.

As the men rushed towards them, another group of men ran around the side of the building.

"Thirty-nine," Doc said after doing a quick count. "We should do it the hard way this time."

"If we must."

"We must," Doc laughed. "Any preference on who you want to keep?"

"The short one on the end," Jervis said. "I can hear his heart from here."

"Done," Doc replied as he carefully, and with very little force, hurled one of his knives. It hit the man's head handle first; and once the man had dropped to the ground, Doc turned his attention to the other goons, sighing when a man crashed into him with a stun gun.

Doc barely felt the jolt of electricity course through him, and he easily tore the gun from his attacker's hand and shoved the probes into the man's neck. The man's eyes widened in shock as the electricity pulsed into him, but as soon as his eyes rolled upward, Doc released the stun gun and snapped the man's neck.

There were already four more men surrounding Doc, stun

batons outstretched. Doc grinned and stalked towards the first one. He slapped the man's baton to the side, hardly noticing when the other batons made contact with his body and electricity jolted into his system.

Doc drew a knife and jabbed his hand forward, stabbing both his knife and his hand through the first man's neck. The body dropped, pulling Doc's hand with it. He ripped his hand free and spun around, snatching one of the batons as he did. Doc stabbed forward with the baton, piercing a man's stomach, then he tore the baton loose and slashed it across another man's face. He threw two knives just to give himself a little room to move about, then shoved the baton through the nearest man's eye.

A wire suddenly dropped over Doc's head and wrapped around his neck, then yanked tightly. Doc didn't fight it, just allowed himself to be pulled backwards for a second. Once he felt that the man dragging him had triumphed enough, Doc wrapped his fingers around the wire, pulled it away from his neck, and sliced through it with his knife. The pole dropped, but Doc turned and caught it with his foot, then flipped it up into his hand.

"Clever," he said as he launched the pole towards the man who'd tried to catch him. The pole speared through the man's chest and into the man standing behind him.

A man grabbed Doc from behind, but Doc broke free, turned, and shattered the bones in the man's face with the heel of his hand. As the man fell to the ground, Doc quickly surveyed the grassy area.

Jervis was sitting on the park bench once more, casually licking the blood from his fingers. He had already killed most of the men, but there were still five of them warily circling Doc.

Doc rushed towards them, crashing into one of them and

falling to the ground with him. Before the man could launch a defense, Doc had already stabbed him through the ear.

Another jolt of electricity tickled Doc's back, but it was nothing compared to the heat that was pulsing out to his body from his tattoo.

Doc rolled off the dead man onto the grass and kicked out with his feet, knocking two of the men backwards. A siren sounded in the distance, and Doc sighed. Playtime was obviously over. He quickly threw four knives, killing the remaining men, and rolled to his feet.

"I thought we were doing this the hard way," Doc grumbled as he slung the unconscious man over his shoulder and followed after Jervis.

"We did," Jervis replied. "It just so happens that your hard way is harder than mine. Besides, you ran out of time, and I didn't."

Doc didn't respond, just grunted. Going on a killing spree with Jervis was very similar to going on a killing spree with Andrew. He could just never move fast enough.

"Exactly five minutes!" Doc crowed a little while later when the man he had knocked unconscious began to offer up information. "Fifteen minutes for you!"

"Be quiet!" Jervis snapped. "Where is Mrs. Foxall?" he asked the bound man.

"I don't know," he blubbered.

The man's face was already a bloody mess, and Doc could barely stand to look at him. Jervis never dillydallied with torture. He had always insisted that it was much kinder to get right to the point.

"We're for hire," the man insisted. "She just contacted us, gave us the job, and the money."

"Where were you going to deliver the package?" Jervis asked.

"Alpha Team Leader was supposed to call her."

"Damn," Doc muttered.

"How did you know where to find us?"

"Someone called us and told us where to go."

The man may have broken in five minutes, but he didn't know anything useful at all. Jervis hadn't made it hard to follow them. The most amateur of amateurs could have achieved it.

"I don't think he knows anything useful," Doc said.

"I realize that," Jervis sighed. "I have a plan," he added.

"And that plan is?"

Jervis didn't immediately respond because he was holding the man's chin and draining him dry of blood. The man's eyes quickly glazed, and Jervis released him.

"I haven't feasted this much since the last time we went out," he said as he dabbed the blood from his face.

"Fun, isn't it?"

"Indeed," Jervis replied. "Now, here's what we're going to do."

It was an interesting plan, one Doc didn't fully approve of. And if it had been anyone but Jervis, he wouldn't have allowed it. But it was Jervis. It had taken more than a hundred Sons of Solomon to capture him. And they'd had to use a whale harpoon to do it.

"Your pant legs are too long," Doc complained as he pulled on Jervis's pants. "And I doubt they know what I'm wearing in any case."

"Stop complaining," Jervis commanded.

Doc tugged Jervis's jacket into place and muttered, "How

on earth did you manage to get so much blood on you? Even my jacket is cleaner than yours."

"I'm a vampire," Jervis said dryly. "I drink blood."

Doc wiggled his shoulders. "Your jacket is nicer than mine," he complained.

"I get our clothing from the same tailor," Jervis sighed. "There's no difference. Maybe your sizing has just changed. I haven't checked it in over fifty years."

"I don't see how my sizing could have changed," Doc grumbled. "I don't gain weight. Or muscle. Or height."

"I thought you were having fun."

"I was. But now you're going to have all the fun."

"For Frankie," Jervis said sternly.

"Fine," Doc grumbled.

"Does this look right?" Jervis asked.

"How should I know?" Doc shrugged. "I don't stare at my face in the mirror."

"Hans."

"Fine," Doc sighed. He stared at Jervis, whose face currently resembled Doc's. It was a strange sight to say the least.

"I don't think my cheeks are that hollow," he finally said.

Jervis's cheeks moved slightly.

"Better," Doc said. "I hope you can remember what your old face looked like. I don't think Sami will like you much if you don't. Besides, I loathe it when you change faces. It always takes me at least a year to get used to the new one."

"Quit griping," Jervis said. "Wait until I text you to let you know I've left the airport. Then you'll board the plane I hired for you."

"I know," Doc said. "You've already told me three times."

"You tend not to listen," Jervis stated. "Be careful."

"They won't be chasing me," Doc retorted. "I almost feel sorry for them. Almost," he added with a grin.

"Enough procrastinating," Jervis chastised. "Get in the box."

"I don't want to."

"For Frankie."

"Stop doing that!" Doc snapped. "It's manipulating."

"Is it?" Jervis asked innocently.

"You know that it is," Doc retorted. "Why can't I just walk off the plane? They're probably not watching yet."

"I can't change your face; just mine," Jervis said. "Get in the box."

"You know how much I hate tight dark spaces," Doc complained.

"It will only take me two minutes to transport you to the empty hangar. Less if you'd stop complaining."

"Fine," Doc growled.

He shoved the porkpie hat Jervis had given him onto his head and climbed into the wooden box.

"No nails!" he yelled as Jervis leveraged the lid into place.

"As if they would stop you. I saw you shove your hand completely through someone; I don't think you'd have much trouble with a crate."

"It's all the witches I ate," Doc replied, trying to fight back the claustrophobia by talking. "Although I had thought it would wear off by now."

"I doubt if something like that wears off," Jervis stated. "Now hush. You can get out as soon as I text you."

Doc forced himself to remain quiet as Jervis wheeled the crate off the plane. The wheels went over a bump, and Doc murmured, "Not a coffin." But, quite without his consent, that memory pulled at him until he was once more lying in his wooden coffin as it was hauled to his grave.

The wagon bumped over the rocky ground, and Doc bumped along with it. He couldn't move, couldn't open his eyes, couldn't open his lips to scream. Señora Teodora had cursed him; he was going to be buried alive.

Inside the fear was a thread of disgust. He'd completely wasted his life. He'd accomplished nothing. He'd frittered away every moment on whiskey and cards. And for what? To die alone in a cold hotel with nothing to show for it.

His father was probably so disappointed. Francisco would certainly be disappointed if he were still alive. And Doc didn't even want to imagine what his mother would think. She'd look at him with sorrow in her eyes and say something like, "I love you, John." The guilt of it would kill him. If he wasn't already dead.

Señora Teodora's voice whispered through his hazy mind. "You may never die."

He liked the sound of that. He didn't want to die; he wasn't ready. He hadn't done much of anything, and there was so much left to do.

He hoped the fact that he could feel the coldness of the air around him meant that she hadn't lied to him, that he was really going to live; but he couldn't be sure.

If he hadn't been paralyzed, he would have gasped in fear when his coffin was dumped into a hole in the ground. At least he assumed it was a hole. That was how they normally buried people. Deep in the earth. So deep that their cries for liberation couldn't be heard.

He was dead. He was a dead man. The pain of it tore at him. The complete uselessness of it. What had he done? Nothing. What mark had he made? None.

A shovelful of dirt dropped onto the lid, and he began to doubt Señora Teodora's promise. Why would she go out of her way to save a man like him? He was nothing special. He was worse than nothing special. He was worthless.

Maybe this was her revenge after all. Maybe this was his hell.

He would have screamed if he could. He would have sobbed and railed against the fates. But he couldn't. He was dead. He was dead.

How long he lay there in his anguish he could not say. But when he heard a shovel crack against the top of his coffin, his heart leapt with relief. Just as his heart leapt with relief at the sound of his phone beeping. He'd been so lost in his memory, he hadn't even realized that Jervis had left him.

Doc pushed against the lid of the box, exhaling in relief when the lid opened easily and the light of the hangar touched his face.

"I hate boxes," he muttered as he pulled himself out. "I swear Jervis did that to me on purpose."

He popped the lid back onto the crate and leapt up on top of it. He sat there, idly swinging his legs against the side as he waited for Jervis's second text.

He wondered how many men Jervis would face when he landed and silently bet himself it would be fifty-five. Mrs. Foxall was a slow learner. She hadn't quite figured out that she wasn't going to win.

Doc always knew when he was going to lose. Except once.

He didn't bother to resist the memory that pulled at him. It wasn't as if he had anything else to do.

"Look, Doc," Lena said, tugging him onto the grass. "It's a swing set. You have to push me."

"I have to?" Doc chuckled.

"You do. You carried my books home from school," she

said, batting her long eyelashes. "And now you have to push me on the swing. Maybe, if you're a very good suitor, I'll let you kiss my cheek later."

She always let him kiss her cheek. And her neck and the spot behind her ear. But if it would make her happy, he'd play out her scene.

She sat primly on the swing and said, "You may push me now."

He leaned down and whispered in her ear. "What if instead we go home, and I kiss that place you like on the inside of your wrist?"

"Absolutely not!" Lena laughed. "I want to swing."

He gave into futility and pushed her gently.

"Harder!" she demanded.

Lena never did anything halfway. If she was doing it, she was doing it all the way. It was one of the reasons he loved her.

Doc's phone beeped, pulling him back into the present once more.

"You may go now," Jervis said. "Wear the hat."

Doc rolled his eyes. As if he needed reminded.

He hopped off the box, removed the lid, and pulled the crate over onto its side so he could reach the hat inside. He'd been planning to wear it; he'd just forgotten.

He shoved the hat on his head, walked to the door of the hangar, and peeked outside. The dark airfield in front of him was completely vacant of people.

He tilted the hat low over his head and walked quickly towards the plane Jervis had pointed out earlier. It was just a small two-seater, and the pilot was waiting for him inside of it.

"Mr. Mackey?" he asked when Doc opened the door.

"That's me," Doc replied.

"Take a seat," the pilot ordered. "And I'll get you to Denver before you can say Jack Sprat."

"Jack Sprat," Doc said.

"Not to be taken literally," the pilot laughed. "The name's Stanley."

"Nice to meet you," Doc said.

Stanley handed him a headset and said, "Let's get going."

The flight was only a couple of hours, and it did go rather quickly. Stanley knew better than to fill the silence, so for the most part, they didn't talk at all.

When they landed in Denver, Doc handed him a card and several hundred dollar bills and said, "If you ever need work, give me a call."

"You already paid me," Stanley insisted, trying to give the money back to Doc.

"This is a tip," Doc said with a grin. "And you can keep the hat."

Stanley laughed cheerfully before saying, "Thanks a bunch, Mr. Mackey. Maybe I'll see you around!"

Doc cast him a wave, then walked towards the unmarked Dulcis van that was waiting for him.

It was after midnight, but Doc didn't want to wait for answers. He wanted answers now. So when he slid into the passenger seat, he grinned at Emily and said, "Take me to the Bakers."

7

"What's wrong?" Babs demanded when she opened the door for Doc a bit later.

"Nothing much," Doc said. "I just need to talk to Frankie."

"Frankie?"

"Frankie."

Her eyes narrowed, but she opened the door wider and allowed Doc to step inside.

"I'll go get her," she said.

It took a few minutes for Frankie to appear at the top of the staircase. Her face was ashen, and she walked down the stairs as slowly as possible. Boudica was trailing behind her, but when they reached the bottom of the stairs, Boudica moved in front of Frankie and growled menacingly.

"Oh hush," Doc said before meeting Frankie's terrified eyes. "You and I need to have a little chat."

"About what?" she asked.

"You tell me, Francesca."

He hadn't thought it was possible for her face to turn whiter, but it did. She swallowed visibly, and Doc instantly regretted not easing her into the conversation a bit more. Just because it was easier for him to lay all his cards on the table, didn't mean it was easier for Frankie.

"Would you like to take a walk?" he offered.

"It's nearly two o'clock in the morning!" Babs exclaimed. "What is going on?"

"I really don't know," Doc replied. "But I'm hoping Frankie will tell me."

Frankie looked between them both before saying softly, "Is it okay if I go outside with Doc?"

"I don't know why you're asking me," Babs grumbled. "You're practically a grown woman, and I've no business telling you what to do. Do you want to go outside with Doc?" she added hurriedly. "Because if you don't, I'll cuff him upside the head and tell him to scram."

Frankie almost smiled. "I'd kinda like to see that," she said. "But I should probably talk to him."

"Go on then," Babs told her. "But when you come back inside, make sure you don't wake me. I've become attached to my beauty sleep."

Frankie nodded, then she and Boudica followed Doc outside. He would have rather sat her down in the library and interrogated her face to face, but he thought she might answer his questions more easily this way.

"I spoke to your grandmother yesterday," Doc said.

A slight intake of air from Frankie told him that she wasn't happy about his statement.

"You didn't... I mean... She doesn't..."

"I didn't tell her anything," Doc said. "I did think it was curious how much she wants to find you though. Her first offer was low. It was only a hundred thousand, but the last time I talked to her, it was up to ten million."

"Ten million?" Frankie gasped.

"A pittance," Doc replied. "I would easily pay a hundred million to find you."

"What for?" she asked.

"Because you're my family," Doc said. "And money is absolutely no object when it comes to family. I made it once; I can make it again, but there's only one Frankie Falon Foxall."

Even in the dark he could tell she was crying, and he reached out and pulled her into his arms.

"I'm sorry," he whispered. "I shouldn't have asked the way I did. I'm just annoyed at your grandmother. She doesn't deserve you. No one in your family deserves you."

"Dad deserved me," she whimpered.

Doc reserved comment. He didn't know anything about her father, so whether or not Wesley Foxall had deserved to be in Frankie's life was yet to be seen.

She continued to cry silently; but after a while, she cleared her throat and stepped away from him.

"Let's go to the treehouse," she suggested. "And I'll tell you what I know."

That wasn't overly promising, but Doc would take it.

They didn't speak as they walked through the dark towards the tree house, but Boudica growled when Frankie started up the ladder.

"It's alright, Boudica," Frankie assured her. "Doc just wants to talk."

Boudica's glowing blue eyes turned to Doc, and he focused on an image of Frankie happy. "That's my goal," he whispered. Boudica glared at him for another second, but she finally stepped out of the way so Doc could go up the ladder after Frankie.

Once they were inside the first room of the treehouse, Frankie lit an oil lamp and set it on a short table. She grabbed one of the beanbag chairs and sat on it, gesturing for him to do the same.

"Did you see Muriel?" she asked.

"Is that your grandmother?" Doc asked as he carefully sat on one of the beanbags.

She nodded.

"No. I just talked to her on the phone. I saw your aunt."

Frankie cringed and asked, "May, April, or June?"

"Really?" Doc asked.

"Really."

"With names like those, what could Muriel possibly have against Frankie?"

"It's was Dad's pet name for me," Frankie said softly.

"Did Muriel and Wesley not get along?"

"You know his name?"

"Muriel mentioned it."

Frankie stared past Doc's shoulder for a long time before she finally said, "They did, and they didn't."

"What does Muriel want from you?"

"What Dad found."

"Maybe you can start at the beginning," Doc prodded.

"Dad's an... was an archaeologist," Frankie mumbled.

"Rats," Doc sighed.

"What?"

"Jervis and I bet. I thought crime syndicate; he thought scientist. If I don't spin this just right, he'll say he won because I'm pretty sure some people consider archaeology a science."

She was staring at him with confusion, so he waved a hand and said, "It doesn't matter. Go on."

"There's an old Scottish legend," Frankie said softly. "It talks about fairies and fae mounds."

"Really?" Doc said evenly, trying to pretend as if he didn't know what she was talking about.

"Look, Jules told me ages ago fairies are real," Frankie said. "But my family doesn't know about the Hidden and cryptids. They can never know about the Hidden," she added a little fearfully.

"On that we agree," Doc said.

"Muriel and Oscar, that's my grandpa," she added before Doc could ask. "They met at some kind of archaeology lecture a long time ago. They started doing digs together, and they uncovered a lot of amazing finds. My dad and his sisters all worked with them. I also have a few cousins," she added in an undertone.

"A few?"

"Nine."

"Foxall Family Archeology," Doc said cheerfully.

"Something like that," Frankie admitted. "About thirty years ago, Oscar was excavating a site, and he found this really strange artifact. It was the only one of its kind that he found there, and he'd never seen anything like it before. No one had. There was this one man though who had been cast out of the proper circles for touting ridiculous theories," Frankie explained. "When Oscar showed him the artifact, he said it was fae."

"So they became obsessed with the fae?" Doc guessed.

"Not exactly. The artifact was pure gold."

"They became obsessed with fae treasure," Doc amended.

"Pretty much. And it's stupid!" Frankie exclaimed. "Do you know how much money they already had?"

"Over ten million?" Doc guessed.

"Exactly!" Her face was angry, but she continued on, "Apparently Oscar and Muriel started hunting down anything they could about the fae, and one of the legends they found suggested that there's an entrance to the fae treasure room in Wales. Like they would have just written that down," Frankie said irritably.

"Did they?" Doc asked.

"No! Muriel's on a wild goose chase!"

"Then why did you run?"

Her shoulders slumped, and she said, "Muriel's on a wild goose chase... in Wales."

"Oh."

"Dad worked with them for years trying to find the entrance, but after Mom left us, he went off on his own. He just wanted to find exciting things that no one else had seen yet," Frankie said, eyes wistful. "He just liked discovering things."

She sighed heavily and said, "He took me everywhere with him. I can't remember anything before Mom left; the first dig I remember was outside of Bagan. Dad could convince anyone to let him dig. Anyone!" She grinned widely and said, "He was a great salesman."

"What happened to him?" Doc asked.

"It was the last dig," she said, grin fading. "He'd just discovered the key, and he knew what it meant. So he hid it, and that night we snuck in to retrieve it. He could have just carried it out, but then it would have been on the list, and he didn't want anyone to know about it. He'd set some charges to blow up the whole site, and he was hoping they'd think we'd died in the explosion."

She stopped here, and Doc knew she was reliving the moment.

"One of the charges blew early," she said. "And a piece of debris pierced his shoulder. He yanked it out, and we ran. We flew to Colorado that same night."

She stopped again, and Doc fought his urge to comfort her and tell her she didn't need to go on. He wanted to help her, and he couldn't unless she told him her story. He needed her to finish.

"The wound made him sick," she whispered. "And he wouldn't go to the hospital, and I didn't know what to do for him. He just sat there at the motel table, transcribing that stupid golden tablet. I don't even know how he knew what it said. I've never seen a language like it. One day, he finished it, I guess, and he left for a long time. When he came back he was barely upright. He handed me his journal, said the key was hidden inside, and then he collapsed onto the floor."

Frankie was crying again, and he barely heard what she said next. "I wanted to call someone, but he'd made me promise that no matter what, I wouldn't talk to anyone. He woke once, and he said, 'never stop running', and then... and then... he died. And all I have left of him is a journal I can't read and a psychotic family that will kill me as soon as they find me."

She snorted and said, "I can't... How could he do that to me?"

"I'm certain he never wanted to leave you," Doc said.

"Then why didn't he go to the hospital?"

"Did he have multiple IDs?" Doc asked.

"Like aliases? No."

"He didn't go to a hospital because Muriel would have found him, and he was trying to protect what he'd found," Doc said.

"Screw what he found!" Frankie snapped. "He should have been protecting me!"

"He should have been," Doc agreed.

"I was fourteen! I walked out of the hotel onto the streets of Denver with two hundred dollars. What was I supposed to do?"

"Find the Bakers," Doc said softly.

"That was a fluke," Frankie muttered.

"So basically a stroke of good luck," Doc chuckled.

"I guess. I mean yes!" she said quickly. "I was just standing in the street in front of their house, and a red-haired woman, Mrs. Baker, walked up to me and grabbed my arm. She yelled at me for dallying, said the children had already had their breakfast, and shoved me inside the house."

A very large stroke of good luck, Doc thought.

"Apparently they were waiting for a nanny from some kind of witch agency, and Mrs. Baker assumed I was the one."

"Serendipitous," Doc murmured.

"Yeah," Frankie said softly. "It really was."

"If your family wasn't always working outside of the law, why isn't there a record of your birth?" Doc asked.

Frankie rolled her eyes and said, "I was born on site just outside Taxila, Pakistan. To two archeologists. I'm sure they probably meant to record my birth at some point, but present-day was never very interesting to them."

Present day was the most important day, Doc thought. The past was gone, and the future might never exist. He was glad Frankie was with the Bakers now. The Baker children existed in the moment, just like people were meant to.

"What do you suggest I do?" he asked.

"What do you mean?"

"I mean what would you like me to do."

"About what?"

"Your family."

"Oh. I dunno."

"Are they all bad?" Doc asked.

"What do you mean?"

"Would they all kill to get what your father discovered?"

"Well..." Her nose crinkled in thought, then she shrugged and said, "Yeah."

"Even your cousins?"

"They're all older than me," she said. "It got kinda bad towards the end there. One or several of them would always show up at digs we were working because they thought Dad had found something. They beat him up really badly one time. Broke his arm," she muttered. "They just couldn't let it go. They couldn't let us go."

Doc cleared his throat and said carefully, "Are you giving me permission to kill them?"

"Do you really need my permission?" she asked.

"I don't want to hurt you more than you've already been hurt."

"Oh." She shrugged again and said, "It would be nice to actually get my driver's license someday."

"I can get you a new identity," Doc said. "You don't have to hide either way."

"I don't want to change my name," she said softly. "It's the only thing I have left of Dad."

"Then I suppose I'll have to kill them."

"I'm sorry I never told you," she said sadly.

"Why would you tell me? It was really none of my business, but I don't want you to be scared of them forever," Doc said. "I want you to be happy."

"I am," she whispered. "And that makes me feel horrible."

"Your father would want you to be happy," Doc said firmly.

"But we went everywhere together," she whispered. "All over the world. I saw all kinds of amazing things. I saw things that no one else ever had. It doesn't really make sense that I would be happy here!" She gestured wildly and added, "With them!"

"Why not?" Doc asked. "They're wonderful. And where else could you see a wardrobe fly? I've certainly never seen that!"

She giggled softly and said, "They are wonderful."

"And loyal," Doc added. "And fierce."

"Yeah."

"You'd have an easier time getting out of a flood than escaping their love."

Frankie laughed and said, "You think?"

"Yes," Doc said sincerely. "For children who never knew love, they give love without reservation. The second you came into their lives, you belonged to them." He paused, struggling to say what he wanted to say. "And the second you came into my life, well, maybe the second second, you belonged to me."

"Why?" she asked.

"Because you're you," he said, grinning at her.

She ducked her head and stared at the floor in front of her, so he changed the subject and said, "Do you know how I can find your grandmother?"

"I can email her and tell her I'm willing to meet," Frankie mumbled.

"Will she actually come?"

Frankie shrugged. "Who knows?"

"I'm sorry about your father."

"Me too. I miss him." Her face scrunched a little, and she looked at Doc, sad expression in her eyes. "At least, I think I do."

Privately, Doc thought she was probably better off without Wesley Foxall in her life, but he'd never say that. He'd never do anything to ruin her memory of him.

"You don't have to tell me," Doc said, "but key to what?"

"I dunno," she said. "I can't read his journal."

"It's in code or just a different language?"

"Both. It's written in Sanskrit, which I can't read, and it's also in some kind of code."

"How do you know?"

"I tried to translate a paragraph, but it didn't make any sense."

"Have you thought about letting Jules look at it?"

Frankie shrugged and said, "They don't know."

"Do you want them to know?"

"That might be alright," she murmured.

"Only if you want to." He stood and added, "But first things first, if we're going to lure out Mrs. Muriel Foxall, we should eat a good breakfast."

"It's probably only three in the morning; Babs will kill us!" she insisted.

"Nah. We'll be quiet."

"You don't know how to cook."

"But you do," Doc pointed out. "I'd like pancakes. My friend Andrew used to put faces on them, so if you could do that, I'd really appreciate it."

Frankie stared at him for a moment before saying, "Seriously?"

"Yes. And maybe extra unicorn breath."

"You're insane," she said sternly, even though she was grinning.

"Maybe," Doc laughed.

He pulled her to her feet, hugged her tightly, then exited the treehouse and waited for her on the ground. Boudica sent him an image of a happy Frankie, and Doc said, "We're getting there."

He scratched behind Boudica's ears while he waited, and once Frankie had reached the ground, they walked silently towards the house. Just as the back door came into view, Dublin stepped out of the shadows.

"Next time you decide to make a midnight visit," he said softly, "you might want to give me a heads up first. I nearly pounced on you at the van."

"My phone is broken," Doc said apologetically.

"Why do you smell like Jervis?"

"I'm wearing his clothes."

"Why?"

"Because he's wearing my face."

"Do I need to know what's going on?" Dublin inquired.

"Frankie?" Doc asked.

"He should," she said softly. "Just in case they somehow find me here."

"They won't," Doc said firmly. "But in any case, we're going to make breakfast. Join us in about thirty minutes?"

"It's three o'clock in the morning," Dublin stated.

"That's why we're having breakfast; supper would have been before midnight," Doc explained with pretend patience.

"I'll be there," Dublin laughed. "Just so long as you're not doing the cooking."

"I'm all thumbs in the kitchen," Doc replied. "But I'll make the coffee."

"You going to make it Andrew style?"

"Is there any other way?"

"Then I'll definitely be there."

"What do you mean Jervis is wearing your face?" Frankie asked after Dublin had faded back into the shadows.

"He's pretending to be me," Doc said.

"Why?"

"Mrs. Foxall was quite insistent on my presence."

"Oh. Is that why you're covered in blood?"

"Yes."

"I'm sorry," she whispered.

"Why?"

"Because this is all my fault."

"Not hardly," Doc said. "I found a can of worms, and I opened it. I'm sorry."

"A can of worms?" Frankie said questioningly.

By now they were inside the kitchen, and Doc ignored her question and said, "Where's the coffee?"

"That cabinet there," she said, pointing.

Doc opened the cabinet and stared at the package of coffee for a moment. It just happened to be Raven's Brew, and that always made him think of Andrew.

Time was an ocean, so they were meeting right now. Forever. He quite liked the idea of them perpetually meeting somewhere on the currents of time.

He grinned, then pushed away his thoughts of Andrew while he filled the pan with water and set it to boil.

"I still don't understand why you won't use a coffee maker," Frankie said. She was breaking eggs into a bowl, and Doc sat on the counter to watch her.

"Babs will murder you if she sees you sitting on the counter," Frankie warned.

"Beauty sleep, remember?" Doc chuckled. "She'll never know. Besides, I'm much too adorable to murder for such a small infraction."

"Why are you so cheerful?"

"I had fun with Jervis," Doc said.

"You had fun killing people?"

"I did."

She cast him a sideways glance and said, "You're kinda weird."

"I try to find joy in the little things," Doc said solemnly.

She snorted as she whisked her pancake batter together. "Get out the griddle," she said. "And put some pats of butter on it."

Doc obeyed her, and while he was at it, he dumped half the package of coffee into the pan of boiling water. For a second it boiled over the sides, but he ignored it because he knew it would eventually settle down.

Doc reclaimed his seat on the counter and asked, "What was your father's favorite meal?"

Frankie shrugged and said, "He didn't care much about food. The only thing he really loved was digging." She shrugged again and added, "And me."

"Did you dig with him?"

"Sometimes, but I don't have the patience. It's really just a whole lot of boring stuff that maybe, maybe, leads up to one exciting moment. They were always a little disappointed that I didn't take to it better."

"They?"

"The family. I'm the only one who couldn't care less about discovering things," she muttered.

"So what did you do on the digs?"

"Wandered off. On this one dig in Dominica I ran into this

local named Dan, and he showed me around the forest and introduced me to all the plants." She smiled wistfully and said, "Plants make sense to me. They are alive in the here and now, and I'm not making up a pretend past for them. You know?"

"Yeah," Doc said.

"Anyway, Dan gave me this book on botany, and I started trying to figure out plants and identify them when we'd go places. I had a whole scrapbook full of plants and flowers, but... Anyway," she said, shaking her head and forcing herself to smile. "I think your coffee is done."

"It tastes better if it burns a bit," Doc said dismissively.

"I smell pancakes," Johnny said sleepily as he wandered into the kitchen. "Doc? What're you doing here? Why're you covered in blood? And how come you get to sit on the counter? I get yelled at if I try to sit on the counter. In clean clothes!" he added irritably.

"I'm grown," Doc said easily. "You're not."

"That's dumb," Johnny grumbled. "You take up more space, and you weigh more than I do. I should get to sit on the counter."

Doc shrugged.

"Whatever," Johnny sighed. "Are we eating pancakes?"

"Yes," Doc said.

"It's still dark out."

"So?"

Johnny opened his mouth, then shook his head and said, "I don't know why I argue with you; you always win."

Doc grinned and said, "I do, don't I?"

"You're awfully cheerful."

"He's been killing people," Frankie said.

"I suppose that would do it," Johnny said as he sat at the

table. "There's always a spring in his step after he goes on a killing spree."

"That is not true," Doc laughed.

"It is," Frankie insisted.

"Prove it," Doc argued.

"Prove it?" Frankie sputtered. "How do you expect me to prove it?"

"Pancakes?" Jules said with a yawn as she suddenly appeared in the kitchen doorway. "Why are we... Oh. Hi, Doc." She shook her head, trying to seem more awake and said, "What are you doing here?"

"Having pancakes," Doc replied cheerfully.

"You're pretty happy for three-thirty in the morning," she muttered. "You must have just killed someone."

"HA!" Frankie yelled. "Proved it!"

"That doesn't prove anything," Doc insisted.

"It does too!" Frankie shot back.

"I'm with Frankie," Johnny said.

"I told you not to wake me!" Babs snapped.

Everyone froze; eyes on Babs's annoyed face.

"Frankie, why are you making pancakes?" she demanded right before growling, "Doc, get the hell off my counter! And while you're at it, pour me a cup of coffee!" She sat down at the table with an irritated huff and said, "Be quick about it or I'll send you all out to clean the stables."

Doc immediately jumped from the counter and poured Babs a steaming cup of coffee.

"You're trouble," she muttered when she took the cup from him. "And filthy. You shouldn't even be inside the house with clothes like those on," she grumbled. She took a sip of coffee and straightened up slightly. "Did you make this?" she demanded.

"Yes," Doc drawled.

"Then you can stay."

Doc winked at her as he poured himself a cup as well, and before long they were all sitting around the table eating Frankie's fluffy pancakes.

"This was almost worth getting up for," Dublin said cheerfully as he drained his third cup of coffee.

"Can I have some?" Johnny asked for the seventh time.

"No," Babs said sternly. "We're all going back to bed as soon as Doc tells us why the hell he woke us up."

"I don't wanna go back to bed," Addison whined. "I like eating breakfast in the dark."

"It's really not that early for them," Doc chuckled.

Babs sighed and said, "Yes, but I'm trying to break them of that unfortunate habit. I've been getting up at four in the morning for nearly three hundred years. I'm ready to sleep in. Now why are you here?"

Doc looked at Frankie and raised his eyebrow. She nodded. "Why don't you start?" Doc suggested.

"Wait," Jules broke in. "What does this have to do with Frankie?"

"Everything," Doc replied.

8

By the time Doc and Frankie had both told their sides of the story, it was bright outside and everyone was staring at them with stunned expressions.

Johnny was the first one to speak. "So you're telling us that you were born into a family of evil archeologists who are searching the world for fae treasure which they totally intend to steal?"

"I guess," Frankie said.

"And your dad discovered the key to the fae treasure?" Jules asked.

Frankie just shrugged.

"Whatever it is he discovered," Babs pointed out, "your grandmother believes it's the key to the treasure."

"Yes."

"And you don't know where it is?" Dublin asked.

Frankie shook her head.

"But you have the journal?" Jules inquired, eyes bright with excitement.

"Yes."

"And you're going to let me read it?"

Frankie leaned back her head as if she was seriously considering Jules's question, but Doc could see the slight tilt at the edge of her lips.

"Please?" Jules begged.

"I suppose," Frankie said slowly. "But..."

"But what?" Jules demanded. "Whatever it is, yes!"

"You'll have to make Boudica's rice mush for a week."

"Deal!" Jules exclaimed.

"So what now?" Dublin asked.

"Frankie's going to tell me how to access her email, and I'm going to set a trap for Mrs. Foxall," Doc said.

"I wanna help!" Johnny burst out.

"I'd better do this one on my own," Doc replied.

"I'm practically a man," Johnny growled.

"Practically," Doc agreed. "That's why I need you here with Dublin. You can help him secure the premises."

Johnny brightened up and said, "I can do that. I've been learning how to make wards."

"Excellent," Doc praised. "I'd better get back to it. I'm sure Jervis has killed all of Mrs. Foxall's men by now, and she's probably ready to meet in person."

Frankie nodded and left the room. She appeared a minute later and handed him a piece of paper.

"I'll need to borrow your truck, Dublin," Doc said as he stood. "I sent Emily home with the van."

Dublin tossed him the keys and said, "If you ruin it, I want it in blue next time."

"Did you just jinx me on purpose?" Doc demanded.

"No," Dublin chuckled. "Why would I do that?"

"Because you want a new truck."

"I like that one. I'd just like it better in blue." Dublin

winked at Doc before saying, "Now if you'll excuse me, I have to go make amends to my wife. She doesn't like it when she wakes up alone."

"Are you sure?" Doc teased. "I'd think she'd breathe a sigh of relief not to see your hairy face first thing in the morning."

"I'll admit, she's a little strange," Dublin said seriously.

They both laughed, then Doc gave the children hugs before walking outside and getting into Dublin's truck. It was time to flush Mrs. Foxall out of her hole.

Doc allowed himself a moment of indulgence by going home to Dulcis. He'd feel more himself if he was wearing his own clothes. He parked Dublin's truck in the top floor parking garage and whistled as he rode the elevator down to his suite.

"Morning!" he said happily as he entered the sitting room.

"Humph," Thaddeus said. "You've either been killing people or fraternizing with a woman."

"Killing people," Doc replied.

"Figures."

"How are you this morning?"

"As well as a plant can be," Thaddeus grumbled.

"I'm glad to hear that, old boy," Doc said.

He patted the side of Thaddeus's pot, which he noticed now had a small painting of a microscope.

"A microscope?" he asked.

"What?" Thaddeus snapped. "Microscopes make me happy."

"Good," Doc murmured, swallowing his chuckle. "I'd hate to see you grumpy," he added under his breath as he walked away.

"I heard that!" Thaddeus yelled. "There's nothing wrong with my hearing, you know!"

"I do now!" Doc yelled back.

He laughed as he dropped Jervis's clothes across the back of his wingback chair. They weren't ruined, just a little bloody.

Doc took a short hot shower, redressed, and headed back towards the parking garage, one of his phones tucked inside his pocket. He picked one of his older cars, the Lamborghini Miura, just because he hadn't driven it in a while, then he headed towards the airport.

Normally Jervis would have made the arrangements for Doc's flight, but Doc figured he was lucky enough that if he just showed up, one of his pilots and planes would be waiting for him.

He drove through the thick Denver traffic, mind considering all the things Frankie had told him. He had no doubt that he was going to end up killing her entire family. It was just the matter of bringing them all together that was the tricky part. They clearly didn't trust each other, and he thought that was a little depressing. What was the point of family if you couldn't depend on them to watch your back?

Francisco had always watched Doc's back. Even when he hadn't deserved it.

Doc grinned as he remembered the time he'd broken his mother's favorite vase. He had been shadow fighting himself down the hallway, pretending he was being attacked by three of the largest boys at school.

He could still feel his horror when he had bumped into the table and the vase had tumbled to the floor. In his mind he watched it fall and break into pieces.

"John!" Mother called out, voice somewhat stronger than normal. "What was that?"

"Nothing, Mother!" he exclaimed as he frantically

gathered the pieces together and ran towards the backdoor. He dashed outside and ran to Francisco's house, sharp bits of ceramic clutched to his chest.

"You have to help me!" he cried as he dumped the pieces onto Francisco's desk.

"This is Mother's favorite vase," Francisco stated.

"I know!" John wailed. "I didn't mean to! I was just... I was..."

"You were lost in your mind again."

"A little," John confessed.

"You're fighting villains in your mind, but you become your own enemy when you do that, pup," Francisco said with a sigh. "You have to be in the moment, you have to live in reality, you have to see with your eyes and hear with your ears."

"I know."

"This is the third mess you've made this week," Francisco added as he tried to fit two pieces of the vase together. "I thought you wanted to learn to fisticuff so you could fight your own battles."

John felt his face turn red. He had wanted to fight his own battles. But every time he did something stupid, he ran to Francisco and asked him to fix it.

"I'm sorry," he muttered. "I'll do better."

"Good. But that doesn't help us with the issue at hand. Run get the glue."

John helped Francisco glue the vase back together, and later when John had presented it to his mother, Francisco had stood right behind him, offering silent support.

"I'm sorry, Mother," John said, trying to keep his tone from wavering. "I broke your vase. Francisco glued it back together, but it's still broken."

"I can barely even tell," Mother said.

John knew she was lying. It was obvious, but she was being kind. She was always so kind.

"Go put it back on the hall table," she instructed. "And stop pretend fighting in the house."

John dropped his head in shame and nodded.

"Run tell the cook that Francisco is staying for tea," she added. "After all, he did an excellent gluing job and deserves a cake or two for his efforts."

With a grin, Doc refocused on the road in front of him. Francisco had never been able to break Doc of the habit of wandering off in his head. So instead, Francisco had taught Doc to split his focus in two. With one side he did whatever it was he was doing, like driving the car and turning towards the appropriate hangar; and with the other side, he wandered off into whatever thought or memory appealed to him at the moment.

Doc parked his car, got out, stretched lazily, then headed towards the hangar. When he was still a few feet away, the side door of the hangar opened and a woman walked out.

"Mr. Holliday?" she said with surprise.

"Indeed," Doc said with a slight bow. "How are you this morning, Tonie?"

Tonie was one of their few witch employees. She was an aerial, and that made her an excellent pilot.

"Jervis didn't call me," she said. "Are you flying out?"

"If you're available. Jervis and I are doing a thing."

"Ah," she said knowingly. "Where do you need to go?"

"You pick," Doc shrugged.

She raised an eyebrow and said, "You want me to pick?"

"Sure."

"Alright, let's go to Orlando."

"Sounds good," Doc agreed. "I like Orlando."

She smiled at him, said, "You can go ahead and board. I'll square everything away, and we'll go."

Doc watched her walk away before boarding the plane. He didn't have much of a plan. He just wanted to get away from Denver before he emailed Muriel Foxall and pretended to be Frankie. He wasn't certain how clever Muriel's people were. They were obviously a little clever because when he'd searched earlier for a Wesley Foxall, there hadn't been a single mention of his death. There were plenty of mentions of Wesley, all of them praising his work as an archeologist, just no mentions of his untimely death.

Doc pulled out his cards, shuffled, and dealt out the tableau for a game of solitaire. He absently moved card after card until he had four foundations, then he shuffled and dealt again.

Since he couldn't do anything more about Frankie until he landed, he turned his mind to Gac. He had Julian, Virgil, Jervis, and Bluegrass all looking for Gac. He had Sydney tracking down something that Gac's original body, Custer, had owned. What other avenues could he utilize to find him?

He finished off another foundation and shuffled again. One part of his mind focused on the game; one part focused on the problem of Gac.

He nodded at Tonie when she walked past him. He felt the airplane leave the ground, and he continued to think. Yiska had said "look to your left", but Doc wasn't even entirely sure Yiska had been talking about Gac because Doc hadn't asked the question to the answer Yiska had given him.

Yiska was becoming nearly as bothersome as Ahanu. He kept popping up when Doc didn't expect him to. The only difference was that Yiska was generally helpful, and his help was free of favors. At least Doc thought his help was free of favors. He should probably ask at some point, but he was a little leery to hear the answer.

He had a suspicion that ancient beings such as Yiska thought on an entirely different wavelength than other people. Even Jervis and Ahanu, who were nowhere near ancient, often saw things in a different manner. They sometimes didn't even seem to recognize the immediate effects because they were too busy looking down the line at a future only they could see.

Ahanu could probably tell Doc every single possible future involving Gac, but Doc didn't work that way. For all of his wandering around in his mind, he was still firmly in the present, the moment of now. He didn't look forward to the future. To look forward meant you were relying more on knowledge than luck, and Doc could not afford to take such a risk.

All he wanted to do was look into the present. He wanted to see where Gac was now, how to kill Gac now, how to finish it now. He didn't care about what Gac might do; he wanted to stop Gac from doing anything. If he believed that Gac might pull off a future event, he might not believe that he could stop him before it happened.

He exhaled irritably. He'd just remembered that he shouldn't even bother looking for Gac. There was no point looking for Gac until he knew how to kill him. And that brought him neatly back around to square one.

He pulled out his phone and texted Jury.

"You know how you put the spirits into the stone? Could you put the spirits into me?"

"That was easily one of the strangest texts I've ever gotten from you," Jury texted back after a few minutes. "The only reason I knew it was you is because no one else would ask such a crazy question. Why do you want to know?"

"Because Gac's not in the stone."

Doc's phone rang, and as soon as Doc answered, Jury snapped, "What do you mean he's not in it?"

"He's not in it."

"How the hell do you know?"

"I saw him."

"You saw him. Saw him where?"

"In the dreaming," Doc said softly.

"Goddamn it, Doc! What the hell have you done? And what the hell are you? In the dreaming, in the Underworld, in the ley lines! People have boundaries, you know! They're supposed to stay put in one plane, one dimension!"

"I'm sorry."

Jury sighed heavily and said, "Why do you lie to me?"

"I'm not lying," Doc said, swallowing a laugh.

"I know you're not sorry."

"I'm sorry you're bothered by my travel choices," Doc replied.

"You annoy me. What was the question again?"

"Can you put a spirit inside me, instead of inside a rock?"

"Not without Bree and Tucker, and even then, I'm not sure. I'm an earth witch; it made sense at the time to use a rock. You're not a rock."

"I see. Jules said there is a spell to pull a spirit inside yourself, but she doesn't know what it is."

"I've never heard of such a thing," Jury said dismissively. "What're you doing?"

"Flying to Orlando."

"Why?"

"To kill Frankie's family."

"Is that the tall one?"

"Yes," Doc ground out.

"You have a problem."

"What's that?" Doc asked.

"You just can't allow people in your life if you don't kill off their entire family first," Jury said.

"That's hardly true," Doc argued. "I didn't kill Bree's or Jervis's families. Most of your family is still alive, and I don't even know if Dublin had a family."

"Everyone has a family," Jury pointed out. "I have to go. I got out of bed to call you, and Gigi's getting cold without me. Have fun killing people."

"I always do," Doc chuckled.

"I know. It's your thing."

Doc laughed as he disconnected, but he sobered as he remembered Jules's description of the world tree and the ormr that lived beneath it. He'd set out to do something that had nothing whatsoever to do with killing, and here he was. Killing people. Lots of people.

He knew better than to think that it was pure coincidence. Some people mistook luck and coincidence for the same thing, but luck had a mind of its own, and it knew exactly what it was doing. Coincidence was just completely random. And in Doc's life, no matter how it seemed, nothing was ever random.

He tapped his fingers on the table for a moment before pulling back out his phone and texting Jervis. "Meet me in Orlando." Then he set down his phone; and while he waited for Jervis's reply, he drifted off to sleep.

When he opened his eyes, he was inside his throne room. He glanced around, somewhat surprised to see that the wall was still there. He hadn't been sure it would be.

He was already sitting on his throne, so he flexed his hand

and wrapped it around the goblet that instantly appeared there. He tried not to think about how his thought alone had simply pulled a goblet of whiskey into existence and took a sip.

"Disgraceful," his father suddenly said as he appeared out of nowhere and sat on Doc's footstool.

Doc stared at him in shock, mind scrambling to say something, anything. "What?" he finally managed, finding it hard just to breathe.

"Drinking whatever it is you're drinking without offering me some," Father said.

His lips were curved slightly, and Doc knew he was in a good humor. It didn't seem like he should still know every nook and cranny of his father's face, but he did.

Doc flexed his other hand and handed his father the goblet that appeared there. Father sniffed it cautiously before taking a drink.

"Decent," he said. "But your decor is ghastly. Bones?"

Doc shrugged. Then he managed to say something he'd always wished he'd said. "I'm sorry."

"For what?"

"For never coming home. For never telling you I didn't die that way. For making you worry. For being a disappointment."

"Who said you were a disappointment?" Father demanded.

"No one. I just..." Doc shrugged and said, "I certainly didn't accomplish much."

"It broke my heart that both of my sons' lives were cut short," Father said. "That you both managed to do as much as you did with the little time allotted you is incredible. That you were able to live your life as fully as you did, astounds me."

"You can't lump me in with Francisco," Doc argued. "He was a business man, a husband, and a father."

"Yes," Father replied. "And you are you. You took what life gave you and wrung it for everything it was worth. Few men have the courage to do that."

"Are you sure you're really my father?" Doc asked skeptically.

"I'm sure," Father replied with a smile.

Doc stopped himself from saying "prove it". He knew it was his father; he just didn't believe it. He couldn't believe he was finally talking to him, finally speaking, not just repeating meaningless phrases.

His father suddenly leaned forward, eyes shiny with excitement. "Now tell me, did you really win a fortune with just a dime once?"

Doc raised an eyebrow in surprise, then laughed softly. "Sure," he said.

"How did you do it?"

"One hand of cards at a time," Doc replied. "Although I did also have to bet my guns, my horse, and the boots on my feet."

Father laughed outright before saying, "More whiskey, and then you have to tell me the entire story."

Doc obliged, only embellishing the story a bit here and there to add a little spice to what was, in fact, not one of his most enthralling tales. By the time he was finished, his father was grinning with delight.

"I knew you'd done it," he crowed. "I told all the gents down at the lodge what a clever boy you are. And of course, they knew better than to argue with me."

"I suppose it might have been more wits than luck that time," Doc conceded.

"You always had a lot of both," Father said.

"Except in anything that counted," Doc murmured softly.

"Perhaps," Father agreed. "But you've turned that around, haven't you? How old are you now?"

"Not quite two hundred," Doc replied.

"That's a long time to live, my boy."

"It is," Doc agreed.

He suddenly woke, leaving his father and his throne room behind. The plane had just landed, but he allowed himself a moment to relive their conversation. He'd always regretted not going to see his father once more. He'd regretted a lot of things when it came to his father. He regretted not trying harder after his mother had died. He regretted not writing more often. He regretted secretly wishing his father had just left him alone instead of trying so hard to turn him into a useful member of society.

He'd carried those regrets around with him for a hundred and fifty years, but no more. His father wasn't angry with him or even disappointed. Doc grinned. His father thought he was a clever boy.

He laughed softly, then stood with a yawn and stretched. It was time to build his trap.

9

The warm humid air of Orlando greeted Doc as he exited the plane. He took a moment to gaze up at the wide blue sky, and then he headed towards the taxi Tonie had arranged for him. Jervis had texted Doc to say he was on his way and to meet him at the Orlando safe house, so as soon as Doc was sitting in the taxi, he gave the driver the address and sat back to watch the city pass.

Cities were like women. They were all beautiful, and he enjoyed them thoroughly. But he'd discovered years ago that he couldn't be away from Denver for long without yearning to return. Although he wasn't entirely certain if it was the city that pulled at him or Dulcis.

The only home he'd ever had before Dulcis was his childhood home, and it was long gone. It hadn't been much of a home after his mother had died, but only because he and his father just hadn't known how to get on without her. She'd linked them together, and once she was gone they'd just drifted apart.

But when he thought of home, the house he'd loved as a

child never came to mind. It was always Dulcis. With Thaddeus waiting irritably in Doc's suite and Jervis somewhere within the building. Dulcis with Doc's lovely rows of supercars. Dulcis, where Jury knew he was always welcome and the Baker children had memorized the code to Doc's door. It was always Dulcis.

He tried to place Dulcis amongst Orlando's glittery buildings, but he just couldn't. Dulcis belonged in Denver, and Doc belonged with Dulcis. He could visit a million other places, but he would always go home.

At the thought of home, his mind shifted to his throne room. He didn't understand why his throne room always came to mind when he was thinking of home. Every time Yiska had said "come home" to one of the trapped Akashii, Doc had seen the same series of images. Jervis, Jury, Bree, Andrew, and the throne room. Over and over and over. There had been flashes of other things as well, like the Bakers and his mother's lap, but it had always ended on the throne room.

Why did his mind consider it part of his home? Why had he made it? When had he made it? Why was the throne made of bones? Whose bones were they? And why did it only exist in the dreaming when everything else existed in both reality and the dreaming?

There were too many questions to answer, and he wasn't even sure he wanted to know the answers. Sometimes it was better not to know the answers.

Doc was pulled from his thoughts when the taxi stopped in front of a building and the driver said, "Here ya go."

"Thank you," Doc said as he climbed from the taxi.

He handed the driver a few hundred dollar bills and walked towards the entrance, waving a dismissive hand over his shoulder when the driver hollered out, "Don't ya want your change?"

Doc entered the building and crossed over to the tall wall of mailboxes. Jervis hadn't actually told him which unit belonged to him so Doc walked along the boxes until he found one marked Hans Degenhardt.

"Why would he make me German?" Doc muttered with a sigh. "He knows I can't speak German worth a damn. There had better be whiskey," he added as he bounded up the stairs two at a time.

When he reached the correct unit, he keyed the code into the code pad, opened the door, and was met with an ear-piercing scream.

"What are you doing?!" a naked woman shrieked as she dashed over to the couch and grabbed a blanket off of it.

"What are you doing?" Doc retorted. "This is my condo."

"Bull crap!" she spat. "I live here! This is my condo!"

"Is your name Hans Degenhardt?" Doc drawled, noting with some amusement how quickly the blood drained from her face. "And do you pay the bills?" he added as he took a menacing step towards her.

"Um... Well, the thing is," she stuttered. "Hans is my uncle, and he's letting me stay here."

"Really? I didn't realize I had such a bewitching niece."

"You can't be Hans," she insisted. "He's owned this condo for over twenty years, and you don't look a day over thirty-five!"

"I'm named after my father," Doc said easily. "Would you like to explain to me why you're squatting in my home?"

"Your home!" she snorted. "I've lived here for five years, and you've never been here once!"

"Interesting," he murmured.

She quickly lost her angry stance and tucked the blanket more tightly around her. "Sorry?" she said.

"That is annoying," Doc murmured.

"What?"

"Being told sorry when it has a question mark on the end."

"There wasn't a question mark on the end," she argued.

"There was. Here's the thing, this is my condo. I own it. I can appreciate you taking advantage of a situation and making the best of it, but I'm afraid the free ride has come to an end."

"You're not going to call the cops?" she asked skeptically.

"No, why would I?"

"I've been living in your house?" she said, eyebrows crinkling in confusion.

"It didn't hurt anyone," Doc shrugged. "I wouldn't even care if you stayed, but I'm about to start a war with some very dangerous people and there's a chance the condo won't make it out alive."

"What?"

"Exactly what I said."

"Who are you?" she demanded.

"My home, my question," he replied. "Who are you?"

"Siofra," she said. "Siofra Relic."

"That is an absolutely fascinating name. You can call me Doc," he added as he took a small step towards her.

"Are you hitting on me?" she asked incredulously.

"I wouldn't use that particular term," he replied. "It's a little too violent for what I had in mind."

"I'm confused," she murmured. "Why are you hitting on me? I broke into your house, and I've been living here rent free."

"I admire your cleverness," Doc drawled.

Thus far, he admired everything about Siofra. She'd figured out his door code, and she'd lived in his safe house for five years without getting caught. And even though she'd just been caught, she wasn't crying or upset or even making excuses. She was rolling with it.

He was close enough to touch her, and he thought she would welcome it, but he needed to be certain. He met her wide blue eyes and said, "You've two choices. You can pack your bags and go, or you can indulge in some mutual pleasure and then pack your bags and go."

"Kicking me out either way?" she laughed. "That's cold."

"As I said, the condo may not survive. It wouldn't be safe for you to stay here."

"You're being for real?" she demanded.

"Yes."

Her grip on the tantalizing blanket had already loosened, and he knew she'd made up her mind, but he still waited for her to make the first move.

"If the condo survives, you can have it back," he said. "I'll even put it in your name."

"But only if I sleep with you?" she asked, grip starting to tighten once more.

"Either way," Doc replied, frustrated with himself for saying such a careless thing. His mind was muddled with need, and he wasn't thinking before he spoke. "As a reward for your cleverness," he added.

His fingers were twitching with desire to touch her, and he knew he'd nearly reached the end of his control so he asked, "Shall I step outside so you can have a moment to dress?"

"You said something about mutual pleasure," she pointed out, eyes narrow. "You didn't change your mind, did you?"

Just then her fingers loosened, and the blanket began to

slide down her body. Doc's eyes followed the edge of the blanket to the floor, drinking in Siofra's absolutely flawless skin. He reached out one hand and wrapped his fingers gently around her hip before tugging her to him.

"You're beautiful," he whispered as he kissed the top of her shoulder.

"You're still dressed," she replied, tone a little breathless.

"You can remedy that for me," he murmured.

He continued to feather kisses over her golden skin as she pushed his jacket from his shoulders. Her fingers made swift work of the buttons on his vest, but then with a slight intake of breath, she pulled away from him.

"That's a knife," she said frankly.

"I did mention that I was going to war," Doc said gently. "I never go to war without my weapons."

"You meant a literal war? As in a killing-people-with-your-knife kind of war?"

"Yes."

"That's insane," she murmured. "Actually, this entire situation is insane." She stared at him for a few seconds, then she shook her head and laughed softly before saying, "But I always was a little crazy."

Doc grinned, dropped his knife harness over the back of a chair, and pulled her back into his arms. She'd soon forget about knives and wars, and so would he. At least for a while.

Doc was kissing the curve of Siofra's thigh when Jervis knocked on the bedroom door.

"Who's that?" she gasped, pulling away from him.

"My friend," Doc said regretfully. "I'll be right out!" he called. He returned his attention to her glistening leg and murmured, "I hate to cut this short."

"Short?" she exclaimed, word ending in a slight moan. "What do you mean short?"

"If I had my way we'd stay in here another day."

Her pleasure-filled eyes grew wide, and she stuttered, "You're serious?"

"Have you known me to be anything less yet?"

She threaded her fingers around his neck and said, "Are you really going to make me go?"

"Yes."

She managed to make a face at him even though his finger was tracing the inside of her thigh.

"Jervis can wait just a minute though," Doc whispered as he moved to kiss her.

"You made me wait for over an hour," Jervis stated when Doc finally stepped out into the living room. "An hour does not qualify as 'right out'."

"It doesn't?" Doc murmured. "How surprising."

"How did you even manage to find a partner between here and the airport?"

"She's been living in the condo."

"She's been what?" Jervis growled.

"If it survives the coming storm, I told her she could have it."

"She will be taking over the bills, I presume," Jervis said.

"Obviously."

"It's difficult to know with you. How did she manage to find it?"

"I don't know," Doc shrugged. "We didn't do much talking."

"Really?" Jervis said, voice rife with sarcasm. "I find that so hard to believe."

"I'm happy to see you have your face back," Doc said cheerfully, hoping to change the subject.

"The world isn't big enough for two of you," Jervis replied.

The bedroom door opened, and Siofra stepped into the living room. She looked just as gorgeous dressed as she did naked, and Doc wanted to pull her into his arms once more, but instead he just smiled at her.

She returned his smile and hefted her small suitcase. "I guess I'll come back later for the rest of it."

Doc handed her a roll of hundred dollar bills and said, "This should be enough for several nights."

"You don't have to do that," she replied, pushing away his hand. "After all, you're just kicking me out of your own home."

"Speaking of which," Jervis said flatly, "how did you discover this particular condo?"

Siofra leaned around Doc to study Jervis. "I think things might have gone very differently if you had shown up first," she said softly.

"Quite," Jervis agreed. His nostrils flared slightly, and he added, "You're not human."

"Neither are you," she said with a grin. "But I don't mind."

"Would someone like to clue me in?" Doc sighed. "Since I can't sniff out species."

"I'm an elf," Siofra said, hand trailing down Doc's still naked ribs. "He's a vampire. Now you're up to speed."

"And here I thought the name was just for fun," Doc drawled.

"It is," she grinned. "Thank you for a wonderful time." She kissed him gently on the mouth and whispered against his skin, "I hope to see you again sometime. Sometime when the vampire is not around to interrupt us."

"The vampire would still like to know how you found this place," Jervis said.

"I worked in the office for about three days," Siofra replied. "Plenty of time to sort through all the files and look at some surveillance footage. I'm not cut out to work with humans," she added with a careless shrug. "They take everything much too seriously. Having a rent-free place to stay really freed me up. Now if you'll excuse me, I don't want any part of your war. Call me when it's over."

She sauntered past Jervis and out into the hallway. She turned back once and winked at Doc before closing the door behind her.

"That still doesn't explain how she figured out the door code," Jervis said irritably. "If I have to hire a team of witches to start warding your safe houses, I'm going to be quite annoyed."

"It doesn't matter if we get a trespasser here or there," Doc shrugged. "It's not as if it hurts anything, and I certainly don't want a handful of witches knowing about my hideouts."

"I suppose," Jervis said. "Strange she is an elf though. I've never met an elf in the States before. And would you put on some clothes? It's hard to take you seriously when you're buck naked."

Doc shrugged and reached down to pick up his pants. "How did it go?" he asked as he began to dress.

"Forty-three, fifty-nine, and sixty-eight."

"I don't think Mrs. Foxall is taking us seriously," Doc said. "Were you followed?"

"Of course not."

"We were both wrong," Doc said casually.

"Really?"

"They're archeologists."

"Technically a science," Jervis replied immediately.

"I knew you'd argue that," Doc sighed. "It's not what you meant though."

"I didn't specify."

"Then I don't know why we both can't have it," Doc argued. "They're basically a crime syndicate."

"But you meant an established crime syndicate," Jervis pointed out.

"I didn't specify," Doc retorted.

"Touché," Jervis said. "Her father?"

"Died from an infected injury."

"Maybe we did both win," Jervis shrugged.

"I suppose we could call the whole thing a wash," Doc suggested rather hopefully. "My fifteen minutes with Winslow cancels out your fifteen minutes with Thaddeus."

"Seems like a fair deal," Jervis said.

"Excellent!" Doc exclaimed. "Now for part two of our act. I'll send an email to Mrs. Foxall from Frankie and ask her to meet."

"You don't think she'll want to talk to her first?"

"Goddamn it, Jervis! I know you didn't just jinx me!"

"Apologies," Jervis murmured.

"Is this payback because I made you wait?"

"An hour of my time is hardly worth mentioning. Especially such a pleasant hour spent listening to your lovemaking."

"Did you learn anything?" Doc asked with a grin.

"Hardly," Jervis snorted. "Are you going to send the email sometime today?"

Doc winked at him, pulled out his phone, logged into Frankie's email account, and drafted an email to Muriel.

I'm sick of running. I'll give you Dad's journal if you'll just leave Marcus and me alone. That was all he wrote before pressing the send button. Frankie hadn't used this email after her father had died because she was scared they'd be able to track it, and Doc was hoping they could.

"Gin?" Doc asked as he placed the phone on the table in front of him.

"Nap," Jervis replied. "In less than twenty-four hours, I've killed nearly two hundred men. That may be an unremarkable occurrence for you, but I've apparently grown soft with age."

Doc chuckled and said, "By all means, let's take a nap. After all, Andrew always said—"

"To sleep when you have the chance," Jervis finished.

"Exactly."

Jervis stretched out on the couch, closed his eyes, and was soon asleep. At least Doc thought he was asleep. Doc watched him with a half-smile, thinking how completely different his life would be if Jervis hadn't been driven to near madness by the murder of his family. The Jervis Doc knew and the Jervis who had returned home to find his family dead were two very different people.

Doc had only ever caught glimpses of the other Jervis. It was there in the gentle way Jervis had braided Bree's hair and the soft smile he always gave her when she walked into a room. It was there in the way Jervis spoiled every child he could without seeming to spoil them at all.

Jervis had been born into a warrior's body, given a hunter's skills, and raised as a lord; but he had never been anything but kind. Kind, wise, and fair. He was still all those things, but there was a hardness to him. An edge. Doc liked the edge, but he was glad the hint of madness that had been in Jervis's eyes so many years ago was finally gone.

We saved each other, Doc thought as he yawned and

stretched out his legs. He couldn't say where he would be without Jervis, but he could say for certain that it wouldn't be anywhere good.

His phone beeped, interrupting Doc's thoughts.

He read the email, sighing in irritation. Of course Muriel had asked for proof of the journal. Goddamn it, Doc thought. Jervis and his goddamn jinxing.

He sent Babs a text and asked her to send him a photograph of one of the pages. "Try to make it an unimportant page," he added.

"How do you suggest I do that?" Babs replied. "It's in code."

"You're a witch. Make some magic happen."

"Remind me to hit you with my broom next time I see you."

"You don't seem to like me as much as you used to," Doc replied, including one of the crying yellow faces.

"You track mud into my house, and you sit on my counters," she retorted. "What do you expect?"

"I made you coffee."

"It was good," she said. "You're forgiven your faults."

He laughed and waited for the photograph to come through. When it did, he looked at it for a moment, trying to decipher any type of meaning, but he couldn't, so he downloaded the photograph and sent it to Muriel.

It was nearly an hour before she responded.

What does it say?

Doc sighed and replied. *I don't know. It's in code.*

Where is the item he transcribed it from?

I don't know.

You useless girl. What do you know?

Doc swallowed his rage and tried to think how to handle Muriel without giving himself away.

I'm sorry, he finally typed. *Dad never taught me how to read his code, and he didn't tell me where he hid the artifact. All I have is the journal. Do you want it?*

This time Doc actually fell asleep before Muriel responded.

Bring it to me.

Where are you?

Home. You know where that is; and if you don't, you're not Francesca.

"Frankie, Frankie," Doc murmured. "Still keeping secrets from me, I see."

He typed up a response to Muriel. *Do you swear to let me leave once I've given it to you?*

He didn't have to wait long for a response.

Of course. What use would you be to me once I have the journal?

Doc didn't believe Muriel Foxall for one second. She'd killed her own daughter to protect whatever she thought this was, and she'd certainly torture her granddaughter just to make sure she didn't know more than she was saying. If it wasn't for Doc's interference, Frankie would be as good as dead.

Muriel would never get the chance to hurt Frankie though. Not ever. He'd handle her just as soon as he knew where she was. He dialed Babs's number, tamping down his irritation at Frankie for not immediately telling him where the Foxall's lived.

"What now?" Babs asked when she answered.

"I thought my faults had been forgiven."

"They were," she stated. "But everyone is in a tizzy over Frankie, and a week ago they were in a tizzy over you. I'm tired of tizzies. The Jury family never had tizzies."

"Having trouble adjusting?" Doc chuckled.

"Yes!" she exclaimed. "I'm not used to... worrying. It's exhausting, and it's all your fault!"

"I'm truly very sorry," Doc said.

He was too. He hated worrying. He hated it so much that he hardly ever did it. Instead he killed people until there was nothing left to worry about. But Babs couldn't do that. She couldn't do that because she was watching over the Bakers so that Doc didn't have to worry about them.

"May I speak to Frankie?" he asked.

"Here," Babs said grumpily.

"Doc?" Frankie said.

"Muriel said to come home, and she said if I don't know where that is, I'm not you."

"Oh."

"Well?"

"Um, well, I guess you have to go home," she said softly.

"Where is that?" Doc replied, trying to damper the tone of command that had crept into his voice.

"Oh, right. It's in Washington D.C."

Doc cringed. D.C. was one of the few cities he considered off-limits. It was a beautiful city, and if it wasn't for the overwhelming sense of desperation and misery that tried to consume him when he stepped a single foot inside its borders, he'd happily go there. But it looked as if he was going to go there anyway.

"Doc?" Frankie asked.

"D.C.," Doc said. "Makes perfect sense."

"Are you okay?"

"Yep. Text me the address."

"Okay."

Doc disconnected and stared at his phone with irritation.

He did not have any interest in going to D.C., but that wasn't the worst of the situation. The worst of it was that he'd just realized he was going to need Jury, and Jury hated D.C. even more than Doc did.

10

Doc had always thought it was best to get unpleasant experiences over with as quickly as possible; and as such, he picked back up his phone and called Jury.

When Jury answered, Doc asked nonchalantly, "Are you busy?"

"Yes," Jury said emphatically. "And here's why, you only ever ask if I'm busy if you're about to ask me to do something you know I won't like. Otherwise you just demand."

"That's hardly true," Doc insisted.

"Really? What is it you want me to do?"

"I was going to ask if you could glamour me to look like Frankie."

"Frankie who?"

"Goddamn it, Jury. The tall one."

"Oh, the norm girl. Sure. Easy. And with pleasure. I mean, why wouldn't I want to glamour you to look like Frankie? So that was only part of it. What's the rest?"

"And go to D.C. with me," Doc said in an undertone.

"No."

"But I need you."

"Absolutely not!"

"I literally can't do this without you."

"Take Frankie with you," Jury countered.

"No."

"You're a little too tall, anyway. And you haven't got any of the natural curves that girls typically have. I doubt if anyone would be fooled."

"They haven't seen her in three years."

"Get another witch," Jury ground out.

"Out of the twelve registered witches inside the United States who can glamour, I've killed at least four of them."

"That leaves eight."

"One of them is you," Doc sighed.

"And seven of them aren't."

"Fine, I'll call your mother."

"She's not into you, you know."

"I know."

"I met her for coffee yesterday," Jury went on. "She's apparently head over heels for Ackley Underwood. Which I suppose is alright. I'd rather her be with him than you."

"There was never any danger of her being with me," Doc reminded him.

"I know, I just... It's very strange to think of her with someone else. It's strange to remember... Anyway."

Doc knew he'd been going to say that it was strange to remember that Phillip Jury was dead. It was strange, but in a good way.

"I feel you've gotten rather off track," Doc pointed out.

"I'm not doing it. Call my mother if you want."

It was time to play his trump card.

"I'm sure she can make a better glamour than you can anyway. Have fun with Gigi."

Doc disconnected and waited.

"I know what you're doing," Jury texted.

Doc sent him a smiley face.

"She can't, you know."

"I guess I'll find out," Doc replied.

"I hate you."

Doc sent him a heart.

"I'm not going."

"I understand. I'm calling your mother now."

"Goddamn it, Doc! I'm coming!"

"You don't have to," Doc texted back.

"Oh, shut up! Where the hell are you?"

Doc texted him the address, then laughed softly as he put back down his phone.

"Is he coming?" Jervis asked without opening his eyes.

"Of course he is."

"You'd think by now he'd know all your tricks."

"He does; he just can't resist them."

"Hubris," Jervis shrugged.

"It's not exactly hubris," Doc replied. "He really is as good as he thinks he is. He just can't stand the idea of anyone else showing him up."

"Hubris," Jervis repeated.

"This'll be fun," Doc said as he propped up his feet on the table. "The three of us killing Frankie's entire family."

"Better than a family reunion," Jervis said tonelessly.

"I'm really starting to enjoy this side of you," Doc said.

"Which side?"

"The side that makes jokes," Doc laughed.

"Who said I was kidding?"

"As if you've ever been to a family reunion."

"There was that time at Solomon's."

"Hardly counts," Doc said dismissively.

"And, well, I suppose..."

Jervis trailed off. Which was completely unlike him.

"Yes?" Doc prodded.

"Sami wants me to go home with her in a few months."

"Don't say it," Doc begged.

"For a family reunion," Jervis finished.

"You said it!"

"It can't be that bad. Can it?" Jervis asked, tone a little desperate.

"How should I know?" Doc shrugged. "I've never been to a real family reunion. Andrew and company was... We were all... We chose each other. Like you and I did. We weren't just born to each other."

Doc studied the beach painting that was hanging on the wall across from him. It reminded him of Ireland and Bree.

"Like Bree picked us," he added softly. "Like you picked Sami."

"Ha!" Jervis snorted. "She picked me."

"But you let her," Doc said. "She's good for you. I haven't ever seen you this relaxed."

"With Eldwin gone, I can finally breathe," Jervis stated. "Each decision is my own. I don't worry about exposing us or having to start over. I don't dream of revenge. I don't avoid sleep because I dream of them. I do dream of them, but now I dream of them before."

"Are they really there?" Doc asked.

"What do you mean?"

Doc hadn't ever told anyone about his throne room. Bluegrass knew about it because she was dead, and Tucker had seen it, but he didn't understand what it was. And Doc had shown it to Tozi because he was irritated at her for being so stubborn, but he didn't just talk about it.

He was suddenly very curious to know about Jervis's dreams though, so he said, "Sometimes when I sleep, I'm in a place in the dreaming where people come to me. Andrew, Francisco; today I saw Father. And they're real. I didn't know for a long time, but it's really them. Francisco said he can feel me, that I call him to me. I don't know what that means, and they won't tell me where they are or how they know when I'm there. I don't really understand it," he added with a shrug.

"Interesting," Jervis said. "My dreams aren't quite like that. I dream of my family, memories of them, times we shared." He paused, seeming to consider his words, then said, "But the memories are never quite the same. The way I remember something and the way I dream it are not quite the same. Sometimes I truly feel that they see me, that they're there with me."

Neither of them spoke for a long time, but Jervis finally said, "Gin?"

"You've had enough napping?"

"Too much more napping, and I'll remind myself of Jury."

"We certainly wouldn't want that," Doc said as he shuffled his cards.

Doc and Jervis played gin for several hours, only stopping long enough to search the condo for whiskey. Doc had won eleven games and Jervis had won five by the time Jury showed up.

"There are pigeons everywhere," Jury said as he sat down on the couch beside Jervis. "Are they just roosting?"

"I'm not sure," Doc admitted. "I had hoped they would

rush in guns blazing, but I actually think Muriel wants Frankie to go home."

"Muriel?"

"Frankie's grandmother."

"Evil?"

"Through and through," Doc said. "She wants some kind of artifact Frankie's father found."

"Yuck," Jury muttered. "Artifacts and D.C.? You must really hate me."

"You get to glamour me to look like a girl," Doc offered.

"That hardly takes the edge off. You owe me stones still, and I'm adding water to the bill."

"There's water everywhere," Doc replied.

"Not the water I want," Jury insisted.

"What do you do with it?" Jervis asked.

"Use it to power things," Jury said easily.

"Things?" Doc prodded.

"You wouldn't understand. Or maybe you would, but you'd pretend like you didn't, and that irritates me, so I'm not going to bother explaining it. Do you have a plan?"

"You glamour me to look like Frankie, you glamour Jervis to look like me, and we go to D.C."

"I want to go on record and say, I'm doing this under protest. You know how I feel about D.C."

"Which part?" Jervis asked, lips tweaking slightly upwards.

"All of it!" Jury snapped. "As you damn well know!"

"I'm not sure we're remembering the same event," Jervis said smoothly. "I had a fairly nice weekend when we went to D.C."

"When did he get a sense of humor?" Jury demanded.

"Sami brings it out in him."

"Note, fire Sami," Jury said in Latin.

"Note," Doc said in Latin. "Pick up laundry."

Jervis snorted, and Jury shot him a look. "Are you laughing? You're away from Dulcis, making jokes, and laughing? Have you checked to make sure that's actually Jervis?"

"It is," Doc chuckled.

"Are you certain? Look how he's sitting!" Jury exclaimed, gesturing towards Jervis. "It's very unJervis like!"

"You're just mad because he had fun in D.C. and you didn't."

"Can we stop bringing it up? I said I'd never go back there, and here I am. Going back! Because I'm a witch and you need a witch."

"I have your mother on speed dial," Doc drawled.

"Lies!" Jury snapped. "You're a girl; Jervis is a less handsome Jervis. Let's get this over with."

Doc glanced down at his legs and grimaced. "Yellow pants?" Frankie's voice came out of his mouth, making him wince. He would never get used to that.

"I was in the mood for the sixties," Jury replied. "I gave you bellbottoms and flowers in your hair."

"You're sadistic."

"You're so goddamn cute I could pinch your rosy cheeks," Jury said.

"Don't even think about it."

"I am thinking about it," Jury said with a wicked grin. "And when you're not paying attention in a few minutes, bam! Cheek pinched!"

"Are the glamours tied off?" Doc asked.

"Yes."

"Good. Then it won't matter if I kill you."

"You wouldn't dare," Jury laughed. "Because if you killed me, you might get stuck looking like a girl forever."

"Are you children done playing?" Jervis asked. "If so, maybe we could get on with it?"

Doc looked at Jervis, who looked like him, and smiled widely. "You know what this reminds me of? That one time in—"

"Don't even say it!" Jervis and Jury snapped simultaneously.

"I'm just saying," Doc laughed.

"Gag him," Jervis suggested. "And then we'll go."

"Excellent idea," Jury said happily. "Done."

A band of air suddenly tightened around Doc's face, and he glared at Jury.

"Let's go," Jervis said.

Doc shook his head.

"I'll take off the gag when we get to the plane," Jury promised.

Doc pulled out a knife.

"It's funny," Jury laughed.

Doc took a step towards him.

"Fine," Jury huffed.

The band of air loosened, and Doc growled before heading towards the door. He made sure to keep his back to them for a moment, just to hide his grin. Whether they liked it or not, it was just like that time.

"Are we killing the pigeons?" Jervis asked as they exited the building.

"Nah," Doc said. "Let them watch."

"You're walking too much like a man," Jury chastised in Latin. "You need to swing your hips a little more."

Doc visualized Frankie in his mind. "She doesn't swing her hips," he said.

She doesn't walk like a man either," Jury retorted.

"I'm Frankie," Doc muttered. "Frankie. Seventeen. Reserved. A little scared. A little lost." He could see her clearly, and he could feel her fear. She wanted to be strong, but she wasn't yet. She wanted to be brave, but she didn't know how. He let himself feel those feelings, and then he adjusted his posture and his walk.

"I hate it when he goes into character," Jury sighed.

"It is impressive though. Remember when he played Lady Macbeth?" Jervis asked.

"Probably the best Lady Macbeth performance ever done," Jury admitted.

"A little water clears us of this deed," Doc said stoically.

"I doubt that," Jury snorted. "We'll have more blood on our hands by the time we're done than Lady Macbeth ever dreamed of."

"But our blood is justified," Jervis pointed out.

By now they'd reached a busy intersection, and Jury hailed a taxi. "I'll sit up front," he said. "You may look like a girl, but I still know you're you, and I've no desire to be squished between you."

Doc rolled his eyes and got into the back, trying to keep his head tilted down like he'd seen Frankie do. It was hard to play someone who lacked confidence. Confidence was just part of his being.

"Take us to the airport," Jury commanded the taxi driver.

Doc grinned at the imperiousness of Jury's tone. It was nice to know that some things never really changed. Jury might know a doorman's name now, but he was still autocratic and a tad overbearing.

"There's another taxi following us," the driver said after a few minutes.

"That's alright," Jury said.

They reached the airport with no trouble, paid the taxi driver, and entered the plane.

Jury immediately flopped into one of the chairs and stared intently at the space in front of him. A wobbly grey hole opened, and Jury shoved his hand inside.

"If we're really going to D.C.," he muttered. "I want to be a little drunk."

He tossed Doc a bottle and kept one for himself. The hole started to close, but then it widened again, and Jury pulled out three more bottles.

"Really drunk," he amended.

Doc chuckled and sat in the chair across from Jury. "It's not really that bad," Doc said consolingly.

Jury made a noise that could have been a snort. It was hard to tell though because he was guzzling down whiskey as fast as he could.

"You do realize this is a trap?" Jervis said dryly as they both watched Jury finish off the bottle.

"Not so much a trap as a proof of life," Doc countered. "I hope you have pickle juice on board."

"Why would I have pickle juice?"

"Because you're always prepared."

"I don't usually plan for the Jury-is-drunk contingency," Jervis retorted. He immediately sighed and said, "I now see how much of an oversight that is."

"I'm right here!" Jury snapped. "Stop talking about me!"

"We're not talking about you," Doc said soothingly. "We're talking about what to do with you once we're there."

"Well stop! I can walk and drink at the same time."

Jury's words were already starting to slur, but Doc didn't point that out. Instead he said, "Muriel won't be there."

"Neither will the journal," Jervis pointed out.

"Exactly. So the question is how do we get to Muriel?"

"We kill everyone and tell Muriel to come to us or else we burn the journal."

"I like it," Doc said. "It has panache. We'll need a book that Jury can glamour to look like the journal."

"We can use the logbook."

"Perfect," Doc said. "I'm still saying—"

"Don't," Jervis snarled, cutting off Doc abruptly.

"You and Jury have no sense of humor," Doc laughed.

"Not about that." Jervis glared at him for another moment before saying, "I'm going to go make sure there's more whiskey on board."

"Don't lie," Doc drawled. "You're going to go call Sami."

"And what if I am?"

"Tell her I said hi."

Doc waited until Jervis was gone to start laughing. The pained look on Jervis's face had said it all. Doc couldn't begin to imagine what it must be like for Jervis to fall in love again after all these years. It was probably a very strange feeling. Like a tree that had seemed dead suddenly blooming.

"I can't glamour the journal if I've never seen it," Jury said sleepily.

"I'll take care of it," Doc said before texting Babs to ask her for a set of photographs showing the covers and the first two or three pages of the journal.

"I don't know why you've always gotta meddle in people's lives," Jury murmured. "Not everyone needs fixed, you know."

Doc raised an eyebrow and said, "You appreciated my meddling."

"I'm not saying I didn't, but maybe some people don't want the all-seeing Doc messing with their lives."

"Frankie doesn't mind."

"Maybe she doesn't," Jury shrugged. "Maybe nobody minds; I just don't know how you can tell who really needs you. Does it ever occur to you not to meddle?"

"No."

"That's what I thought."

Jury's eyes weren't even open, and he almost seemed to be sleep talking, but Doc knew he was still awake.

"I just don't get you," Jury mumbled. "When you first saw me, what made you think 'that man needs my interference'?"

"I didn't think that at all," Doc said.

"What did you think?"

"I saw a man who was staring over a cliff edge, and I'd been there. And frankly, it's not much fun to stand on the edge of a cliff all by yourself."

Jury snorted and said, "What do you see when you look at Frankie?"

"A young girl who's lost and doesn't really know who she is yet. She's a little confused, and she's scared. I can't help with the confusion, but I can take away the fear."

"I don't see people that way," Jury said. "To me Frankie is just a girl who isn't old enough to be long-legged. I didn't see Tucker any particular way either until you dragged him into our lives. If you want to bring home strays in the future, Jervis and I should get a vote."

"Would you have voted no on Tucker?"

"Absolutely!" Jury declared. "He's a norm. And he's a little annoying, but it's too late now. You've already put him on the team; it'd be impossible to get rid of him."

"What about the Bakers?"

Jury lifted his hands and gave two thumbs down.

"Really?" Doc drawled. "Why?"

"The tall one's a norm; the little one pouts too much; the boy is alright; but the girl still stares at me, and it's annoying."

"Dublin?"

"Jurys don't intermingle with shifters. They're not our kind," Jury said. He tried to affect a haughty tone, but he couldn't quite manage with as drunk as he was.

"But what if I'd let Jervis and Andrew vote about you?" Doc asked.

"Ouch. Point taken," Jury said with a shrug. "Wake me when we get there."

"I'll bet you ten merlins Jervis wakes the both of us," Doc said softly.

Jury didn't respond, and Doc watched him for a moment. In a way, Jervis and Andrew had voted on Jury. They'd each taken one look at him, privately rolled their eyes, and not said a single word against him. They'd never seen him quite the way Doc did, but they hadn't turned their backs on him either. Just like Jury would never turn his back on Dublin or Frankie. He might not admit that to himself, but Doc knew it was true. Jury was loyal through and through, so anyone Doc loved, Jury would protect without question.

"Fourth luckiest day," Doc muttered softly. "Tozi, Andrew, Jervis, and Jury." After that he didn't bother trying to order how lucky he was. There was really no point. He hated to admit it, but he was a marionette and Lady Luck was the one pulling his strings. He refused to believe, however, that anyone or anything else was pulling them as well.

His mind didn't quite accept his refusal though; it wanted to follow that rabbit hole, wanted to think about trees and dragons. But instead of letting his mind run wild, Doc yawned widely, changed his chair's position, closed his eyes, and fell asleep, right into a memory dream.

Doc and Andrew were lying on top of a hill watching the moon sail above them, but Doc wasn't thinking about the moon and how lovely it was. He was thinking about how much things were changing and shifting.

Bill was out courting some lady. Janey had disappeared over a week ago, and all she'd said before she'd left was something vague about Wolf Heart. And when Andrew had said 'let's go riding', it was just Doc and Andrew who went. Doyle, Joe, and Charlie had stayed at the ranch.

Andrew didn't seem bothered; or if he was, he wasn't letting it show, but Doc hated it. He always hated it when things changed. Things could only be perfect for a moment, just one gossamer moment, and then it all fell away.

"I can hear you thinking," Andrew chuckled.

"You can't," Doc retorted.

"It's okay, you know. Life is constantly moving forward. It doesn't go backwards, and it doesn't stand still. It can't, and even if it could, it wouldn't want to."

Doc rolled his eyes and said nothing. He was feeling rather irritated about things in general. He'd left thinking... He wasn't sure what he'd been thinking, but he'd gotten caught up in Jervis's war and stayed gone far longer than he'd intended. Four years was nothing to him. But four years seemed to make a difference to everyone else.

"We'll all die eventually," Andrew said softly. "It's part of the cycle, but it doesn't mean it's the end of us."

"Shooting star," Doc lied, hoping to distract him.

"I already got my wish," Andrew said carelessly.

Doc rolled his eyes again. Andrew wanted him to ask, but he wasn't going to.

"Oh, come on," Andrew laughed.

"Look, another one," Doc said.

"That time I was looking, and there wasn't," Andrew stated, tone still full of humor.

"Fine," Doc sighed. "What was your wish?"

"That you would find someone like you. And you said Jervis will live just as long as you will."

Doc was quiet for a long time. "Did you really wish for that?" he finally asked.

"Couple times. You look just the same as you did the day I met you. What's it been, twenty-five years now?"

Doc didn't respond.

"Janey says I'm just finally starting to look like a man," Andrew added with amusement. "I think I'm about sixty now. I never could really figure it out, but Ahanu would probably know."

"You look the same," Doc insisted.

"I do, basically," Andrew agreed. "But still."

"It's Charlie, Doyle, Joe, and Two Stones," Doc murmured.

"I know. Janey goes out every night and sings to Brings the Rain," Andrew said softly. "It's been ten years. But it's been over forty years since I've seen Pecos, and I still miss him."

"Are you trying to help?"

"My point is that I got my wish. Told you shooting stars work."

"It wasn't your wish," Doc snorted. "It was my luck."

"Maybe," Andrew chuckled. "Maybe so. You know what I was thinking just the other day?" he went on without pause.

"No, but I'm sure you'll tell me," Doc drawled.

"Would you still love me if I didn't?"

"I might love you even more," Doc offered.

"I doubt that. This'll blow your mind," Andrew promised. "I was thinking that I'm not special."

"You're insane," Doc said flatly.

"No, seriously. Hear me out on this. Everyone has the potential to be me."

"That makes absolutely no sense," Doc said.

"Imagine that we each have unlimited power inside of us." Andrew paused and after a few seconds he said, "Did you imagine it?"

"Yes," Doc lied.

"You didn't," Andrew laughed. "But I still love you. Anyway, so you have the power, and it's unlimited, infinite, complete, right?"

"Alright."

"And everyone can touch it, but they've been told all their lives that they can't, so they don't."

"No one ever told me I couldn't touch the power," Doc argued.

"Sure they did. They told you people get sick, people break their bones, people need help to heal, people need shelter, people need medicine, people need tools and weapons and cupboards full of food. They told you you can't make something out of nothing. They told you you can't really affect reality. They told you you're not that significant. You follow?"

"Not really," Doc admitted.

"You'll work it out someday," Andrew promised. "They put all these limiting beliefs on you, all these finite measures, but you're so much more than that. Everyone can touch the power. Everyone can wield the power. Everyone could be like me. All they have to do is tear out the well of disbelief."

"What about Bill?" Doc asked.

Andrew burst out laughing.

"What?"

"That boy plays everyone for a fool," Andrew chuckled. "He's exactly like me; he just chooses not to advertise it."

"I don't believe you," Doc said, mind quickly sorting through all his memories of Bill, looking for signs of greatness.

"He's better than the rest of us," Andrew said, voice proud and sad at the same time. "He once told me that he wasn't born into war, and he didn't feel the same need to fight as we do. And he asked if that disappointed me. Silly boy," Andrew murmured. "How could he ever disappoint me? Every time he smiles I know I did okay."

Doc tried to imagine what that must feel like. The knowledge that you'd done something good and protected something beautiful. But he couldn't quite grasp it.

"All I'm saying," Andrew suddenly said, "is that all you have to do is tear down the well."

"Wake up," Jervis ordered.

"I'm awake," Doc replied, eyes still closed as he tried to hold on to Andrew's words. Not for the first time he wondered if Andrew was right. If everyone could just tear down the well and be gods.

11

"At a quick count, I'd say there're eighty-three," Jury said in Latin as the three of them walked slowly up the grass-lined driveway towards the gaudy-looking Foxall mansion.

"One hundred and five," Jervis stated.

"I said it was a quick count," Jury snarled. "And besides, I'm half-drunk; I wasn't exactly aiming for perfection."

"No fighting," Doc tsked. "And you do realize that we're dealing with archeologists? Chances are they know Latin. And every other language we know."

"I bet they didn't bother with French," Jury said in French. "After all, it's not a dead language."

"Maybe," Doc conceded.

He was walking between them, mind constantly reminding himself that he was Frankie. Uncertain, worried, upset. He schooled his face into the appropriate expression and knocked on the front door.

A man answered it, and Doc said softly, "Where's Muriel?"

He had no way of knowing whether or not this man was

one of Frankie's many relations, but he didn't figure they were close, so it didn't really matter if he called anyone by name.

"She's waiting for you in the study," the man said as he stepped aside to let them through.

This was an unexpected complication. He may look like Frankie, but he didn't actually know where the study was. He'd just have to let Lady Luck lead him. He started walking forward, then turned left down a hallway. After passing a few doorways, he opened the door on his right.

It was certainly the study, but Muriel was nowhere to be seen.

"Trap," Jervis muttered.

"Proof of life," Doc replied in French, pointing towards a small monitor that was sitting on the desk.

A woman's crease-lined face suddenly filled the screen, and she snapped, "Come closer, Francesca."

Doc took two steps towards the desk.

"Well, I suppose you've grown into yourself a bit," Muriel muttered.

Doc didn't respond.

"Where is the journal?"

Doc lifted the logbook that Jury had glamoured to look like Wesley Foxall's journal.

"Bring it closer," Muriel ordered.

Doc glanced back at Jury. Jury's face was creased with concentration, but after a moment he gave Doc a sharp nod. Doc stepped forward and held up the journal once more.

"Open it."

Doc opened it to the first page.

Muriel visually examined it before saying, "I'm rather ashamed of you, Francesca. I would have thought a Foxall would be too smart to bring the actual journal."

Doc allowed himself to grin and said, "I'm actually very smart. In about fifteen minutes everyone here will be dead."

Jervis cleared his throat.

"In about eight to ten minutes," Doc corrected. "Everyone here will be dead. After that you have one hour to personally retrieve the journal. If you're not here within the hour, I'll burn it."

"Don't be stupid, girl," Muriel snarled. "Even Mr. Nettle doesn't stand a chance this time."

"We'll see about that," Doc said as he stepped backwards.

Without a word, Jury drew his gun and shot the monitor to pieces.

"Now for the fun part," Doc said cheerfully.

"Finally," Jury sighed. "I need a distraction; the whiskey's wearing off."

He waved his hand in a circle, and the walls began to tremble; and then all of a sudden, strands and lengths of wire tore through the plaster all around the room.

"Cameras disabled," he said languidly.

Jervis raised an eyebrow, but didn't say a word.

"We should set some ground rules," Doc said as he sat on the edge of the desk. "You," he pointed at Jury. "No magic. And you," he pointed at Jervis. "Try to slow it down."

"How about I go out the window and take care of the outside ones?" Jervis offered.

"Deal," Doc said, but Jervis was gone before Doc had fully spoken the word. "I think he's actually faster than he used to be," Doc sighed.

"Or you're getting slower," Jury snorted. "I'm feeling lazy, so I'm just going to sit down and let you handle it."

"You mean you're feeling drunk."

"Exactly."

Jury plopped into the Chesterfield chair near the desk and muttered, "Wake me if you need me."

The study door suddenly swung open, and the man who'd let them into the mansion stepped into the room.

"Don't be stupid, Francesca," he said softly. "Come without a fight, and Muriel'll take it easy on you."

"You're lying," Doc said.

"Why would I lie to you? You've been running from the family for far too long. It's time to stop."

"Don't forget to keep one alive," Jury mumbled.

"I'll keep this one alive," Doc said. "I think he's one of the uncles," he added as he stalked a little closer.

"Don't you recognize me?" the man demanded.

"Afraid not," Doc shrugged.

And then he pounced, plowing into the man with enough force to take him to the ground; and before the man could mount any sort of attack, his wrists and ankles were already bound with zip ties.

"What the hell are you doing?" he growled.

"Saving you for last," Doc replied as he slapped a piece of duct tape over the man's mouth and rolled him over by the wall.

Doc headed towards the study door, but stopped himself. As much as he wanted to rush out into the house and just start killing them, he was certain Muriel had cameras throughout the house; and he didn't want to give her any clues that he wasn't actually Frankie. So, unfortunately, he'd have to wait for them to come to him.

He stared at the door and said softly, "Come into my parlor, little flies."

Just as he'd finished speaking, the door swung open and several men walked into the study.

"It's time to go, Francesca," a younger man said, tone harsh.

"You're all very slow on the uptake," Doc laughed.

He threw three knives, one right after the other, watching in satisfaction as they all hit their marks. As the three men fell to the floor, heat poured into Doc's tattoo.

A face peeked briefly into the room before disappearing, and a voice drifted back in. "The bitch killed them."

Doc decided to take offense on Frankie's behalf, and he searched the room for a more painful way to kill the next wave of goons, grinning widely when his eyes settled on an ancient broadsword mounted behind the desk.

He walked over to the sword and ripped it from its mounting, then ran his finger gently down its blade. It was too dull to even cut him. "Perfect," he drawled.

"I'm setting the journal on fire!" he yelled once he was positioned against the wall by the door.

"Shit!" someone hissed. "We've got to get in there. If we lose the journal, we're all dead."

"You first," someone else said.

The door swung open, and a man stumbled into the room. Doc waited patiently. Seven men crept in slowly behind the first man, guns clutched in their shaking hands.

"Francesca?" the first man called out.

"I prefer Frankie," Doc said as he rushed forward.

He swung the sword with full force, watching in amazement as the blade ripped through three necks and one torso. Blood and body bits spewed across the room, showering the other four men.

Doc heard Jury sputter something, but he focused on the four remaining men, stalking towards them with amusement. He jabbed quickly forward, skewering one of them from nearly four feet away, but instead of pulling the sword out, Doc ripped it to the side, splitting the man in two and cleaving through the other three men. Heat soared into Doc's tattoo as three legless torsos dropped to the ground.

"I feel practically medieval," Doc said cheerfully as he hefted the broadsword and spun towards the door, ready for the next wave of men.

Doc stared at the door, waiting, but nearly dropped the sword in surprise when Jury suddenly bellowed, "THERE'S A GODDAMN FUCKING HEAD IN MY FUCKING LAP!"

Doc glanced over his shoulder, just barely managing to swallow his explosion of laughter when he saw Jury sitting stiffly and staring down at the bloody head gazing up at him.

"Get it the fuck off!" Jury commanded. "Right the fuck now!"

Doc couldn't help it; he snorted, then burst out laughing.

"I know you're not fucking laughing right now!" Jury snarled as he flicked his hand.

The head spun off Jury's lap and flew through the air right towards Doc's face. Doc ducked, but a trail of lukewarm blood splattered across his face.

"I'm sorry," Doc chortled. "But you should've seen your face."

"You're about to see your face," Jury snapped. "Behind you," he added.

Doc spun, sword in hand, and sliced through the three men trying to sneak up on him.

"You know I hate D.C.," Jury went on, blue magic bursting off his fingers into the other men who were just coming through the study door. "And now I hate D.C. even more. Because I woke up to a goddamn bloody head on my lap! Do you know how disgusting that is?"

"I don't know why you're so bothered; you come from a long line of decapitators," Doc pointed out.

He surged forward to stop Jury from killing everyone before they entered the room, but he was finding it difficult to use the broadsword in such a limited space. He speared the sword through the nearest man, pinning him to the wall, then leaped forward and snapped another man's neck.

Before Doc could take another step though, all the remaining men's heads exploded, showering blood and gore everywhere.

"That was payback for what you just said," Jury growled irritably. "How do you like being covered in bits of brain?"

"It's underneath the glamour," Doc said flippantly. "I can't even tell it's there."

He turned casually, readying himself to catch Jury if he collapsed, but Jury was fine. He was fine because one of his hands was inside a grey hole that Doc assumed was allowing him to touch the earth somewhere.

"That's a really nifty trick," Doc said with a grin.

Jury shrugged and said, "It's alright, but I'm not going to give you credit or anything. It's not as if you had the idea."

"It's exactly as if I had the idea," Doc drawled.

"Prove it."

Doc laughed softly and said, "I don't suppose I can."

"Exactly," Jury said, tone smug.

Jury withdrew his hand from the grey space and shook the water from it with a careless movement. And just like that, his hand was completely dry, and Doc knew he'd used magic to do it.

"If you're an earth witch," he asked, "why do you put your hand into a lake?"

"I put it on the bottom of the lake," Jury replied. "That

way I'm touching both water and earth. Not to mention that doing it that way keeps some idiot from wandering along and stepping on my hand or cutting it off or something ridiculous like that."

"Ah," Doc murmured. "You've certainly refined your magic skills in the last year."

"Magic skills?" Jury snorted.

"What would you call it?"

"I don't actually know," he admitted. "Jervis is coming down the hallway."

"You heard him?" Doc asked in surprise.

"No. I can see him."

"Through the wall," Doc stated just as Jervis stepped over a headless body and into the study.

"Yeah," Jury said with a yawn. He dropped back into the chair he'd been sitting in and closed his eyes. "Through the goddamn wall," he muttered.

Doc wasn't particularly surprised. Jury could sense life, and it followed that he could sense life through a wall, just like Andrew had been able to. But Doc was surprised at the ease with which Jury could suddenly do things he'd never been able to do before. His short time with Phillip Jury had definitely changed him. After all, he'd not only sensed a life force through the wall, but he'd also somehow known it was Jervis's life force.

"This room is a mess," Jervis said flatly.

"I didn't do it," Doc replied.

Jervis gestured towards where the sword was stuck firmly inside the wall, corpse hanging off of it.

"Alright, I made part of the mess," Doc admitted. "But not the exploded heads part. Jury was throwing a fit, and he snatched all my kills."

"He did a rather spectacular job of it," Jervis admitted.

"That he did," Doc agreed. "Did we get them all?"

"Yes."

"So Muriel has fifty minutes to show up, which gives us plenty of time to torture Frankie's uncle."

Doc stepped over an unidentifiable body part towards the wall where he'd left the bound man, then sighed heavily.

"What?" Jervis asked.

"Apparently, Jury wasn't very specific when he cast his spell to kill everyone." Doc ran a hand over his neck, shuddered, and said, "But I still have my head so I guess he was specific enough."

"So no torturing?"

"No torturing. Do you want to play gin?"

"No," Jervis said. "I want to see what's in the hidden room."

"There's a hidden room?!" Doc exclaimed. "I love hidden rooms. Where is it?"

Jervis pointed at the fireplace, and Doc hurried over to it and began to look for secret switches. He eventually pushed the right little bit of moulding and the inside of the fireplace jolted backwards, then slid to the side.

"Jules and Johnny would love this," Doc said as he stepped inside.

"Frankie would not," Jervis said definitely.

"She'd much rather be out in the garden," Doc agreed.

He felt the wall for a light switch and flipped it when he found it.

"Pinch me," he whispered.

Jervis pinched his arm so hard that Doc actually flinched.

"Nope," Doc breathed. "Not dreaming."

"It's not that impressive," Jervis stated.

"I've never seen this much gold in one place. Look at it! It's just... gleaming."

"It has no real value," Jervis insisted.

"Maybe not, but it's gorgeous. Just like a super car, so don't try to ruin this for me."

Doc walked forward and ran his finger over a golden goblet. It was every bit as gaudy as the goblets from his throne room, but this one was real. He lifted it and stared at himself in the sheen of gold, almost startling because he'd quite forgotten he was wearing Frankie's face.

"Jury really is very good at glamours," he said thoughtfully. "How do you think it works?"

"I've read no less than two hundred books on magic," Jervis said, "and I still don't understand how it works. I think perhaps to understand magic you have to be a witch."

"That's what I've always thought," Doc murmured as he dropped the goblet and picked up a golden crown encrusted with rubies and emeralds. "It's a goddamn crown," he laughed. "I'm putting it on."

He slipped it onto his head and turned with a flourish. "How do I look?"

"Like you were made to wear it," Jervis said. "Or Frankie was made to wear it; I'm not sure which."

Doc chuckled and turned to examine more of the treasure. It bothered him a little how well the crown fit him. It must have been made to fit a specific someone so it really shouldn't have fit at all. But he forced thoughts of that away and picked up a handful of golden coins.

"I've never seen coins like these," he said, studying the relief of a tree that was on the face of one.

"Elf coins," Jervis said. "I can't imagine how the Foxalls got their hands on them. Elves are very reclusive."

"There's a lot about the Foxalls that doesn't make sense," Doc agreed. "But I'll take my time with Muriel so I can figure it out."

He dropped the coins and picked up a sheet of gold with runes inscribed on it.

"Nordic," Jervis stated. "It's describing a visit with the fae."

"I'm starting to notice a theme," Doc said.

"Besides the obsession with gold?" Jervis asked dryly.

"Besides that," Doc chuckled.

"It's really rather strange that Frankie ended up within the Hidden after all," Jervis mused.

"She belongs there," Doc said. "The rest of the Foxalls don't."

Jervis tilted his head and said, "Someone is here."

"Excellent," Doc said. "I'm nearly bored with this particular caper."

"Too easy?" Jervis inquired.

"Too easy. I've gotten used to a little bit of a challenge."

He and Jervis stepped back out into the study and closed the treasure room behind them. Then Doc sat on the desk once more, completely ignoring the fact that it was splattered with blood.

"Francesca?" Muriel's voice called out. "Are you here?"

"In here, Muriel!" Doc called back.

He heard a short gasp when Muriel entered the hallway, and he composed his face into a bland expression with a slight smile.

Muriel appeared at the doorway and stared inside the study. "What have you done?" she asked, face pale.

"I didn't do it," Doc said with a shrug. After all, he didn't have a speck of blood on him. At least not visibly. "And I did warn you," he added.

"Where's the journal?" Muriel demanded.

"It's nice to see how much you care about them," Doc murmured. "Didn't even shed a tear."

"They were obviously useless," Muriel said disdainfully. "And most of them were hired, so why would I care?"

"My uncle wasn't hired," Doc said.

"He knew the risks. Where is the journal?"

"Right here," Doc said, picking it up off the desk behind him and dangling it in front of her. "But if you want it, you have to come get it."

Muriel stared greedily at the journal, but she didn't move further into the room even though Doc could see her fingers twitching with the need to touch it. He knew she had a plan; he just didn't know what it was, and he was waiting for her to reveal it.

She took one cautious step inside the room, eyes darting around it. Her eyes stopped briefly on Jervis and Jury, and then for just the slightest moment they skittered across to the window.

"Oh hell," Doc muttered as he pushed himself off the desk.

At that exact moment, a sharp stinging pain tore through his skull, and he suddenly couldn't see. He felt his body move forward; he felt his mind shut down. Everything turned black, and Doc felt a heaviness settle on him as he collapsed.

This couldn't be it. He refused to die from a bullet to the brain. That was too easy.

His finger twitched, and he grinned. At least he grinned inwardly. He couldn't actually feel his lips, but he knew without a doubt that he wasn't dead.

Another finger twitched, and he forced his eyes to open. Jervis was staring down at him, concern clear on his face.

"Did you get the shooter?" Doc asked, a little surprised his lips could still move.

"Yes," Jervis replied, relief briefly filling his face before his normal stoic expression took hold again.

"Do I look alright?" Doc inquired hopefully.

"You did before Jury dropped your glamour," Jervis replied. "Not so much now."

Doc ran a hand over his face, flinching when his fingers touched the ragged edge of the hole in his forehead.

"Muriel killed Frankie," Doc growled. "That's nasty for anyone, but especially nasty for a grandmother. How long was I out?"

"A minute, maybe two, but I left you Mrs. Foxall."

"Excellent," Doc said as he pushed himself to his feet. "I have a score to settle with her."

When Doc finally got his bearings, he was pleased to see that Muriel was already tied to a chair and looking rather frightened.

"You are a very nasty woman," he said irritably.

"Who are you?" she whispered. "And where's Frankie?"

Doc turned around and caught Jury's eyes. "Did she see me when you removed the glamour?" Doc mouthed.

Jury shook his head.

"So for all she knows, Frankie is dead?"

Jury nodded.

Doc turned back around and snapped, "You murdered her."

"Did I?" she murmured. "I wasn't sure. Why aren't you dead?"

He was missing something; he could just tell.

"There were three snipers," Jervis murmured in Doc's ear.

Doc cast another look at Jury.

"He apparently had a shield up," Jervis added. "I, however, had a horrible headache for at least one second, maybe two."

"You're terribly annoying," Doc said.

"Are you talking to me or her?" Jervis asked.

"You. One second? I completely blacked out."

"I know. If Jury hadn't been here to protect you, you might have lost your head," Jervis said, tone slightly amused.

"Go away," Doc demanded. "I'm trying to focus, and it's difficult with you breathing in my ear."

He returned his attention to Muriel and said, "I'm not dead because your sniper missed the important parts. Now, tell me where the rest of the family is hiding."

"Are you going to kill me?" Muriel asked, voice wobbling.

"Yes."

Her shoulders slumped, and she suddenly seemed very old. Her ploy didn't fool Doc one bit though. He'd seen poker players pull that very trick, and it never moved him. Age made no difference at all to him; character did.

"You murdered your own daughter, you murdered Frankie, and you'll stop at nothing to feed your greed," Doc said firmly. "You will die today, but it's up to you how painfully you die. Tell me where the rest of your family is, and I won't torture you... much."

Tears rolled down her lined cheeks, and she sobbed, "I was only trying to fulfill my husband's dying wish."

"I don't have the patience for games," Doc said as he pulled his knife, leaned forward, and stabbed it through Muriel's shoulder.

She screamed in pain and started sobbing in earnest.

"I've no sympathy for you," Doc stated. "You're a cruel,

cold woman; and you have no love for others. I'll not be the least bit bothered to chop bits and pieces from you."

He twisted the knife before yanking it free.

"Tell me where the others are."

She just continued to sob so Doc laid her hand flat on the arm of the chair and chopped off one of her fingers. Her wail of pain and terror echoed through the study. If she had been anyone else, Doc might have pitied her. But Frankie was his. He loved her, and Muriel had tried to end Frankie's life. For no reason whatsoever. He felt nothing but righteous anger and the need to exterminate the entire Foxall line so that Frankie could finally be free.

"Tell me where they are," Doc ordered as he raised his knife once more.

"They're at the connecting estate!" Muriel screamed.

"I'll handle it," Jervis said.

With that, Jervis was gone, and Doc was left with a sobbing Muriel and a snoring Jury.

"Does anyone else know about Frankie and the artifact?" Doc asked.

"No," she whimpered.

"Are you sure?" he drawled as he lightly dug the tip of his knife into her bleeding wound.

"Yes!" she screamed.

"Yes?" Doc asked.

"I'm sure no one else knows!"

Doc studied Muriel's weeping face as he considered what to ask her next. He found he didn't really care how the Foxalls had amassed their fortune or how they'd managed to steal the elven gold; and since he wasn't in the mood just to torture her, he decided to ignore her while he waited for Jervis to return.

Doc wandered around the study for a moment looking at all the various artifacts, but he soon wearied of that and picked up a handful of paperclips off the desk. He took careful aim and flicked one with his finger, grinning when it landed on top of Jury's sleeping head.

"Ten merlins says I can get this entire handful in his hair before he wakes up," he whispered to himself.

He'd flicked half of them by the time Jervis returned.

"What are you doing?" Jervis demanded.

"Trying to annoy Jury," Doc replied.

"Is it working?"

"No," Doc sighed. "He refuses to wake up and yell at me. I bet you a hundred merlins he doesn't notice they're there until we get home."

"I'll take that bet," Jervis said. "The neighboring estate has been swept clean," he added.

There were fresh splatters of blood on Jervis's face, and Doc grinned at him widely.

"What a pair we make," he chuckled. "Jury's going to have to glamour us just so we can make it home without causing a fuss."

"I miss the olden days," Jervis said with a shrug. "No one ever used to even notice it when I got blood on my clothes. Half the time they just assumed I was a careless butcher."

Doc laughed before saying, "There should have been at least two women."

"There were five," Jervis replied. "Eighteen men and three teenage boys."

"Good enough," Doc said cheerfully.

There wasn't any way he could be completely positive that they'd killed Frankie's entire family. He was certain they'd killed most of them, and he was even more certain that only a complete madman would seek out Frankie after witnessing the trail of death and destruction Doc and Jervis had left in their wake. And if anyone ever did, Frankie had Boudica.

Doc turned to face Muriel Foxall once more and said, "Is there anything else I should know? Any family members left unaccounted for, any strings left unsnipped?"

"No," she said, voice barely audible.

"I'd better put that to the test," Doc murmured as he cut off another finger.

"No!" she screamed. "There's no one else!"

"Very good," Doc said. "I'll leave you with these parting words. Frankie is safe. The fae are real. I've personally met two of them, and they possess more power than you could ever dream of."

Muriel's eyes widened, and for a moment greed and hatred overcame the fear and pain in her eyes. "Where are they?" she demanded.

"You'll never know," Doc whispered. And then he shoved his knife through her rotten black heart.

12

They didn't burn the house. Instead they called the local Worms to come clean up, and Jervis brought in a team of his own to clear out the artifacts. The elven gold would be returned to the elves, but everything else would be moved to a storage unit for Frankie. By the time they were done cleaning up, the Foxalls would be nothing but a distant memory.

"That was fun," Doc said as he, Jervis, and Jury finally boarded Doc's plane.

"Ehh," Jury grumbled.

"It was so much better than the last time we went to D.C.," Doc insisted, trying not to snicker about the paperclips that were still sticking every which way out of Jury's hair.

"I don't want to talk about it," Jury stated. "In some ways it might have been better; if you don't count waking up with a head on my lap, but D.C. is still on my don't-visit list."

"You can hardly blame him," Jervis said. "It took us over three hours to get the tar off of him."

"I said I don't want to talk about it!" Jury snapped. "So

shut up or I'll rip a hole in the side of the plane and kill us all."

"I'm not sure I would die," Doc pointed out. "Especially if I killed you on the way down."

Jury glared at him and said in a menacing tone, "One more word, and I'm giving you a permanent Frankie glamour."

Doc opened his mouth. Blue magic flared on Jury's hand. Doc grinned. The blue magic swirled into a spiral.

"You're really good at that," Doc mouthed.

"I'm going to sleep," Jury growled. "Don't wake me when we get there."

"Testy, isn't he?" Doc chuckled once he was sure Jury was asleep.

"Quite," Jervis said. "I'm beginning to miss the days when he didn't know how powerful he was."

"But he was so arrogant back then," Doc said with a cringe.

"He's not the least bit arrogant now," Jervis stated.

"Nope," Doc agreed. "He really is every bit as powerful as he thinks he is."

"Maybe a little more so."

"Don't tell him," Doc said, allowing a pained tone to color his words.

"I never tell anyone what I truly think," Jervis said easily.

"Never?"

"Never."

Jervis was actually grinning, which Doc found harder to read than when he wasn't grinning.

"I like seeing you happy," Doc said.

Jervis's eyebrows tightened for a moment before he said softly, "I rather like feeling happy."

"Is it all because of Sami?" Doc asked, knowing how

dangerous it was to pin all of one's happiness on another human being.

"No," Jervis replied. "It's because after all this time I finally gave myself permission to truly live, to feel, to be happy. There will always be a part of me that wishes I had died with them, but they wouldn't want me to live in continual sorrow, not like I have been. I didn't die that day," he said firmly. "And it was a gift, even if I didn't see it that way at the time. If I had died, I wouldn't have met you, I wouldn't have helped you raise Bree, I wouldn't know the Bakers, and I wouldn't be confounded by Sami."

He cast a sideways glance at Jury. "And I also wouldn't have had the pleasure of watching a young, arrogant, and foolish Thomas Jury turn into the man he is today." Jervis smiled slightly and added, "He's rather grown on me over the years."

"He doesn't know that," Doc said.

"Doesn't he?" Jervis asked with surprise.

"No. He thinks your only interest in him all these years is because of your loyalty to me."

"Ah," Jervis murmured. "So perhaps he's still a little foolish."

"Just a little," Doc agreed with a chuckle.

"I'll try to find a way to tell him, but you know that words don't come easy to me."

"Me neither."

"Sami considers it my only failing."

"Your only?" Doc snorted.

"Just that one," Jervis said.

"I'll have to give her a list."

"It wouldn't matter. She's quite blind when it comes to me. She said just the other day that my stern manner is delightful."

"Delightful?"

"That's the word she used."

"You're one of my favorite people," Doc said, grinning widely, "and not even I would call you delightful."

"Neither would Bree. She told me so herself. She said I was steadfast and constant and comforting and loving."

"But not delightful?" Doc prodded, swallowing a laugh.

"She said I could be considered delightful depending on which definition of delightful we were using."

"I imagine that's the point of the conversation where Winslow needed you."

"How right you are. He wanted to discuss the dress code."

"Whatever he wanted, no."

"Actually, in this case, his idea had some merit," Jervis admitted.

"Strange," Doc said.

"And delightful," Jervis added.

They both suddenly laughed, and Doc savored it. Jervis rarely laughed, and Doc quite liked the sound of it. He'd even go so far as to say that he found it rather delightful.

As soon as they were back in Denver, Doc went to see Frankie. He found her in the Baker estate forest, sitting with Boudica next to a flourishing raspberry bush.

Without a word, Doc sat beside her. Boudica lifted her head and put it onto Doc's lap, and he scratched behind her ears while he waited for Frankie to speak.

"You're covered in blood," she finally said. "Again."

"I am," Doc agreed. "Jury flatly refused to put a glamour on me. He said that if I was going to fight messy I had to suffer the consequences."

"That wasn't very nice."

"There was this incident with a decapitated head and some innocent paperclips, and consequently, he was in a really bad mood," Doc chuckled.

"Paperclips?" Frankie asked.

"Yes. I won that bet," he added with a grin.

"Is Muriel dead?" Frankie whispered.

"Yes."

He didn't miss the relief that flashed through her eyes, followed instantly by guilt.

"You killed her because of me," Frankie gasped, eyes suddenly widening.

"No," Doc said. "I killed her because she used her significance to hurt others. She wasn't a nice person," he went on. "She shot you in the head. And for what? There was absolutely no reason for her to do that. She was rotten, some people are."

"She shot me in the head?" Frankie asked in confusion. "I don't understand."

"Jury glamoured me to look like you. Only he gave me yellow bellbottoms, and I looked ridiculous."

Frankie laughed before she thought better of it and quickly sobered.

"Muriel tried to kill me," she said softly.

"Yes. I still have a bit of a headache," Doc admitted.

The color left Frankie's face. "She shot you in the head?!"

"Right here," Doc said, tapping his forehead.

"Are you alright?" Frankie asked fearfully.

"I'm fine," Doc assured her. "Mostly. I mean every now and then I feel a garbly-goo basencoming," he said, deliberately garbling his words.

Her face turned even whiter, and Doc laughed and said, "I'm only teasing you. I'm fine."

"Doc!"

"I'm sorry," he chuckled. "I shouldn't have done that."

She glared at him, but then she threw her arms around him and hugged him tightly. "Thank you," she whispered.

"Anything for you," Doc said softly, meaning it wholeheartedly.

Frankie pulled away from him, rubbing her eyes as she did. Boudica moved from Doc's lap to Frankie's, and they were both silent for a while.

"Are they all dead?" she asked eventually.

"I can't swear that I got them all," Doc admitted. "I definitely killed Muriel, and Jervis killed five women at the connecting estate, so I assume we got all your aunts. I highly doubt that anyone will come looking for you though. I made my thoughts on the matter pretty clear, and Jervis will locate any Foxall assets and transfer them into your name," Doc added offhandedly.

"Oh," Frankie said. "I... I don't... He doesn't need to do that."

"Better for you to have it," Doc said firmly.

"That would make me..."

She didn't continue, so Doc said it for her, "Filthy rich judging by all the gold I found in the secret room. There was a crown," he said with a grin. "I wore it."

She laughed, and it made him happy to hear it.

"Thank you," she said once more. "I didn't ever think... I don't know what I thought exactly, but I didn't ever think I'd be free of them. Not really."

"You are," Doc assured her.

"It's... It's a strange feeling."

"A good feeling, I trust?"

"Yes," she said, smiling at him. "A very good feeling."

"I don't want you putting this on yourself," Doc told her. "Even if they hadn't been after you, I would have still killed them. They're the type of people I kill."

Frankie nodded, then said abruptly, "Jules wants to see you. She finished translating Dad's journal, and we found the artifact."

An odd tingle ran down Doc's spine at her words, and he found himself wishing they hadn't found it, but he didn't know why.

He stood, offered Frankie his hand, and pulled her to her feet. They walked silently back to the house, Boudica trailing behind them. When they reached the kitchen, there was a flurry of hugs and yells.

Johnny said, "Hi, Doc!"

Addison said, "Is my horn any longer today, Doc?"

And Jules said flatly, "You're covered in blood, Doc."

Babs gave him a consoling smile, pulled a bottle of whiskey from one of the cabinets, and gave it to him.

"For me?" Doc asked in surprise.

"It's only fair," she replied with a shrug.

"Careful," Doc drawled. "I might start to think you like me."

"You can think whatever you like," Babs replied with a grin. "It doesn't make it true."

"We found the artifact!" Johnny said, cutting off Doc's response.

"And it's pure gold," Addison said. "It's so pretty. I like to just sit and look at it."

"I just have to assume Wesley's translation is accurate," Jules broke in. "I can't read Fae yet, but I've been using Wesley's notes to figure it out."

Doc popped the cork off the whiskey bottle and took a

drink. When he had drank enough that he was certain he could handle a longwinded Jules's lecture, he said, "Tell me more."

"It's a warning," Jules said excitedly. "Come out to the treehouse and look at it."

Doc followed the excited children outside and up into the treehouse into Jules's special room. There was paper everywhere, but in the middle of one table there was nothing but a chunk of gold that was covered in strange symbols.

"Isn't it pretty?" Addison said as she tugged Doc over to look at it.

He wasn't sure. At a glance he didn't particularly like it, but it was just gold. He'd been thrilled to see the gold inside the secret chamber, and he'd be hard-pressed to explain what the difference was, but there was a difference.

"Wesley translated it in sections," Jules was saying. "He started with the top, then the bottom, then he did the four sides. I'm not sure how he figured out the order."

"Interesting," Doc murmured.

"If his translation is correct, it says that only trouble will come to those who seek the treasure of the fae. Variations of this warning are all over it. One says the treasure will completely destroy a mortal being. Another says that no mortal man or creature can hope to understand or contain the treasure. Which is curious," Jules added, voice laced with confusion. "I don't think they're speaking of gold at all because you can't contain gold, can you?"

"I don't think he translated that part correctly," Johnny broke in. "Maybe it should have been carry or store. Like it's so much gold no mortal man can hope to store it."

Doc somehow knew that Johnny was wrong, and so did Jules because she was shaking her head and saying, "I don't think so. Besides, Wesley underlined the word 'contain' three times."

"Well, maybe you screwed up your translation," Johnny said. "It's in code so it's not like you can be certain what it says."

"You take that back, Johnny Baker," Jules ordered.

"I'm just saying," Johnny shrugged. "It is possible."

"Frankie said something about a key before," Doc broke in, hoping to avoid an all-out war.

"Right!" Jules exclaimed. "So the top and bottom are the warning bits, and the sides contain some sort of spell or something that should hypothetically reveal the treasure."

"Have you tried it?" Doc asked.

"Of course not," Jules snorted. "It's far too complicated for us to pull off. Jury could do it, but not us."

"In that case," Doc said, "here's what we're going to do. We're going to burn the journal and melt the gold."

"What?!" Jules gasped. "We can't do that! Then it will be lost."

"It sounds to me as if it should have never existed," Doc said. "Furthermore, if something like this is in existence, there's always a possibility that someone evil, someone like Gac or Phillip Jury or Muriel Foxall, will find it and use it. The world is better off without it."

"But—"

"No buts," Doc said firmly. "We're destroying them both."

"I agree with Doc," Frankie said. "And since it's technically my property that means we do it."

"But then we'll never know what the treasure is," Johnny and Jules said simultaneously.

"Who cares?" Frankie said. "It's never been anything but bad for me."

"Fine," Jules sighed. "We'll take it outside and melt it."

"I don't wanna melt it!" Addison shrieked as she grabbed the gold off the table and ran into a corner. "It's pretty, and I like it!"

"Addison," Doc said sternly. "Give me the gold."

"I won't," she pouted.

"Then I'm afraid I'm going to have to call Unicorn Central and cancel your unicorn breath delivery," Doc said.

Addison's face went white, and she stuttered, "You wouldn't, would you?"

"I would. It's up to you. Gold or unicorn breath?"

Addison whimpered as she looked down at the gold she was clutching in her hands. "It's so pretty."

"Liadawn would be very hurt if you chose gold over her breath," Doc said carelessly.

"You would tell her?" Addison gasped.

"I'd have to."

Addison's little shoulders slumped in defeat, and she shuffled over to Doc and handed him the gold.

The second it touched his hand, Doc wanted to hurl it out the window. He could feel it moving, just barely, vibrating in his hand.

"Let's go," he urged, gesturing towards the ladder.

Once they were all on the ground, Jules walked over to a fire pit surrounded by chairs and said, "Put the gold in the pit."

Doc dropped it on top of the ashes, shuddering slightly as it left his hand.

"It really is pretty," Jules murmured. "I hate to destroy it."

"I don't," Doc said. "Can you and Johnny do it?"

"I can do it," Jules sighed. "But let's save it for last. We'll do the journal first."

Frankie laid the journal on top of the gold brick. There were tears gathered in her eyes, and Doc knew that no matter what she said, this was hard for her. The journal was the only thing she had left of her father, but she was willing to burn it because, just like Doc, she felt uneasy around the artifact.

Jules stood, stared at the journal, and muttered a few words in Gaelic. A purple ball of magic formed inside her hand. Another word, and the magic turned into a ball of fire. Jules knelt and placed the fire on the book, and the journal instantly burst into flames.

As they watched it burn, Doc said, "Did you make any copies?"

"Just the pages I sent you," Jules replied, voice subdued.

"Good," Doc said, feeling an acute relief once the final bits of journal had crumbled into black ash.

"Do I have to melt it?" Jules asked plaintively.

"Yes!" Doc and Frankie replied at once.

Doc cast Frankie a look, and she said, "I hate it. I don't know why, but I do. I always have."

"It's gold," Johnny sputtered. "How can you hate it?"

"I don't like it either," Doc said. "Melt it," he ordered, tone leaving no room for argument.

Jules sighed heavily, but she began to mutter in Gaelic. After the purple magic had gathered in her hand, she reached out and touched the gold brick. A few seconds later it began to melt, and in another couple seconds, there was a puddle of gold in the bottom of the fire pit.

"Can we at least keep the gold?" Johnny asked.

"Yes," Doc replied, staring at a bit of black that was lying in the center of the molten gold. "What's that?"

"I'm not sure," Jules said. She plucked it free with her

other hand and studied it curiously. "It's a ring," she finally said. "It has fae writing on it, but it's really tiny."

"Melt it," Doc said, more horrified at the sight of the ring than he had been at the gold.

"I can't," Jules replied.

"What do you mean you can't?"

"I can't," she said, shrugging. "Whatever it is, it's not meltable."

"That's not even a word," Doc said grumpily.

He didn't want her touching it, so even though the very thought of touching it himself sent chills down his spine, he reached out and snatched the ring from her hand.

"I'll take it to Jury," he said. "He'll know how to destroy it." The curiosity in Jules's eyes reminded him so much of Thaddeus that he added, "Not all mysteries need solved, and not all phenomena need explained; some things are best left alone."

"I know," she sighed. "It's powerful. I can feel it. What are you doing?" she suddenly asked.

"What do you mean?" Doc replied.

"Why are you putting it on?"

"I'm not," Doc retorted as he glanced down at his hands.

Icy horror filled him as he watched his own hand slip the black ring onto one of his fingers. And then the entire world turned black.

13

Voices swirled around Doc. Strange voices. Voices he'd never heard. Voices layered with mystery. Voices layered with wisdom and years beyond understanding.

"He wears the ring."

"Rather unexpected."

"I thought the ring lost."

Doc tried to open his eyes, but something, a force, a burden, something, was holding him still, keeping him frozen. He struggled against it, but he couldn't budge at all.

"He is just a man," a voice laced with disappointment said.

"Look again, sister."

There was a slight pause, then the woman said, "I see now. I was only using my eyes."

"Do you think this is wise?" another voice asked.

"The choice is not ours to make."

"The choice was made long ago."

"When the ring was forged."

"It chose him."

"We cannot unchoose him."

"The ring should not have been forged," a new voice said. "This pathway is not wise."

"I agree, but there is nothing to be done."

"We could leave him in the plains," the new voice suggested.

"That would break our oath."

"Better to break the oath than to be unwise."

"I vouch for this man," another voice suddenly said, a voice Doc vaguely recognized.

He searched his mind, looking for the face that went with it, but before he could find it, the disagreeable voice said sharply, "You are no longer a member of this council. Your voice carries no weight here."

"I am willing to hear what she has to say," another voice broke in.

"As am I."

"And I."

"You are all fools! The oath is five thousand years old. Why hold to it like this? It was forged in a moment of weakness."

"Silence!" a stern voice ordered. "Fiona, what have you to say?"

Fiona. Rachelle's sister. The fairy Doc had saved from Gionta's painting. That was the voice he was hearing.

"This man is just," Fiona said with conviction. "He sees truth, and he cuts through lies. He does not hesitate to put his own life at risk to protect others. He protects. That is his nature."

"The question is not whether or not he is just," the stern voice said. "The question is whether or not he is capable of completing the task."

"He is strong enough to complete any task," Fiona stated.

"Are we looking at the same man?" the disagreeable voice spat.

"You have only to truly look at him to see the power within him," one of the other voices said. "I fear you have been corrupted by your time with the humans, brother. I do not think you see clearly anymore."

"Are you suggesting that I am no longer pure?" the disagreeable one snarled.

"I am merely suggesting that there is no clear reason to object to honoring our oath."

Doc was through listening to disembodied voices arguing about his fate. He was not a puppet. He was not a tool or a chosen vessel. He was Doc Holliday. Lucky gambler. Good friend. Exceptional lover. And he wasn't about to let a bunch of ancient fairies decide they knew what was best for him.

He focused on the force holding him in place, searching for its weakness. At first it was just a blank wall, but as he studied it, the crevices became clear, just like the tics of an opposing gambler.

In his mind, he wedged a knife inside one of the crevices and kicked the handle with his foot. The wall shattered, and he was instantly free.

"I've really no interest in your oath," Doc said as he stood.

As one, the fairies surrounding him took a startled step away from him.

"I was holding you in place," one of them said, face and tone confused.

"I was over it," Doc shrugged. "I don't want this ring, and I didn't put it on. It put me on. You can have it back, and you can do whatever you want with it, but it doesn't involve me."

"You cannot unchoose yourself," Fiona said gently.

"Like hell I can't."

"You do not even know what is being asked of you," the man with the stern voice said.

"I'm not a pawn," Doc replied.

"No one is asking you to be a pawn," the man said. "If you will walk with me, I will explain."

Doc scanned their faces, eyes locking onto the one he was certain had the disagreeable voice. A quick study told Doc everything he needed to know.

"Kill him," Doc said, gesturing towards the man. "And I'll walk with you."

"Done," the stern-voiced man said.

Doc knew enough about fairies to know that they were full of tricks, but the pain he saw cross the disagreeable man's face before he dropped forward onto the marble floor wasn't fake, and the horror he saw on the other faces wasn't pretend.

"How could you?" one of them gasped.

"Silas gave himself over to corruption," the stern man replied. "You should have been able to see it. The human saw it, and he does not have near your senses. Come," the man said. "We will walk in the garden."

Doc followed him out of the marbled courtyard into a wild explosion of plants. It wasn't a garden in the traditional human sense. It was nature, doing what it wanted; it just happened to be right outside of a door.

"How did you know that Silas was corrupted?" the man asked.

"It's so nice to meet you," Doc replied. "You can call me Doc."

The man chuckled and said, "Please forgive my rudeness. My name is Mattasavi. Would you please tell me how you knew that Silas was corrupted?"

"I could see it in his eyes," Doc replied. "There was a cruelty there. It's easy to spot if you know what you're looking for."

"You are the man who released Fiona from her prison," Mattasavi said.

It wasn't a question, but Doc still said, "Yes."

"I am grateful. She was missed."

They were walking past a stand of trees, and a trio of nymphs ran over to Doc and hung garlands of flowers around his neck.

"Thank you," Doc told them. He ignored their inviting caresses though. It didn't matter how beautiful they were, he knew better than to get distracted while he was talking to a fairy. Fairies were sly. Like a mix between Ahanu and a jinn.

"You are not mortal," Mattasavi stated.

Still not a question, but Doc still answered. "No."

"You are human, but not what is known as a witch or a shaman."

This time Doc waited for Mattasavi to continue.

"Why are you this way?"

"I simply am," Doc replied.

"I see. Let me tell you about the oath."

Doc wasn't overly interested in the oath, and he briefly considered demanding to be sent home, but he knew better. He was among the fae, and they didn't take kindly to demands. So he'd listen to what Mattasavi had to say, and then he'd ask firmly to be returned to the same time and place as he'd left.

"It was more of a contract," Mattasavi said. "But we gave our word we would fulfill our end of it when the time came. And the time has finally come."

"What time?" Doc asked, curiosity finally roused.

"Five thousand years ago, give or take," Mattasavi said with a shrug, "a man came to us to ask a favor. He had nothing to offer in exchange, he had no favors owed to him. We were not indebted to him."

Mattasavi stopped talking, but he continued to walk through the garden and down beside a lake with a sandy beach. He stood at the edge looking out at the water for so long that Doc had to bite his tongue not to speak.

"It was not Fiona who vouched for this man, but I," Mattasavi said softly. "I had not met him before, but I felt an instant kinship with him, as if he were part of me, as if he and I had somehow been split apart the moment we were brought into being. And indeed, even his name was mine. He was called Ivasattam."

He turned from the lake and started walking along it, although his feet rarely touched the ground. Doc followed him silently. Only when they were within the shaded depths of a forest grove did Mattasavi continue.

"Ivas and I spoke for many days about his request, and in spite of my reservations, I believed him so completely that I convinced the council to grant him his request. They agreed on one condition. Should the request be granted and turn out to be detrimental, I would pay with my own life."

He shrugged carelessly and said, "It was an easy promise to make."

"What was Ivas's request?" Doc asked, trying to lead Mattasavi back to the ring and why Doc was wearing it.

"I forget how impatient young ones are," Mattasavi murmured. "I do not remember what it was like to be young. I am forever in between."

"Unless Ivas's request costs you your head," Doc pointed out.

Mattasavi chuckled lightly. "This is my favorite portion of the woods," he said, gesturing in front of them. "The trees here tend to twine together."

They were silent for another long while as they walked beneath and beside twisting trees, and Doc once again bit his tongue to keep from demanding answers, telling himself that he could easily keep silent as long as a five-thousand-year-old being. He wished there was a younger fairy who could tell him the story of the oath. One who spoke a little faster, and one who got to the point much quicker.

"Ivas was what you call a witch, a scryer. He had scryed the future many, many times. Every single version was different he said. Every single version had twists and turns. But every single version came to a single point. Always and always he said.

"He would tell no one, not even me, what that point was. All he would say was that all the versions came to a point, but this particular point had the potential to go one of two ways. One reality would create good, the other evil."

"The end of the world?" Doc asked incredulously.

"No," Mattasavi said easily. "There is no end. There are ends; there are shifts; there are changes. But there is no end. This was not an end. Just a shift."

Mattasavi's words skittered over Doc's skin, and Doc controlled the shudder that tried to follow them. He didn't want to continue this conversation, but he wasn't sure why. Mattasavi's words didn't really affect him. In fact, he was planning on walking away as soon as Mattasavi was done. But he wanted to walk away now, without hearing another word.

Mattasavi began to speak again, and Doc pulled himself from his thoughts and listened. The sooner Mattasavi got to the end of his story, the sooner Doc could leave.

"Ivas said that the world would go on as it was if we did not interfere. He said it would make very little difference in the larger scope of things. But he said, and he said it quite insistently, that within the scope that it did change, it would change everything."

"So how did you interfere?" Doc inquired, still hoping to direct the conversation.

"Ivas asked us to choose a champion. A warrior. A knight."

A strange feeling of inevitability settled over Doc. This moment had always happened. This path had always been walked. This choice had always been made. Just like Andrew had always won.

"To do so, we forged a ring of onyx," Mattasavi said.

"You can't forge rock," Doc interrupted. It was a silly thing to argue over, but it was all he had at this point.

"You cannot forge rock," Mattasavi said, tone slightly condescending. "You also cannot manifest gold. These are talents that belong to the fae alone."

Doc made a gesture of acceptance and said, "Please continue."

"We forged a ring of onyx, as I have said. And we encased it in a warning so severe that only the bravest man would dream to seek out the treasure. The gold passed from hand to hand and room to room for many, many years. And now it has chosen."

"And what exactly did it choose?"

"A champion."

"I'm not a champion," Doc insisted. "I don't go riding into battle at other people's demand."

"If you did, you would not be a champion," Mattasavi replied calmly. "Let us make an arrangement, you and I. I will tell you the task I would ask you to complete. If you wish to leave after you have heard what I say, I will take the ring from you. If you wish to complete the task of your own volition, you may keep the ring. Is that agreeable to you?"

It was a trap. Doc knew it was a trap. But that was what made a trap a trap. The knowing you couldn't get out of it without losing a limb.

"Go on," Doc said.

He'd felt the hand of fate before. It was very different than the hand of luck. He much preferred luck.

"As a people we rarely involve ourselves in the affairs of mortals," Mattasavi said. "They are too transient. Humans especially. We have seen too much to bother with your wars and your strange ways. The path that Ivas predicted did not directly affect us, not really, but it was a ripple in the ocean. A ripple seems a very small thing at first, but as you watch it, it continues to move out and out and out, affecting everything in its path."

This conversation felt familiar, but Doc couldn't ever recall having it.

"If left unchecked, this particular ripple will turn things wrong, out of place, off-balance. The harmony will be lost. There is nothing sadder than a song that no longer makes beautiful notes," Mattasavi said softly. "I would ask you to preserve the song, stop the ripple, keep the harmony," he said.

"Could you possibly be more vague?" Doc drawled irritably.

"If I choose. There is a tree analogy I've been itching for a chance to use for more than a hundred years now."

Doc raised an eyebrow. "Was that a joke?" he asked skeptically.

"It is better than my moss analogy," Mattasavi said with a grin. "Even Fiona falls asleep during my moss analogy, and she finds my company enjoyable."

"I see," Doc said.

"I cannot be overly specific because I do not know the cause of the ripple. All I know is the point of origin."

Doc gestured for him to continue.

"I can only tell you a location."

A swell of irritation overtook Doc, and he snapped, "A location? That's it?"

"Ivas told me everything I have told you, and then he died, having traded his life for what he had seen," Mattasavi said solemnly. "A location might not seem like much, but if this is the moment he saw, it will be all you need."

"If?" Doc snarled, forcing himself not to be drawn in by Mattasavi's evident sorrow about Ivas's death.

"If," Mattasavi said with a shrug. "I do not know the time, just the place."

"What if the moment has already past?" Doc demanded.

"It has not passed."

"How could you possibly know?"

"The ring knows. Ivas imbued it with everything he knew. The ring chose you at the right time. Ivas chose you."

For the first time since he'd placed it unknowingly onto his finger, Doc looked down at the ring. It was still black, but now there was golden filigree breaking up the solid blackness. He stared at it, and the filigree moved, turning into letters, then into words that he could read.

"The way is never unclear," it read. "Just follow your inclination."

Doc frowned, wondering if the message was for him specifically or for anyone who wore the ring.

"We should retire for the evening," Mattasavi suddenly said. "It will give you time to think. Would you like to join me for a repast or shall I send it to your room?"

"I'm not hungry," Doc replied.

He didn't normally concern himself with being poisoned, but he was within the realm of the fae, and the rules were quite different here. He'd only entered the fae realm once before, and he'd not regretted it for an instant, but this was a very different occasion.

"Something to quench your thirst?"

"No."

"Very well," Mattasavi murmured. "Celestial will show you to a room."

Doc nodded and followed the nearly naked fairy who suddenly appeared beside them. She took him to a villa, but the distance to it was not nearly equal to the distance he and Mattasavi had walked. Doc tried not to focus on it too intently, but it troubled him. The entire fae realm troubled him. It was magic in its truest form, and he didn't like it one bit.

"Your chamber," Celestial said as she opened a door for him. "I am happy to keep you company."

"Thank you," Doc replied with a smile. "Any other night I would commit myself to pleasing you, but not tonight."

"Are you certain?" she asked, pressing her lithe body against his.

"Quite."

He pulled away from her and closed the door between them. He glanced quickly around the room before walking over to the window. The trees were spread out beneath him; and far, far away he could just barely see the edges of a rocky coastline.

He'd never thought he would return to the eighth continent. Once had really been enough. Not that he didn't find it beautiful. There was no place on earth quite as lovely, but that was the problem. Where on earth was it? How could such a vast place be so completely hidden? It spoke of the power of the fairies that they'd been able to hide and maintain something so massive, something so impactful; and he'd never been able to fully resolve himself to such a thing.

The only reason he'd been able to leave the first time was because he'd tricked Lexi into showing him the way. When she had invited him in the first place, she hadn't bothered to tell him that once inside, mortals weren't allowed to leave so he considered them even on the tricking score.

It made him feel a little bit more in control to know that he could sneak out the door and leave anytime. He wasn't going to sneak out, but he liked knowing he could.

He already knew what he was going to do, and so did Mattasavi. Giving Doc time to think it over was merely Mattasavi's way of testing Doc's mettle.

Doc sighed in frustration. He hated it when a task was shoved upon him without his consent, but he hated it even more when he couldn't just walk away from such a task.

He pushed away his frustration and turned his attention to the ring. The words had faded away, and it was once again pure black. He tried to pull it off, but it wouldn't budge. He hadn't expected that it would.

There was a soft knock on Doc's door, and he went to answer it, smiling when he saw Fiona.

"Am I disturbing you?" she asked softly.

"Hardly," Doc replied.

"May we talk?"

Doc held the door open wider and gestured for her to

come inside. Fiona was not available so he didn't mind inviting her into his bedchamber.

"I was surprised to see the ring on you," she said after she had curled up inside the window seat.

"Not as surprised as I was," Doc said dryly.

She laughed merrily, sound like the trickling of a cheerful brook.

"Do fairies have children?" Doc asked. "Or have they always been?"

"What a clever question, Mr. Holliday."

"Please, call me Doc."

She smiled and said, "What a clever question, Doc."

"Are you going to answer?"

"Certainly. We have always been. Whenever one of us dies, which is very unusual, another is birthed from the earth so that the balance is maintained. There are never more of us, and never less of us."

"I see," Doc said softly, trying to wrap his mind around such a concept.

"For many years we watched the other species, trying to determine the difference between us, but eventually we turned inward and focused on our own sphere of influence. That is why it was so out of character for us to have entered into an oath with Ivasattam."

Doc controlled his impulse to demand answers and waited for her to go on.

"Mattasavi truly believed every word Ivasattam said," she went on.

"And you?" Doc asked.

"I had no reason to distrust him," she said easily. "I do not particularly see why it matters. It is only a shift. I have seen more than one end, and everything begins anew. It is the balance of things. Too far out of balance one way, and things must reverse to the other side. Eventually, everything settles in the middle."

"Until some fool comes along and pushes the swing again," Doc pointed out.

"I enjoy your mind," she said. "It is rare for humans to have much thought. They are very brutish in nature. Eat, sleep, and copulate."

Doc raised an eyebrow.

"We are endless," she replied with a slight grin. "We have plenty of time to eat, sleep, copulate, and consider the mysteries of the universe around us. Humans have very little time, and they waste it entirely."

Doc didn't have any rebuttal for her words. He'd often thought that humans frittered away their lives on rather pointless things, but he also knew that it was easy for him to think such a thing since he was on the outside of it.

"You, however, have denied all those things in the time you have been here," she went on.

"I know better than to get distracted when I'm facing an opponent," Doc replied.

"Mattasavi is not your enemy."

"I never said he was."

"Will you accept the task?" Fiona asked.

"You already know the answer."

"I did not think there was any danger of you refusing it," she said. "But Mattasavi has not witnessed your true nature; he did not know."

"What is my true nature?" Doc asked.

Once more her lips curved into a grin, and she said, "I mustn't ruin the surprise for you. If you have any questions, the ring will answer them."

She stood as she spoke, and as soon as the last word had left her mouth, Doc felt the air around him tighten.

"I do enjoy your company," Fiona said. "And I hope we meet again."

And then she was gone. Or he was gone. He wasn't entirely sure yet because his vision hadn't stopped spinning.

14

"You still haven't answered me," Jules said irritably. "Why did you put it on?"

"What?" Doc asked, head feeling completely muddled.

"I asked you why you put on the ring," Jules ground out. "You said you didn't like it." She paused, then demanded, "Why are you looking at me like that?"

Doc turned slowly, confused eyes taking in the presence of Frankie, Johnny, and Addison and noticing the still molten gold in the fire pit.

He turned back to Jules. "You just melted the gold," he said slowly.

"Yes!" Jules snapped. "What is wrong with you?"

"Nothing," Doc said. "I'd better get this ring to Jury. I'll see you soon."

He walked away without another word because he was too off-balance to manage a normal conversation. He had expected some time to have passed; he hadn't expected never to leave, never to miss a single second. Or maybe he'd never even been gone; he didn't know. It bothered him greatly, but at least this way he didn't have to try to explain his absence to anyone.

He had thought that Fiona would just drop him into the location where the ripple was going to occur, and he didn't understand what he was doing here if this wasn't that moment. How was he supposed to find the moment? They hadn't told him the location; they hadn't told him anything. The whole situation was confounding him, and he needed a moment to think it out.

He rounded the corner of the house, relieved to see that Emily was still waiting for him. "Take me home, please," Doc said as he climbed into the passenger seat of the van.

"Are you okay?" she asked.

"Fine," Doc replied, trying to control the shortness of his tone.

They didn't speak again as Emily drove through the traffic towards Dulcis. Doc found himself unable to make small talk; and as much as he trusted her, he couldn't possibly tell her about the ring or the fae. He'd never told anyone about the eighth continent. It wasn't the type of thing you told people. It was the equivalent of telling norms about the Hidden for no reason whatsoever. There were only two people he could trust with a secret like that. Two people who were still alive anyway.

He tried to reason out the problem of the ring, but he couldn't quite get his thoughts to focus. For some reason, everything seemed brighter and louder and more intense than normal. There was something else too, something beneath the overwhelming intensity of everything. He was feeling feelings that didn't belong to him.

It was all so disorienting, that when they finally reached

Dulcis, Doc had to remind himself to tell Emily thank you before he walked towards the parking garage's elevator. He reached out his hand to touch the elevator button, feeling as if he were moving through molasses. It wasn't just that the electric lights were overwhelming; they felt wrong. The elevators felt wrong. The cars in the garage behind him felt wrong.

Everything that he was so used to and had learned to take for granted seemed unreal and out of place. Everything was so changed to him, so altered, that he felt as if he'd been with the fae for a thousand years.

He managed to get inside the sub-subbasement before he collapsed onto the fainting couch. All of a sudden the entire world was too overwhelming. It was completely unlike him to long for the calm cadence of a forest far away from the city, but that was all he could think about. And then the forest became Andrew's ranch, and all was finally quiet.

Doc breathed a sigh of relief. He'd never truly appreciated the quiet of Andrew's ranch until now.

"You alright?" a rough voice said. "You look a mite green."

Doc frowned in confusion and slowly opened his eyes. Pecos was standing just in front of him.

Doc took a step backward and whispered, "What the hell?"

"I was just 'bout to ask you the same thing," Pecos said.

"I don't understand," Doc murmured, glancing wildly around him at the rolling green meadows of the ranch. "I was in the basement. And then I was thinking of Andrew's ranch, and then..." He trailed off, horror filling him.

"I'm asleep," he said desperately.

"Seems like I've had this conversation before," Pecos chuckled.

"But I really am asleep," Doc insisted. "And all I have to do is wake up." He closed his eyes and imagined the sub-subbasement. When he opened his eyes, Jervis was staring at him in concern.

"Whiskey," Doc croaked. "I need whiskey."

Jervis quickly found a bottle and handed it to him. Doc popped the cork and drank the entire contents before he spoke.

"When you walked in, was I here, sleeping on the couch?"

"No," Jervis said slowly.

"Shit," Doc hissed. "I was afraid you were going to say that. Where was I?"

"I couldn't possibly say," Jervis replied. "You weren't, and then you were."

Doc leaned forward and put his head between his legs. "I think I'm going to vomit," he muttered.

"Not on the Louis XV Savonnerie, you're not."

"Do you have any idea what this means?" Doc moaned.

"No."

"I can't... I want... Call Jury! I want this ring off of me!"

He hadn't felt this sick in over a hundred years, and it was taking all of his willpower not to vomit. Everything was spinning. His head was spinning, his mind, his stomach, everything; and he felt absolutely wretched.

"I hesitate to mention this..." Jervis said slowly.

"Then don't."

"It's just that..."

Doc wrapped his hand over his mouth. He was certain he wasn't going to like whatever it was Jervis was trying so hard to say.

"Your smell is... altered."

"For fuck's sake, Jervis," Doc whispered. "What does that even mean?"

"You don't smell quite... human anymore."

Bile climbed up Doc's throat, but he forced himself to swallow it. He wasn't going to vomit. He wasn't going to vomit because if he ruined the carpet, Jervis would kill him. He held onto that thought until the shock of Jervis's statement had passed. Then he said very carefully, "What do I smell like?"

"A little bit like a..."

In his mind, Doc crossed his fingers and prayed to the goddess of luck. He never prayed to gods, but in this case he felt it was warranted.

"Like a fae," Jervis finished.

The goddess of luck clearly hated him. Or she had simply abandoned him the second he'd put on that goddamn ring. Correction, the second the goddamn ring had put itself on him.

"Have you ever even smelled a fae?" Doc demanded, grasping at the only straw he could think of.

"Yes."

"Well, shit."

"Winslow just texted," Jervis said tonelessly. "Pecos Bill is apparently in my office."

"Take care of him," Doc ordered. "I can't deal with anyone right now. I'm... I'm... Just tell him I'm fine."

"I rather doubt he's going to listen to me."

"You're not going to give him a choice."

"Interesting theory," Jervis murmured.

Doc heard him move towards the door, he heard the door open and close, then everything was silent once more. Only it wasn't. He could hear the city outside. He could hear the hum of the electric lights. He could hear the murmur of mice in the alley.

"No, no, no," he murmured. No one could hear mice in the alley. That was insane.

Everything felt wrong. He felt wrong. His skin was prickling, and his throat was raw. He could feel everything. He could hear everything. And he was very much afraid that if he tried, he could go anywhere he could visualize.

He tore at the ring once more, trying to get it off, but it absolutely refused to budge. He had no idea if Jervis had already called Jury or not, but he couldn't wait. He needed the ring off now.

He moved to one of the tables and laid his hand flat on the surface. Then he took out his knife, placed the edge of the blade on top of his finger, and pressed down. The knife didn't budge, and his finger remained firmly affixed.

"No," Doc growled as he sawed with all his might. "I do not accept. I don't want it. I don't want this. I'll do the task, whatever it is, but I don't want this ring. I don't. Take it back!"

"I shall assume you're talking to yourself," Jervis said blandly.

Doc had heard the door open, so it didn't surprise him to hear Jervis speak; but he didn't bother to acknowledge him because he only had eyes for the cursed ring.

"Jury is on his way," Jervis reported. "And Pecos and his wife are headed up to the White Coyote suite. He refuses to leave until he speaks with you."

Doc wanted to scream, but his throat was too dry. He turned and said, "Cut off my finger."

"If you couldn't do it, I doubt if I can," Jervis replied.

"Try!" Doc ordered.

Jervis studied him for a moment, but moved to take the knife from Doc's hand. Doc put his hand back onto the table and stared at it, hoping against all hope that Jervis would succeed where he had failed.

Jervis placed the blade on Doc's finger below the ring and attempted to slice down. Doc could feel the pressure, but the skin on his finger didn't even cut.

"The hand!" he insisted.

"No."

"The hand!"

He could hear the panic in his voice, but he couldn't help it. The ring was infecting him with a sickness. He would happily loss his hand if it would rid him of the disease.

"No," Jervis said firmly.

"Jervis—"

"No!" Jervis interrupted. "You will sit down, and we will wait for Jury. I will not cut off your hand just because you're unhappy about the kiss of the fae."

"I don't want it!" Doc yelled. "I didn't choose it! It chose me! I didn't teleport to Pecos's ranch! It teleported me to Pecos's ranch, but it used my thoughts, my mind, to do it! Do you understand that?!"

"You're so goddamn stubborn sometimes that it makes me want to kick you!" Jervis snapped.

Jervis's tone cut through Doc's panic, and Doc frowned at him. "Did you just say you want to kick me?" he asked.

"Yes."

"Like a donkey?"

"Why not?"

"Interesting," Doc said.

Jervis's calm, no-nonsense tone and the steady look in his eyes helped Doc focus. He didn't need to panic. Jervis and Jury would help him. Between the three of them, there was nothing they couldn't do.

"Sit down," Jervis ordered.

"Not because you told me to," Doc muttered. "But because I'm sick of standing."

"Understandable," Jervis said.

In hindsight, he was glad Jervis hadn't tried to cut off his hand. Having only one hand would slow him down in several of his favorite pastimes. Not by much, but still, knife throwing and love making wouldn't be quite the same with only one hand.

Someone pounded on the sub-subbasement door, and Jervis stood with a vexed sigh.

"That will be Jury," he said as he walked over to open it.

"What's wrong?" Jury demanded as soon as the door was open enough for him to wiggle through. "What the hell is wrong with you, Doc? You look ill."

"I am ill," Doc retorted.

"He's not," Jervis cut in.

"I am!" Doc snapped. "I've been infected with fairy!"

"What?!" Jury inquired with agitation. "What the hell does that mean?"

"It doesn't matter," Doc replied. "Just get this ring off of me, and it'll be fine."

He held out his hand; and Jury took it, forehead creasing in concentration.

"What is this?" he asked.

"A ring," Doc said shortly.

"Yes, but what is it?"

"You tell me."

Jury was silent, and Doc could feel the magic feathering over his hand. What was worse was that he could see it. Nausea rolled in his stomach as he watched Jury's strands of magic poke and prod at the ring. He wanted to close his eyes, but he couldn't. He'd seen magic before, but he'd also been able to remove the witch fetish any time he wanted. Unlike the ring.

"Stop wiggling," Jury snapped.

"I'm not wiggling," Doc argued.

"You are. Doesn't matter though. I can't take it off," Jury said as he dropped Doc's hand.

"What do you mean you can't take it off?" Doc demanded.

"It's part of you," Jury said with a shrug. "It's basically fused to you."

"It's what?"

Doc stared at his finger. The ring was no longer a ring; it was a band of onyx skin. He dropped to the couch in despair, head spinning.

"What exactly is going on?" Jury asked.

"Hans has inherited a fae ring that is making him just a little bit fae; and in typical Hans fashion, he's throwing a fit about it," Jervis said briskly.

"Wait," Jury said. "That's a fae ring?"

"Yes."

"What do you mean it's making him a little bit fae?"

"Just what I said."

"There has to be a way," Doc broke in. "If we cut off my hand—"

"We are not cutting off your hand!" Jervis snapped. "Besides, you're already altered, and I don't think cutting off your hand will change anything."

"But we can try," Doc insisted.

"You're being a child," Jervis growled.

"You don't understand; you couldn't possibly understand!" Doc shot back. "I've a tattoo that turned me into a mythical dragon, and I'm apparently collecting souls for the mother or who knows what. And now I'm a slave to a fae ring that's wearing me, not the other way around! I want it gone!"

"I knew you were going to overreact!" Jervis spat. "There's just no reasoning with you."

"No reasoning!" Doc shouted. "I'm being very reasonable! I will not be used! I am not a pawn! I do not adhere to other people's demands and wishes. My will is my own! And I did not put on this goddamn ring!"

"And never once does it occur to you what possibilities are open to you because you have the ring, what lives you could change because you suddenly have abilities you never had!" Jervis yelled back.

"I can change the world without the goddamn ring!"

"But without the tattoo, you'd be dead!"

"That's completely beside the point."

"It's not! The tattoo made you into a different being, but you are the man beneath the tattoo. The ring is making you into a different being, but you are the man beneath the ring," Jervis insisted.

"I didn't ask for it!" Doc spat. "It's using me without my permission!"

"Shut up!" Jury suddenly shouted.

"I wasn't talking to you!" Doc snapped.

"I said shut up," Jury snarled.

A band of air tightened around Doc's mouth, and he reacted instantly. In less than a second, his knife was in his hand and his hand was at Jury's throat.

"Are you going to kill me?" Jury taunted. "Because you don't like having a magical gag? At least you don't have a hand up your ass."

Doc narrowed his eyes and pushed the knife forward slightly.

"Jervis is right," Jury stated flatly. "You're acting like a spoiled brat. You don't have the slightest idea what it's like to be controlled, what it's like to be used as a puppet."

Doc raised his hand enough so that Jury could see the ring.

"That's nothing," Jury laughed. "I hate to repeat myself, but Jervis is right. You are the man beneath the ring. The ring isn't making you do anything or changing who you are. It's just changing your physical form."

Jury stepped away from Doc and said, "Come upstairs with me."

Doc gestured towards his mouth.

"You'll have to kill me if you want it off," Jury said with a shrug. "I'm leaving it on until you've listened to what I have to say."

Doc's fingers twitched. He would never kill Jury; but there was no reason why he couldn't wound him. Before Doc could do anything though, Jervis's hand wrapped around his wrist.

"Go with him, Hans," Jervis whispered in German. "Please."

Doc closed his eyes and exhaled tightly. It was downright devious for Jervis to pull out the please because he knew Doc would never deny him anything. Doc put away his knife and gestured for Jury to lead the way.

Once they were inside the elevator, Jury said, "If it's any consolation, I've glamoured your mouth to look normal. Otherwise, you'd look like you were gasping for air."

Doc rolled his eyes.

"And as a courtesy, I've glamoured away your filthy clothes. You really need to start taking more care when you kill people. What are you going to do someday when I'm not there to cover up all the blood?"

Doc was only half listening. The sensations weren't quite as bad as earlier, but he was still having trouble with the elevator and the lights. There was something inside him that kept insisting it was wrong. All of it was wrong. Discordant, off-balance.

He closed his eyes and opened Francisco's box. He struggled to capture all the overwhelming sensations coursing through his body, and then he shoved them into the box and slammed the lid.

Just then the elevator stopped, and Doc opened his eyes and followed Jury out into the lobby.

"Let's sit," Jury said conversationally as he walked over to a bench near a pot of pink orchids.

He sat and splayed out his long legs in front of him, looking shockingly like a king on his throne.

"You've never been controlled, Doc," he said softly. "And I can prove it to you. See that man behind the counter? He looks cheerful so I'm guessing it's Winslow. Sami thinks she can talk to me now, and she told me all about him. I hate it when people tell me things, but Sami doesn't seem to get that."

Jury sighed slightly before saying, "Winslow is now going to come over here. Not because he needs to, but because I told him to."

A chill ran down Doc's back at Jury's tone, and it crawled into his spine when he saw Winslow drop the papers he was holding and walk towards them.

"How can I help you, sir?" Winslow said.

He was talking to Jury, not Doc; and his eyes were hazy.

"I'd like you to go to the kitchen and get me a snack," Jury said. "Coffee too. Make it snappy."

"Yes, sir," Winslow said, usual cheerfulness lost behind the mask of his compulsion.

As soon as he was gone, Jury said, "Oh, look. It's Emily. What do you think she's doing? I think she's going to come over here and offer to run her fingers through my hair."

Doc grabbed Jury's arm, and Jury laughed. The sound was harsh.

"As if that could stop me," he said bitterly. Doc tightened his grip, and Jury said, "Relax; I'm just telling you what she's going to say."

Emily was already walking towards them, and as soon as she was near, she said, "May I run my fingers through your hair, sir?"

"No," Jury said flippantly. "But you can go get me a snack."

Emily trotted off immediately towards the kitchen, but she wasn't Emily anymore. She was just a woman being controlled. What made her Emily was lost, just like Winslow's cheerfulness.

"You have never been controlled," Jury said flatly. "You can't be controlled. You have no idea what it feels like to have your choice ripped from you. You have no idea what it's like to be a puppet on a string, dancing to your master's orders."

Doc felt a whisper of magic tickle over his scalp, and he glared at Jury.

"You're fighting me," Jury said easily, blue eyes unusually hard. "I'm one of the most powerful witches in the world. Do you really think you can hold out against me?"

Doc's fingers itched to reach for his knife, but this wasn't a fight that could be won with steel. It had to be won with his mind. The magic tried to burrow under his skin, and Doc pushed against it.

"Hold on a moment," Jury said. "I'm going to make that

man over there go get me a snack too. Turns out I'm hungry."

Another Dulcis employee suddenly walked towards the kitchen, then Jury returned his attention to Doc.

"Cynric was the only witch who's ever been recorded as capable of holding more than one compulsion at once," Jury said. "Of course, I'm not asking them to jump off a cliff or anything," he went on. "But it's still pretty impressive."

His face twisted, and he said bitterly, "Even with the artifact, Phillip could only control me. He could use persuasion, but he could only compulse me. That was enough though, because once he had control of me, I could compulse others on his behalf. You have no idea what it's like, Doc."

Jury's magic skittered over Doc's face and tried to worm its way into his eyes.

They were just staring at each other now, fighting a battle with no words and no obvious weapons. Doc could feel the little drills of magic trying to work their way inside of him. He could even see them trying to work their way inside of him, but he refused to let them. He would not be compelled. He would not.

"Your snack, sir," Winslow suddenly said.

"Put it on the floor," Jury replied, without ever breaking eye contact with Doc. "You are free to go."

Winslow jolted backwards, shook his head, and said, "I'm sorry; I seem to have forgotten why I came over here."

"You got me a snack," Jury said dismissively.

"Oh. Well, enjoy!" Winslow exclaimed before trotting swiftly back towards the front desk.

The magic force trying to worm its way inside Doc increased.

"Your snack, sir," Emily said.

"Thank you," Jury replied. "Put it on the floor, go back outside, and then you are free to go."

Emily placed the food on the floor and walked towards the revolving doors.

"Your snack, sir," the other employee suddenly said.

"Place it on the floor, return to the front desk, and you are free to go," Jury replied, lips curling slightly.

The employee did as he was told, and then the magic attacking Doc began to twist and bore. The pain wasn't nearly as intense as the pain Doc had suffered when Eli Gac had tried to remove his soul, but it was still a very unpleasant feeling. It was crawling all over him, searching for a way in, but Doc refused to let it infiltrate, refused to give way.

"The thing is," Jury said softly. "You know I'm trying to compulse you. You knew the second the magic touched you. I've been trying to compulse you for five minutes now, but I haven't made any headway, and I'm giving it my very best try. Five minutes is plenty of time for you to figure out who's trying to compulse you and how you can kill them. You could have killed me ten times over by now. You cannot be controlled. It isn't possible to control you. You're uncontrollable."

A bead of sweat formed on Jury's brow, and the pain in Doc's head pulsed.

"I'm ten times more powerful than Phillip ever was," Jury spat. "But he gained control of me without my even noticing it. You knew right away, Doc! And you fought it. You're fighting it right now."

Jury's eye flared a bright blue, and for a second Doc felt as if his head might collapse under the pressure of Jury's gaze.

"You may feel as if something was put on you when Señora Teodora changed you," Jury said. "You may feel as if something is being put upon you now; but you, and only you, have ever decided what you do. You, and only you, have always been in control of your actions."

Jury suddenly dropped back onto the bench with a sharp exhale, and the magic boring into Doc and the muzzle of air keeping Doc from speaking faded away.

"You're exhausting," Jury sighed. "Hand me a plate, will you?"

Without a word, Doc handed Jury one of the plates. He was furious with him, but he couldn't deny that Jury had made a pretty valid point. He wasn't going to admit it though. At least not yet.

15

"I'm annoyed at you for making me do that," Jury said once they were back inside the sub-subbasement. "I had to pretend I was Phillip for minute, and now I need a boiling shower to get his filthy taint off of me."

"I didn't make you do it," Doc countered. "I didn't even know you could do it."

"It's not as if I advertise it," Jury muttered. "It's not exactly a skill I'm proud of."

"But you are good at it."

"I don't want to be good at it, but I was trying to make a point."

"Did it work?" Jervis asked from his perch on top of a marble sarcophagus.

"I don't know," Jury sighed. "Did it, Doc?"

"Maybe," Doc allowed.

"Maybe?" Jervis prodded.

"I will admit that I am difficult to control."

"Impossible," Jury corrected.

"Somewhat impossible," Doc amended.

"Completely impossible," Jury stated.

"But I still maintain that I wouldn't be right here if Señora Teodora hadn't pushed me this way," Doc said stubbornly.

"Is that really such a bad thing?" Jervis asked.

Doc glanced up at him. He and Jervis had been friends for over a hundred years now. And even though Doc had sworn a long time ago that he would never ever depend on another person, he depended on Jervis. Jervis was home. No matter where Doc went, no matter what trouble he got into, he knew that Jervis was waiting for him here at Dulcis with a whiskey in hand. He knew Jervis was keeping an eye on everyone that Doc couldn't watch while he was off battling witches or freeing trapped Akashii. Jervis made it possible for Doc to be whatever it was he was.

Would he still know Jervis if Señora Teodora had merely healed him, patted him on the head, and said, "Go have fun"? He doubted it.

He moved his gaze to Jury, thinking as he often did how it was all interconnected. Andrew, Jervis, Jury. One led to another and so on. Jervis kept him sane, and Jury kept him connected with the world at large. Jury refused to hide from the world, and he accepted advancements and changes with ease because he knew that given enough time, he could figure out a way to thwart them if he wanted to.

"No," Doc finally said, grinning at them. "It's not a bad thing. I'm sorry I ever implied that it was. Apparently, I'm a soul-devouring dragon who is turning into a half-fae."

"That was the strangest fucking sentence I've ever heard," Jury said. "And completely out of context. Would you care to explain?"

"The artifact Frankie's father found was a chunk of fae gold, and it was covered in fae writing, which he translated."

"Why do they always translate it?" Jervis sighed. "What did it say?" he asked before Doc could reply to his first question.

"Part of it was a warning; and it said, 'Only trouble will come to those who seek the treasure of the fae. The treasure will completely destroy a mortal being. No mortal man or creature can hope to understand or contain the treasure.'"

Doc silently cursed his perfect recall. He had rather hoped that burning the journal would erase the words from his mind, but it hadn't.

"And what was the rest?" Jervis inquired.

"Jules said it was a spell that would reveal the treasure."

"And?"

"She said it was too complicated for them to try."

"And?" Jervis prodded once more.

Doc sighed and said, "You know how much I hate warnings and cursed treasure and what not. I told them to burn the journal and melt the gold."

"You did what?" Jury exclaimed. "Fae treasure, Doc! What is wrong with you?"

"Don't need it," Doc said. "Certainly didn't want it."

"What do you mean didn't want it?" Jury demanded.

"Jules melted the gold, and there was a ring inside. She couldn't melt it, so I said I'd bring it to you to destroy. And then it put me on."

Jervis and Jury both stared at Doc silently for a few moments, then Jervis said softly, "Put you on?"

"The ring put itself on my finger. I did not do it. It did it."

"I see," Jervis murmured.

"I don't," Jury said. "How could it do that? You're you!"

"I don't know," Doc said. "But the second the ring was on me, I went to the fae realm."

"The eighth continent?" Jervis asked.

"You know about the eighth continent?" Doc replied in surprise.

"The eighth what?" Jury sputtered. "What the fuck? Are you seriously saying... No, you can't be. You're just fucking with me, right?"

"It's the home of the fae," Jervis said. "At one time it was visible, and all creatures could access it, but over time, the fae withdrew from the world of men, and they shielded their home so that no one could ever discover it."

"You're serious?" Jury demanded.

"Completely."

"And you went there?" Jury asked, turning to Doc.

"Twice," Doc replied. "But just once today."

"Twice," Jury said softly. "I used to think it was fine that you didn't tell me everything, but if you continue to keep shit like an eighth fucking continent and the Underworld secret from me, I'm going to glamour your toes to look like lobster tails."

Doc imagined such a thing and cringed. "That might actually be hard to work with," he admitted. "Especially now that you can tie off your glamours."

Jury grinned widely. "I've written a list."

"A list?"

"Of all the physical manifestations I think you'd be hard-pressed to seal the deal with."

"Really?"

"Lobster tails as toes is only number fifty."

"That's a little frightening."

"I can't wait to get to number one," Jury said with a laugh. "It's really good. So the eighth continent?"

"The home of the fae," Doc said.

"I thought they lived inside fairy mounds," Jury stated.

"Fairy mounds are just doorways," Doc replied.

"I'm beginning to think my education was lacking," Jury murmured. "So the ring took you to the fae?"

"Yes. A long time ago they made a deal with some human witch to choose a..." Doc paused here because the idea of calling himself a champion just didn't sit right with him. "A warrior," he finally said. "To correct an upcoming event that he had scryed. The ring was forged, and it chose me."

"I can see why you were annoyed," Jury said.

"I was only a little annoyed at that," Doc admitted. "What really annoyed me was when I accidentally transported myself to Pecos's ranch."

Jury stared at him. "You what?" he finally said.

"Yep," Doc said. "And then Jervis said I smell a little fae-like, and I can see the strands of your magic, and I can hear the goddamn mice in the alley. They're about to send out a scouting party to the dumpster. That's a loose translation, but you get the idea."

Jury's face no longer held any amusement whatsoever.

"That's not possible," he said flatly. "You're human. You cannot become a different species. That's just not possible."

"In fact, it is possible," Jervis broke in.

"What the hell do you mean?" Jury demanded.

"I mean that it is possible. Not plausible, but possible."

"Well?"

"There are stories among my people..." Jervis frowned briefly and said, "My father used to tell us a bedtime tale about a boy who was chosen by the gods to carry out a task. They imbued him with the essence of the gods, but once the task was completed, he returned to his previous state."

"I like the sound of that," Doc said.

"They were gods," Jury put in. "Why did they need someone else to carry out their tasks?"

"Who knows?" Jervis shrugged. "That's hardly the point."

"Why not? They're not very godlike if they can't even handle their own business."

"You were chosen to complete a task and given the essence of the fae," Jervis said, completely ignoring Jury's statement. "What next?"

"I've no idea," Doc said. "They said all they knew was a location; they didn't tell me the location; they didn't tell me the event; they didn't tell me anything except that if it goes one way it's bad."

"I see," Jervis sighed. "How like them."

"They did say if I had any questions I could ask the ring," Doc said hesitantly. "Apparently, it's infused with the spirit of the scryer."

"Have you asked it anything?" Jervis inquired.

"No."

"Well?"

"You know how much I hate magic," Doc sighed.

"Are you denying the task?"

"No," Doc grumbled.

"Then ask the ring."

"This is stupid," Doc muttered. "Ring, where is the location of the event I am supposed to stop?"

Doc stayed firmly in the room with Jervis and Jury. He could see them; he could even hear Jury muttering about how gods should handle their own goddamn business, but he wasn't completely there. Part of his mind was someplace else. And someone was there with him.

"You are the champion the fae chose?" a tall, slender man asked, voice unsure.

"Unfortunately," Doc replied. "You're Ivas."

"Yes. Your question is incorrect."

"Why?"

"There is not an event to stop."

Doc waited for Ivas to go on, but he didn't.

"Yes?" Doc finally prodded.

Back in the sub-subbasement, Jury tossed a merlin at Doc's head.

"Are you listening to me?" he snapped.

"Not right now," Doc said as he caught the merlin. "I'm busy."

"I am not loving this day," Jury muttered. "Things get messy when you start dealing with the fae, you know."

"Hush," Doc ordered.

He returned his attention to Ivas and said, "You were saying?"

"You merely need to adjust the flow," Ivas said.

"Fine," Doc stated, controlling his desire to sigh in frustration. "Where?"

"The time is not right," Ivas said. "Not quite."

"How will I know when the time is right?"

"The ring will show you."

Doc's vision refocused, and he was fully in the basement once more.

"Interesting," he said.

"Interesting?" Jury growled. "You just told me to hush!"

"I was busy," Doc said.

"You were sitting right here," Jury retorted.

"I think I was inside the ring," Doc replied.

"That's it," Jury said. "I'm giving up on this day. I'm going home, taking a hot shower, eating the contents of my refrigerator, and taking a nap. If you can figure out how to explain this to a six year old, you're welcome to come over. If not, I don't want to see you."

With that, Jury stood and headed towards the door.

Jervis cleared his throat.

"Um, Jury?" Doc said.

"What?" Jury snapped.

"You're not busy tonight?"

"Not yet."

"So dinner?"

Jury turned and said, "What's the catch?"

"No catch," Doc said solemnly. "Dinner at Jervis's. Sami invited us."

"I see," Jury ground out. "You're both going to owe me."

"I already owe you," Doc reminded him.

"You're going to owe me more."

"Fine. Seven," Doc said.

Jervis cleared his throat again.

"Make it eight," Doc amended. "And dress nicely."

"I always do," Jury snarled, and then he left the room.

"He's no fun at all, is he?" Doc drawled.

"He acquiesced more easily than I expected."

"He would've put up more of a fight if he hadn't been exhausted from compulsing all the employees at Dulcis."

"All the employees?" Jervis demanded.

"Just three," Doc replied. "Winslow, Emily, and someone I haven't met."

"What did he do to them?"

Doc could hear the anger in Jervis's tone, so he waited just a moment before saying, "It's like this... He made them all get him... snacks. And he didn't pay for them."

"Snacks?"

"Snacks. And some coffee."

"He compulsed my employees and made them get him snacks?"

"Yes."

"Only Jury would compulse someone to bring him snacks," Jervis snorted. The anger was gone, replaced with amusement.

"I feel strange," Doc said. "Do you really think it won't be permanent?"

"The fae have a set number of people," Jervis said offhandedly. "You cannot be added permanently to their number without one of them dying."

That was no comfort at all since Mattasavi had killed Silas at Doc's request; and Fiona had said when one fae died, another was birthed.

"You're looking green again," Jervis pointed out.

"I'm fine," Doc lied.

"Hans."

"I know there's no point in lying to you," Doc said. "Just let me have it."

Jervis jumped from the sarcophagus and studied Doc for a moment before saying, "Since you've no particular mission at the moment, you may want to consider getting cleaned up for dinner."

Doc glanced down at his chest. He had completely forgotten that he was coated in dried blood and other bits of humanity.

"You don't think Sami would approve of my appearance?" he drawled.

"Hans."

"I'm going," Doc laughed.

He stood and headed for the door. Just as he was touching the door handle, Jervis said, "And don't forget about Pecos.

He doesn't strike me as the most patient of men, and I'm fairly certain the steel-plated door leading into here wouldn't have stopped him."

"I'll handle him," Doc replied.

In addition to hearing and seeing too much, he was feeling guilty for resenting Pecos's appearance. He liked Pecos. But when he'd thought of Andrew's ranch, he'd meant Andrew's ranch, not Pecos's ranch.

He stepped into the elevator, pushed the lock button so no one else could access it, then pressed the button for the floor below his. That entire floor only had four suites.

The White Coyote Suite for Pecos. The Raven Suite for Andrew. Jury's suite or the Veneficas Suite. And an open suite for whoever might show up at any given time. Lena had insisted upon naming it the Pomegranate Suite for some reason, and Doc hadn't argued with her.

As the elevator slid upwards, Doc tried to harness all the sensations once more. They kept slipping out of the box at the most inopportune times. For instance, he could hear the moving cables of the elevator. He had never given the elevator a single thought, but now he couldn't ignore it.

He shoved everything he could into Francisco's box, but before he closed it, he tried to shove in his resentment of Pecos as well. Pecos couldn't help it that he wasn't Andrew. Besides, Pecos was family. He'd been Andrew's family, so he was Doc's family. And he clearly felt the same way about Doc or else he wouldn't have showed up at the hotel just minutes after Doc had accidentally appeared at the ranch.

The elevator door opened, and Doc slammed the lid on Francisco's box and locked it tightly. "Stay," he hissed before walking down the hallway and knocking on Pecos's door.

After a few seconds, Aylen opened it, and Doc just stared

at her. She said something; she was touching him, searching for wounds, he suspected, but he couldn't be sure. He couldn't hear her. He was too overwhelmed by her presence. She was absolutely glowing. Not figuratively. Literally. Light was pouring off her, infiltrating every single crack and surface. He could feel the heat of it, the purity of it, the power of it.

"Doc!" Pecos snapped.

Doc tore his eyes from Aylen and tried to focus on Pecos.

"What the hell's wrong with you?" Pecos demanded.

"Nothing," Doc managed to say.

Pecos frowned.

"I'm fine," Doc said. "I've just inherited some fae powers, and I'm trying to get used to them."

"What?"

The look on Pecos's face was so incredulous that Doc laughed.

"I'm sorry," Doc chuckled. "You look like you've just swallowed a live hornet."

Pecos raised an eyebrow.

"If you have a couple hours, I'll explain it to you."

Pecos gestured towards the sitting room, and Doc headed towards it. It wasn't what he wanted to be doing right now. He'd much rather be upstairs taking a shower, followed by a nap.

But Pecos had come all this way just because he was worried about Doc. Doc could actually feel the worry pulsing from him, and he knew Pecos was worried about him because Andrew would have worried, and that was something Doc could fully understand. And since he had nothing but time, it didn't hurt him at all to use some of it explaining the Hidden and the world that was unseen to Pecos and Aylen.

16

By eight o'clock that night, Doc was shaved, showered, dressed in blood-free clothes, and knocking on Jervis's door, Pecos and Aylen in tow. Sami had been delighted to include them; he'd known that she would be.

Jervis opened the door, raised one eyebrow, and said, "I suppose that explains the extra place settings. Do come in."

Even though Doc wanted to laugh, he just smiled and said, "Thank you; I'm so looking forward to the evening."

"Don't you dare," Jervis said flatly.

"Dare what?" Doc asked cheerfully.

"Make this into a thing."

"I'm not making it into a thing; you're making it into a thing."

"Shut up and go get your drink."

"I must first greet the hostess," Doc said smoothly.

"I will kill you if you do not remove yourself from my sight."

With a chuckle, Doc moved into the suite, taking Aylen with him. He figured that wherever Aylen went, Pecos would follow, and right now they were both rather stiff and needed some gentle guidance.

"Sami," Doc drawled as he took her hand and kissed it.

"Doc!" Sami exclaimed happily. "I'm so glad you could come. And this must be Aylen and Pecos. I'm delighted to meet you both."

She smiled brilliantly as she spoke, and even without the fae sight, Doc could see that her song was beautiful and sweet. She was happy, and it was resonating off of her in little bursts of sunlight. He wouldn't have been able to see that without the fae sight, but he would have been able to sense it either way.

"Any friend of Doc's is a friend of mine," Sami went on. "Our families go back to the 1940s."

"I met Pecos's family in 1888," Doc said confidentially.

"Really?" Sami said. "That's amazing! You do have a tendency to meet the most amazing people."

By this point, Sami had taken Aylen's hand. "I just have to show you the art piece I purchased for the dining room," she gushed. "It's utterly resplendent."

Aylen cast Pecos a panicked look, but she allowed Sami to usher her out of the room.

"Does she ever shut up?" Pecos asked softly.

"Not that I'm aware of."

"You really didn't need to bring us."

"You may as well get used to it," Doc said firmly. "You're part of it now."

Pecos grunted.

"Although we typically do more killing than dining," Doc added.

"That's good 'cause I'm a bit more comfortable with a gun in my hand than a fork," Pecos muttered.

"You and me both," Doc chuckled. "We should probably go save Aylen. By this time Sami's probably pried all your secrets from her."

Pecos shuddered visibly and hurried into the dining room, and Doc followed him with a laugh.

When Jury arrived a few minutes later, he was so charming and personable that Doc might have wondered if he was really Jury except he could see quite clearly that he was. A gift of the fae sight, he supposed.

It didn't take long for Sami's cheerfulness and Jury's charm to fully infiltrate Pecos, Aylen, and Jervis; and soon everyone was conversing and laughing and generally enjoying themselves.

Doc watched them with a grin, feeling slightly outside of it. He usually felt a little outside of things, but tonight was more pronounced than normal because he could barely look at them without seeing what he was certain were their auras floating about. Not only was it making him a little lightheaded, but it was also showing him a layer of them he'd never seen before, a layer he couldn't unsee. It made him feel pansophic, and he didn't like it.

Sami was yawning behind her hand and it was after midnight by the time all the courses had been served. Aylen and Pecos excused themselves after dessert, thanking Sami for a lovely time as they did and inviting both her and Jervis to the ranch.

As soon as they were gone, Doc stood and said, "Thank you, Sami. It was a delightful affair."

"It was nice, wasn't it?" she said happily.

"I've never seen a better hostess," he said with complete sincerity as he kissed the back of her hand.

She blushed and giggled, and he could tell his words had

pleased her. He winked at Jervis and headed towards the door.

"I need a drink," Jury said from right behind Doc.

"You know the way home," Doc said.

"Your place is closer," Jury pointed out.

"It's late."

"That's never bothered you before."

"To be honest, your aura is a little unnerving."

They were in the elevator now, just staring at each other.

"I wish you hadn't said that," Jury finally muttered. "The thing is, Jervis and I decided not to leave you alone."

"Jervis and you decided," Doc stated.

Jury shrugged.

"I'm too tired to argue with you," Doc murmured. "We'll argue in the morning."

"And that's why I'm staying with you," Jury said. "I have never, ever known you to be too tired to argue."

"Shut up," Doc said as he pressed the button to open the elevator onto his side of the hallway.

Jury followed him down the hallway and into Doc's suite. Once there, Jury flopped onto the couch, yawned, and said, "See you in the morning."

"It is morning, you reprobate," Thaddeus grumbled.

"He means the morning with light," Doc replied, trying not to stare at Thaddeus's rather astounding aura. "Goodnight, both of you."

He walked into his bedroom and fell onto the bed. He was exhausted. It was no wonder the fae didn't leave their home very often. There were too many sounds, too many people, too many everything.

He could hear Jury breathing in the other room. He could hear Jury's heartbeat. He could hear Thaddeus's heartbeat.

He'd never even realized Thaddeus had a heart. How could a plant have a heart?

He rubbed his hand over the ring, but he couldn't feel it anymore. Jury was right; it was part of him now. Besides the color, there was no distinguishing it from his skin. He didn't want it, but he was stuck with it. And that annoyed him.

There had been so many times as a boy that he'd not had a choice in what he did. He had had to leave his mother's side when he hadn't wanted to. He'd had to leave Francisco. He'd had to learn a trade he had no real interest in. He'd had to get sick and die.

He loathed not having a choice; and after his rebirth, he'd made sure that he always chose one way or the other. He never let anyone else make his decisions for him. At least he'd never thought he had. But now he was putting on rings without wanting to, he was going on a quest he had no interest in, and he was turning into a fairy. He was feeling things and seeing things that he didn't want to see or feel. And he hated it. It made him feel powerless, just like he'd felt as a boy.

He stared at himself in the mirror above his bed, trying to see if he looked any different, but he didn't think that he did. It repulsed him that he smelled different to Jervis. It was as if he was being scrubbed away and replaced with someone else.

"No," he muttered. "I'm fine. Jervis is right. This is a gift."

He didn't believe it, not really, but he thought if he said it often enough it might make it true.

He closed his eyes and forced himself to sleep, hopeful that in the dreaming he could pretend he was still human. His body fell asleep, but his mind wandered into a memory, one that did nothing to help him forget what had happened.

"Come home with me," Lexi whispered in Doc's ear.

"There is a waterfall that is so clear you can see the crystals inside of it."

"This waterfall is clear enough," Doc replied as he wound a strand of her radiant hair around his finger.

"One drink of the water, and you can taste all the waters that ever existed in their purest forms."

"I'm not that interested in water," Doc chuckled. "I have to meet my friend tomorrow," he added for good measure. "I promised him I would."

The last time Doc hadn't showed up on time, Jury had ranted and raved about it for three hours. Doc usually found Jury's rants highly amusing, but he didn't trust Lexi's intentions so he was willing to arrive on time.

He kissed her neck, trying to distract her; and she leaned against him with a sigh.

His method of distraction worked for some time, but when she had finally moved away from him and was fastening her loose garments, she murmured, "It's a different continent."

"What is?" Doc asked in spite of the fact that he knew he shouldn't.

"The fae world."

"Different than Europe," Doc replied.

"No. Different than any continent shown on a human map. It is the eighth continent."

A frisson of excitement tore through Doc, and he leaned forward with interest.

"A hidden continent?" he asked.

"Yes," she murmured, trying and failing to hide her smile of victory.

But Doc didn't care about her motivation anymore; he was too entranced with the idea of a hidden continent. She had discovered his greatest weakness, his relentless curiosity.

"Take me there," he said, completely heedless of his words.

The dream shifted before Doc watched himself follow Lexi willingly into a fae mound, but the new dream was not a memory of his own.

He was young, only a boy. He knew this because the hands attached to his arms were small and smooth. They were grasping a shiny obsidian plate, and Doc's eyes, or at least the eyes pretending to be his, were staring into the plate intently.

The black of the stone faded away, and Doc saw two armies facing each other, each ready to die for some lofty notion passed down from a ruler who was nowhere to be seen.

"Ivas," a soft voice said. "You must put that away. You shouldn't use it this way. Come; come and eat."

"Soon, Mother," Doc's lips replied. "I must see what happens next."

"You know what happens next," she chided, worry clear in her tone. "You cannot keep looking. Your hair, child. It's already streaked with grey."

"I have to look," the boy insisted. "There is something I must see."

The memory abruptly shifted, but Doc was still the child, only now he was fighting against someone's restraining arms.

"NO!!!" Doc screamed, tears streaming from his eyes as he watched them break his precious obsidian plate.

"It's for the best, Ivas," a worried voice whispered in his ear. "Please. You're killing yourself."

Doc fought until he had no energy left, and then he fell against the man holding him, sobbing with sorrow and fear. They had taken his sight. They had stolen his sight.

The memory left, replaced with another. The boy was

older now, stronger, and no one stopped him when he waved and walked off into the woods. They liked it when he left their dwelling. They thought the fresh air was good for him. If only they knew.

He walked deep into the woods, using his senses to make sure he wasn't followed, then he entered the cave and dug free the stone plate he'd torn from the earth with his own two hands.

He had to know; he simply had to know.

The surface of the black stone shimmered, and a scene opened before him. Doc watched it hungrily, watching for something; but he didn't know what.

After a long time, his heart began to patter with excitement, and he whispered, "This is it. This is the moment."

Everything was suddenly so clear. Everything made sense. Everything was arranged, placed in neat order; and he finally knew what to do. He knew what to do.

Doc sat upright with a gasp. The sensation of elation was still coursing through him, filling him with satisfaction, but he wasn't sure why. What Ivas had seen and what Ivas knew was not clear to Doc. All he'd seen was a forest on fire, and it didn't make any sense to him.

He could easily ask the ring to explain what he'd just seen, but the emotions he'd felt from Ivas were so close to the surface that he decided not to. He was already struggling to maintain his own sense of self, and he didn't want to muddy the waters any more than they already were.

What he really wanted was to talk to someone who understood time.

He tried to stop it as soon as the thought popped into his head, but it was too late.

"This is an interesting turn of events," Ahanu murmured when Doc popped into the space beside him.

"Shit," Doc hissed. "I did not mean to do that."

"Nonetheless," Ahanu said easily. "You are here now. You may as well sit down and have a smoke."

Doc frowned, and Ahanu shrugged before saying, "I know you do not smoke; you've told me often enough. Smoke was code for have a conversation. If you want. I assume you did want, because you are, in fact, here. With me."

"Not on purpose," Doc growled.

He could easily think himself home, but he didn't. Instead he sat beside Ahanu on the cabin's steps.

"It is balmy today," Ahanu said vaguely. "It always is here."

"What are you doing?" Doc demanded.

"I thought perhaps some idle conversation regarding the weather might warm you up to things," Ahanu said.

"It is balmy," Doc agreed.

"See? Isn't that nice?"

"I don't know."

Neither of them spoke for a long time, and the only noise was the soft shush of Ahanu's smoke rings drifting into the air.

"How do you know when to stop looking?" Doc finally asked, still remembering the insane drive he'd felt to hold the plate in his hands and look at the future.

Ahanu shrugged a shoulder and said, "I have only ever allowed myself to look at the events surrounding Meli, and I stopped when I saw the outcome that needed to be manifested."

A smoke ring drifted out past the porch and into the forest beyond.

"If I had allowed myself to look at everything, to try to

understand everything, I am certain I would have gone insane."

Doc didn't think Ivas had crossed into insanity, but he had certainly not been entirely sane when he'd walked into the cave. Something had been driving him, something he couldn't quite control.

"Why do you ask?" Ahanu inquired.

"A scryer apparently foretold a future event that would make an impact within its sphere, and I'm supposed to stop it." Doc paused and shook his head. "That's not right. I'm supposed to adjust the flow of the event."

"Ah."

"And that's all I know."

"Knowing too much would destroy your intention," Ahanu said.

"What do you mean?"

"If I had told Andrew that he and Pecos would lose, would he have fought as hard as he did to win? And if he had not fought as hard as he did to win, would Meli have slept so long, would she have slept at all? Would she have been there for you to wake up when the time was right? Would Andrew have even been the man he needed to be if he had not already given it his all to defeat her once before?"

"So you're saying I'm better off not knowing," Doc said.

"If you know, you may change your own course, and your course is the very reason you were chosen."

"I don't suppose you'd care to clarify?" Doc drawled.

"The ring on your finger sought you out. It sought you out because you both resonate with the same song. It was attracted to you."

Doc thought about arguing with Ahanu, but there was no point. There was no point because he was right. Doc could see the waves of vibration pulsing out from the ring, and they were no different than his own vibration. He could also see the melody surrounding Ahanu. It danced with every breath Ahanu took, as merry and mysterious as its creator. He wished he couldn't see those things, but he could.

"I don't know why I thought you'd clarify things," Doc sighed.

"That is a rather silly idea," Ahanu replied with a light chuckle.

"I never actually said anything about the ring," Doc pointed out.

"My powers are not limited to zapping and scrying," Ahanu replied, tone amused.

"I see."

Doc wished that witches and shamans came with labels telling him exactly what they were capable of.

"If you know the event you are supposed to affect," Ahanu went on, "you would try to employ logic to it and formulate a plan. And if you did that, your song would change. If you do not know the event, your song will stay the same, and you will move forward in your same way."

Ahanu smiled as if he'd just told Doc something marvelous and was quite proud of himself.

"I suppose one could consider that clarified," Doc murmured.

"It was very clarified," Ahanu said. "If it were a lake, you would be able to see every stone on the bottom."

"Maybe," Doc muttered, trying to work out exactly what Ahanu might mean. He found it interesting that both Mattasavi and Ahanu had mentioned the song. Maybe seeing the song was part of being fae, and maybe that was how he'd know when it was time to act. If he focused, if he bent his mind to it, maybe he'd see the song start to shift, he'd see the melody stumble.

He'd always been able to tell how his mother was feeling by the song she would play on the piano. If she was feeling well, she never missed a note and the song she was playing would be cheerful and fun. If she was feeling unwell, notes of discord would sneak in here and there, making an already sad song even more melancholy.

It was always obvious when a musician missed a note, and Doc was beginning to suspect that if he paid close attention, it would be just as obvious when life missed a note.

"Do you mind if I stay here for a while?" he asked. "It's not as overwhelming."

Ahanu tilted his head and replied, "You want to stay here? With me?"

"If you don't mind. Jury's heartbeat is hammering, and Thaddeus's heartbeat is tripping all over itself. And they're both snoring. I can hear the traffic outside even though my suite is soundproof; I can hear the electricity in the walls; I can even hear Pecos and Aylen murmuring back and forth beneath me."

"I see," Ahanu said.

"Do you play poker?" Doc asked.

"Me?"

"There's no one else here," Doc replied with a grin.

"I have never played poker."

"Would you like to learn?"

"I suppose," Ahanu said, voice hesitant.

Doc laughed softly, thinking that it was a strange turn of events that had brought this about. He was hiding away with Ahanu in a nowhere place, and this time he wasn't the least bit upset about it.

Doc taught Ahanu to play poker, and they played many silent hands. Ahanu turned out to be a fascinating opponent because he didn't ever project honestly. And then sometimes, just to muddy the waters, he did project honestly. And Doc couldn't tell the difference; he couldn't tell when Ahanu was lying.

They eventually took a break and sat on the porch again, staring at the unmoving woods beyond the cabin. The longer Doc gazed at the trees, the more a feeling of familiarity crept over him; and without asking, he knew they were the lost woods of Ahanu's childhood. Even from here he could see the patch of flowers Meli had been gathering the day they had been murdered.

Doc grieved for Ahanu and his sisters. They'd died in truth that day and had never been able to move past that moment. They were tied to it in a way that bound them; and only Aylen, with Pecos's insistence, had been able to step past it.

There were moments in a person's life that were unquestionably defining. If it hadn't been for those greedy Europeans, Ahanu would have lived out his life in his native land not knowing the power that lurked within him. And he would have died some four hundred years ago. Likewise, if it hadn't been for the death of young Ahanu, Andrew would have never known the power that lived inside him. A moment in one person's life then became a moment in another person's life. And so on and so forth.

"It is unwise to think as much as you are without drinking coffee to fuel it," Ahanu said at some point, interrupting Doc's thoughts. "I will make you some."

While Doc waited, he thought about his own moment. Jervis was right. Doc could have taken Tozi's gift and settled down to live a normal life, one without coughing and blood. He could have returned home and lived by his father, seen his brother's children, and gone back to dental surgery. But he'd been happy to leave that life behind and start a new one. He'd been happy to step into the role of the dragon. He'd never regretted it. Not once.

And he didn't regret it now. He was who he was. Tozi had marked him, but she hadn't made him.

The scent of burnt coffee brought Doc back to the moment, and he grinned as Ahanu handed him a steaming cup.

Doc took a sip and said, "This is definitely Doyle approved."

"I did learn from watching them," Ahanu chuckled.

"Did you search for other champions before Andrew?" Doc asked.

"I'm too good at observing the patterns to waste my time on others," Ahanu replied. "I knew Pecos was needed, and I thought he was the champion. My original hope was that Andrew would help Pecos become more than he was, because I also knew he needed to be more. I did not expect Pecos to change Andrew so much. There is only so much you can observe, and it is difficult to account for people's will and choices when there are at least a hundred variants for every moment."

"It sounds exhausting," Doc admitted.

"It is."

"Do you stay here all the time?" Doc asked. "It seems a little... quiet." He'd been going to say lonely, but he managed to stop himself.

"I stay here in between," Ahanu said.

"In between meddling," Doc chuckled.

"Exactly."

"If you'd ever like to stay somewhere else, you are always welcome at Dulcis."

Ahanu turned to stare at him, unreadable face still unreadable, but eyes full of confusion. "You are inviting me into your home?" he said slowly.

"Truth be told, I... like you," Doc managed to say.

"You like me?"

Ahanu was clearly not used to people telling him they liked him, and for some reason the pure disbelief in his eyes made Doc laugh.

"Yes," he said between chortles. "I actually like you."

Ahanu's eyebrows furrowed, and he said, "Surely you're joking."

"I'm not," Doc replied, forcing his mirth to subside.

Ahanu didn't seem to know how to respond so Doc said, "Poker?"

"Yes."

They played many more silent hands, but eventually Doc felt it was time to return.

"Thank you," he said as he put away his cards and leaned back in his chair. "I needed this."

"You are welcome," Ahanu said softly. "A word of advice?"

"Yes?"

"Make sure to think yourself back to the same moment in time."

Doc stared at him for a moment before starting to laugh, and this time Ahanu joined him. They laughed for several minutes, but Doc finally wound down enough to say, "The same moment in time; that's good. I would have never thought of it."

"I have made that mistake several times," Ahanu said with a grin.

"Never admit to it," Doc advised. "It makes you look like less of a god."

"A god," Ahanu said thoughtfully. "I never thought of myself that way, but I suppose it takes one to know one."

"No!" Doc exclaimed. "I'm not a god. I'm just god adjacent for a moment. As soon as I don't need them, the god powers are returning to the fae."

"Why wouldn't you want them?" Ahanu asked.

"I don't need them," Doc said frankly. "And they're very distracting. I'd rather stick with doing things the old-fashioned way."

"I see. Remember, same time."

Doc grinned widely at him, said "stop by anytime", and visualized himself back in his bedroom at the same moment he'd left. He felt the mattress give beneath him, and he held his breath for a moment until he heard Jury's snore from the other room.

"Same time," Doc said, laughing softly to himself.

The idea that it was possible for him to move through time was absolutely sickening, but if he focused on the amusing side of things, he could ignore the nausea that wanted to roll through him.

He stretched out and turned onto his side so he could gaze out the window. It was still dark, but the city was never really dark, and the silhouettes of tall buildings filled the skyline.

He gazed at the buildings, not sure what to do next. It apparently wasn't time for him to shift any currents, but he wasn't excited about the idea of running around in fae form. He wished he could don it like a hat or a glove when the time was right, but he knew there was no point allowing his thoughts to wander down such a path because it was what it was. There was no changing it.

He wasn't going to just sit here and wait for the moment to occur though. He had to keep moving, or he'd think too much about the ring on his fingers and the powers soaking into his bones.

He pulled out his mental to-do list and quickly reviewed it. Frankie was taken care of so he should probably turn his attention to the trapped souls and Gac. As if his thoughts had summoned it, Doc's phone suddenly rang and the screen showed that Virgil was calling.

"I was just thinking of you," Doc drawled when he answered.

"You've nothing better to do at four in the morning?" Virgil responded.

"No. Do you?"

"I should be asleep," Virgil grumbled, although his tone lacked any bitterness. "But I had this idea, and I went chasing after it."

He paused, and Doc knew that was his cue. "What did you find?" he asked.

"I found a trail," Virgil said triumphantly.

"A trail?"

"A money trail. People are never as careful with their money as they should be," he said condescendingly. "I'm only embarrassed with myself that I didn't think of it earlier."

"The easiest ways are always the most difficult to remember," Doc agreed.

"Isn't that the truth?" Virgil sighed. "As I was saying, I found a trail. I'll send you over the information in the morning, and hopefully you can glean something useful from it."

"I'll send a courier now," Doc replied.

"Impatient?"

"Extremely."

"You should never reveal your hand, you know that," Virgil chided.

"But I already paid you," Doc pointed out. "Someone will be there soon."

He disconnected and started to call Jervis, but stopped himself when he remembered the look he'd seen in Sami's eyes when he'd left. It was better if he went for the papers himself anyway.

He stood and quietly slipped out of his bedroom, through the sitting room, and into the hallway beyond his suite, leaving Jury behind. Jury and Jervis might have decided not to leave him alone, but he hadn't agreed to it so he didn't feel bad for giving them the slip.

He used the stairwell to access the alley and headed towards Virgil's. The night air was brisk, and he savored the feeling of it on his skin. He wasn't sure he'd ever felt the wind quite this way, and he suddenly longed to touch a woman. What would it be like to make love to a woman when he could hear her heartbeat quicken? Desire shot through him at the thought, but he pushed it away. Now was not the time. Right now he was hunting Gac.

He walked down another street, nodding cheerfully at the few people he passed, trying and failing not to study their auras as he did. He'd never seen an aura before today; but even without being told, he knew these people's auras were not quite right.

They weren't energetic like Sami's or full of power like Jury's. They were unvaried and just a little bit grey. The mere idea of eating someone with an aura like theirs turned Doc's stomach.

"Gift," he snorted. "As if."

As he walked, he began to notice something he'd never felt before, and he didn't like it. He'd always been able to feel the cadence of the cities he went into. That was the very reason he didn't like D.C.. He knew Denver's cadence was a little desperate, but he'd always thought it was because of the people living there. But maybe it wasn't because he could actually feel the city.

It was alive; it had breath and a heartbeat and an energy all its own. It was a little desperate and a little harried. He could feel the greed of it, but he could also sense its desire to protect its own. It was holding all these people in its arms, trying to shelter them, trying to comfort them, but it couldn't quite manage. No one was ever satisfied, and their dissatisfaction was infecting the city as well.

The city was weeping. He could feel its sorrow; he could feel its fear, and he didn't know how to help it, how to comfort it. He tried to turn his senses inward so he couldn't feel it anymore, but he couldn't block it out. He was part of it; it was part of him; he knew it; he was it.

Even though he was fighting an entire barrage of overwhelming sensations, when he was about a block from Virgil's home, Doc's senses suddenly sharpened and narrowed down to the street in front of him. Something was wrong. He could tell something was wrong. The song was wrong.

He ran forward quickly, springing up Virgil's front steps, but the door was locked. He broke the lock, but the door still didn't budge, and he remembered that Virgil had locking bars on the inside of all of his doors. Instead of breaking through the door, Doc just moved to the side and hurled himself through the window.

Magic slithered over his skin, stopping at Jury's bracelets; but Doc ignored it, instead listening for sounds of movement.

"I told you I don't know!" Virgil suddenly exclaimed.

His voice was laced with pain, and Doc didn't waste any time in moving swiftly towards him.

"I don't believe you," a heavily accented voice replied. "What is he looking for?"

"A man! That's all I know."

"Why?"

"How should I know? He hires me to do a job, and I do it."

Doc leaned on the doorjamb, quickly assessing the scene. Virgil was bound by magic to his desk chair, and three male witches were surrounding him. The one who had spoken was also the one holding the pair of tin snips in his hand, and the tip of one of Virgil's fingers was lying on the floor in a puddle of blood.

"This is what comes of doing business with Baudelaires, Virgil," Doc drawled, grinning slightly when the three men spun in surprise. "Not much in the way of witches, are you?" he murmured. "I would have never been able to sneak up on Jury like that. For crying out, I even broke a window."

"You're paying for that window," Virgil growled. "I have this under control."

"Your severed finger tells a different story," Doc stated, pretending not to notice that the witches were readying themselves to attack.

"Just go!" Virgil demanded.

"I am so hurt right now," Doc said, shaking his head. "You of all people should know that I can't be in the same room with a Baudelaire without killing them."

"Killing them!" one of the men snorted. "Who do you think you are?"

"Doc, Doc Holliday," Doc said cheerfully. "Surely you've heard of me."

The color fled from the speaker's face, and he lifted his hands in a show of submission. "We were just having a conversation with old Virgil here," he said. "Just a conversation between friends."

"Again, I refer to the severed finger."

"I hated that finger," Virgil said.

Virgil was no longer bound, and Doc watched him warily from the corner of his eye just in case he did something tremendously stupid. Virgil was a business man caught in between two very powerful and dangerous clients, and he wasn't sure what to do.

"We were just leaving anyway," the man said.

"I'm afraid not," Doc replied.

"Doc!" Virgil snapped.

"The problem is I know Baudelaires, and I know that if I'd sent over one of my employees to pick up the papers tonight, I would have never seen them again. That may not bother you, Virgil, but it doesn't sit well with me. Are you working with Alex?"

"You know I don't discuss my clients," Virgil growled.

"I wasn't asking you; I was asking them," Doc replied.

"We're not looking for trouble," one of them said. "We really were just leaving."

"No," Doc said firmly.

He could feel Virgil's anxiety, and he knew Virgil was wishing he would just leave. But Doc couldn't do that. The Baudelaires were on the list. And furthermore, in spite of their insistence that they were leaving, Doc could tell that they were readying themselves for an attack.

"It's cheating," he sighed. "That's what it is. I like being surprised when the big solid wall of invisible air slams into me."

The words had barely left his mouth when, as predicted, a big solid mass of air slammed into him and shoved him against the far wall. And before it even happened he knew that the other two witches were about to hurl all the metal in the room at him, pointy ends first.

It was as if time had slowed down, but he could see into the future as well. He could see what they were doing; he could see their magic moving, he could see what it was going to do, and it was distracting as hell.

Doc closed his eyes for a second, trying to reset his vision, but even then he could see. He could see the heat of them moving across the room towards him.

"Actually," he murmured. "I think I can work with this."

He kept his eyes closed and moved to the side along the wall, easily breaking past the barrier and hardly feeling it when a piece of metal pierced his arm. He drew a knife and hurled it towards the closest form of heat. The form jerked backwards, and Doc knew he'd hit his mark.

He drew another knife, intending to kill the next man, but heat suddenly rammed into him, completely overwhelming his mind and body. The heat was so intense he fell against the wall, accidentally opening his eyes as he did.

He could see it. He could see it all. The aura of the witch he'd just killed was crashing into Doc, filling him, making him stronger; and at the same time the essence of the witch was twisting free of his body and being sucked towards Doc's.

Doc watched in frozen turmoil as both the aura and the essence disappeared inside his tattoo. His senses sharpened even more, and he realized that he was still being crushed by air and there was also a fire poker sticking out of his chest.

"Goddamn ridiculous," he muttered.

He ripped the poker from his ribs and used it to slash through the wall of air. He stepped through the shattering magic wall and strode forward, ramming the poker through the first witch's head as he did. He tore the poker from the remnants of the skull and slammed it into the second witch's head, completely destroying the man's face.

He tried to close his eyes, but didn't quite manage it before both auras started swirling into him. The heat was overwhelming. The power was overwhelming. He was so hot he felt that if he touched something it would go up in flames. Through his shirt, his tattoo was glowing so brightly that it hurt his eyes to look at it. Both men dropped to the floor, and their essences started to flow into Doc as well, leaving behind oddly grey-colored bodies.

It wasn't that these witches were more powerful than any of the other witches he'd ever eaten because they weren't. It was that he was simply feeling everything so much more.

Virgil was yelling at him, and Doc turned to look at him, suddenly noticing how frail Virgil was, how delicate.

"Hush," Doc said. "I'm busy."

Virgil's face paled, and he stepped away from Doc.

Doc forced his lips to grin before returning his attention to the power pulsing through him. The witches were fully empty. He could tell because they didn't have any more color and nothing was moving from them to him, but the energy of their life force was bouncing down his limbs like a new spring lamb. He watched it in fascination as it mixed with his own life force, then he turned his attention to his tattoo.

For just a second when he'd watched it earlier, it had

opened, like a mouth. It looked completely normal now except for the three different strands of color that were skittering back and forth along the outer ring. They weren't the only souls inside the ring either. Not only could Doc's fae eyes see the tattoo through his shirt, but he could also see past the flatness of the tattoo into the deep inner depths, and there were thousands of souls there.

He gazed at them, noting immediately the difference between the new souls he'd just gathered and the others. The new souls were bright and sparkling, but some of the old souls were so faded he could barely see them anymore, and it occurred to him that he was slowly killing them.

I am the dragon, he thought with sudden clarity. And I am the only way to kill a spirit.

Virgil made a slight noise behind him, and Doc pulled his attention back to the present moment and turned to face him.

"You may tell Alex Baudelaire that this was entirely my doing," Doc said. "I'm sure you have a video camera hidden in here that will confirm your version of events."

Virgil had wrapped up his bloody hand and was studying Doc with a mixture of apprehension and curiosity.

"Just one question, and then our business dealing will be complete," Doc went on.

He felt like he was speaking from far away. He was disconnected from this moment, playing it out because he knew he needed to, but in his mind it was already past.

"Were they inquiring about me?"

Virgil made a nearly imperceptible nod.

"Give me the information you found about Gac, and consider yourself fired," Doc said.

It was the last time he'd ever fire Virgil. He had no interest in working with people who also worked for the Baudelaires.

At least in the capacity that Virgil did. Bennie had worked for anyone who had money, and Doc had never minded, but perhaps that was because Bennie was simply more honest about who he was.

But even if Doc changed his mind one day and wanted to hire Virgil again, he would be dead. Doc could see the cup of Virgil's potential and it was nearly empty. Virgil had but months to live. Doc felt a wave of sadness, but the man he'd so enjoyed had never truly existed, so Doc wasn't actually losing anything.

"You should take some time off," Doc advised as he took the file from Virgil. "Spend some time with your family."

Doc turned and left the room, exiting through the same window he'd come in through. He was still just running through the motions; he didn't know how to bring himself back into the moment, but he had to figure it out. He couldn't survive like this, not even for a minute. It was taking all the joy out of living.

17

"What are you doing?!" Jervis demanded.

Doc wasn't the least bit surprised by Jervis's sudden appearance in the sub-subbasement. He had heard him coming. Which was insane because in a hundred years, he'd never heard Jervis's approach, not once. And he didn't need to remove the silk tie he'd tied around his eyes as a blindfold to know that Jervis's face was creased with irritation. He also didn't need his eyes to know that Jervis's irritation hid a great deal of concern.

"I'm acclimating," Doc said calmly.

"Acclimating?"

"I'm having just a little difficulty existing in the moment."

"And the blindfold helps this how?"

"With the blindfold on I can only see the heat of your body. I can still hear everything that I shouldn't be able to hear, and I can sense a shift in the room from more than fifty feet away, but at least I can't see auras or life force or magic or anything else."

"I see."

"I ate some witches earlier," Doc said offhandedly. "I saw their auras get sucked inside my tattoo, followed by their souls and whatever else goes inside me when I kill someone. It was absolutely horrifying to watch."

"I—"

"That really wasn't the worst of it," Doc interrupted. "The worst of it was that the sensation of eating them was so magnified, so intense, so mind exploding, that I had to exert all of my control not to just fall on the floor and shake like a man who'd just survived a most singular la petite mort."

"Fascinating," Jervis murmured.

Jervis sat. Doc felt it and saw it and sensed it.

"How do people live like this?" Doc demanded.

"It's difficult to say," Jervis replied. "My senses have always been superior to yours. I don't know what it is like to be human."

"Apparently it's a rip off," Doc muttered.

"You seem to do alright."

"I do really prefer it," Doc sighed. "By the way, Virgil is permanently fired. He's been working with the Baudelaires."

The noise Jervis made would have concerned Doc if he hadn't already known that Virgil didn't have long to live.

"This is going to sound ridiculous," Doc said, "but I feel like I'm up on Mount Olympus staring down at all the puny mortals. I feel distant; I feel all-knowing; I feel as if this moment has already passed, and I know everything that is going to happen."

"The fae are, by strict definition, gods," Jervis replied.

"I don't want to be a god!"

"It's only for a while," Jervis said soothingly.

"Did I happen to mention that the leader killed one of the fae not long after I arrived?" Doc said bitterly.

"You did not mention that."

"Yeah."

"In that case, you should figure out how to utilize it instead of locking yourself away like the fae have done," Jervis advised. "All their power is quite useless to them because they've neither the spirit nor the will to live in a way that makes an impact, and that is not you."

Doc wished he could think of a pithy comeback, but he knew Jervis was right. For a moment, or a lifetime, he had the powers of a god. He should probably see what he could do with them.

He picked Virgil's file folder off the floor and handed it to Jervis. "See if you can make heads or tails out of this," he said. "It's all money talk, and you know I don't do that."

He wanted to give himself another minute, but he didn't suppose it would matter in the end, so he removed the blindfold from his eyes and tossed it onto the floor behind him.

Jervis was looking over the paperwork with a practiced eye. "It's really too bad about Virgil," he said distractedly. "This is good work."

"But does it help?"

"Maybe. I'll let you know."

"And what should I do in the meantime?" Doc asked, not caring that his tone sounded petulant.

"Surely you have a list," Jervis replied.

"I do," Doc admitted. "But everything on my list involves Tucker. I'm supposed to be teaching him how to fight, and I need him to summon up the soldier I killed so I can interview him."

"I see. Do you think you can handle Mr. Tucker in your... advanced state?"

"I don't know."

"Trust me when I say you can't," Jervis stated.

"Then what do I do with myself?"

Normally, he would just go out and see what happened, but he felt like he needed a purpose or a directive to get himself moving. He'd much rather stay tucked away in the basement, but he didn't want to turn into the completely disconnected and hidden away fae.

"Finish cleaning house," Jervis advised, handing Doc a carefully folded piece of paper.

Doc unfolded it and read the names. Some of them, like Preston Harrow's name, were already marked out, but there were still five names waiting for their visit from death.

"Oh goody," Doc murmured. "More witches. Do they all still live in Denver? That's rather bold of them, isn't it? I thought I made my intentions pretty clear."

"You haven't exactly been out and about," Jervis replied. "And they are witches. Arrogance is their stock-in-trade."

"True, but unlike Jury, most of them really can't afford it," Doc said.

He almost asked Jervis what time it was, but he didn't need to. He already knew. He could feel the darkness outside the building. He could hear the soft murmur of night insects.

"I'm a little surprised you and Jury let me sit down here all day," he said.

"Jury was mad at you for sneaking out, and I told him I'd know if you tried to leave."

"But you wouldn't know if I teleported."

"That is true," Jervis allowed.

"Which I did when Jury was sleeping in the other room."

"I'll be sure to let him know."

"I'd rather you didn't," Doc said. "I guess I'll go out. It says here that Frank Isaacs regularly patronizes the Pink Flamingo."

"Perhaps you should start with a quieter place," Jervis suggested. "Since you're still acclimating."

"Good point. Who's likely to be at home?"

"Elmina Comey," Jervis replied. "She hasn't gone out much at all since Phillip Jury's death. She's apparently an extremely powerful aerial inferno witch."

"Is there any particular reason why they can't just say air and fire witch?"

"It doesn't sound nearly as prestigious," Jervis said dryly.

Doc rolled his eyes, surprised at the amount of colors that flashed behind his eyelids.

"By the time you've finished with her, Joseph Goodling is also likely to be home. He is married and has two half-grown children. I leave it up to you to decide which of them need to die."

"Very well," Doc said as he stood.

He exited the basement rather slowly. He was struggling to find his normal joy in the hunt or anything else for that matter, but he knew he couldn't become like the fae. He couldn't lose his zeal for life. So what if he could see magic forming its spell? So what if he knew when someone was going to die?

He should be excited. It was really no different than discovering the secret door in Muriel Foxall's home and touching all the treasure within. He'd just been given a roomful of treasure, and he intended to enjoy it to the fullest.

He closed his eyes and mentally shook off the weight that was bearing down on him. He was in complete control of himself. He couldn't control his senses right now, but he could control his reaction to them, he could control his attitude. He felt ridiculous even saying such a thing, but he was trying to remind himself.

He hadn't just wasted his day down in the basement; he truly had been attuning to his new senses. He hadn't figured out how to turn them off; he wasn't sure they could be turned off, but he had figured out how to turn down the volume. And turning down the volume helped everything not be so overwhelming.

He still felt emotions and sensed things he'd rather not. He could still see auras and strands of elements or magic. He could still hear the elevator cables. But for the first time in over a day, he felt like he could probably work with it.

He opened his eyes and grinned slowly. He was a soul-devouring dragon. And right this moment, he possessed the powers of a god. It was time to put them to good use.

Driving to Elmina Comey's house was both exhilarating and exhausting. There were so many things he'd never noticed before, like how the air currents wafted over the road and how little bits of debris were constantly assaulting everything. He'd never truly heard the many varied sounds of hundreds of vehicles running all at once before, and he'd never realized how completely deafening it was. He'd also never realized how many variations to the color green there were. Even amidst the concrete and asphalt lanes of the interstate, there was an abundance of life, and it shocked him to see it.

When he finally parked at the end of Elmina's lane, he turned off his car and heaved a sigh of relief. He was glad he'd taken Jervis's advice and come here first.

Since he already needed a moment of respite after the chaos of the road, he was certain he couldn't have handled a raucous place like the Pink Flamingo. Elmina lived in a large mansion just on the edge of a national forest, and it was pleasantly quiet here. So quiet, in fact, that Doc couldn't even feel the city anymore. He inhaled deeply, just enjoying the calm energy of the area.

After a moment of steady breathing, Doc stepped from his car. A strange surge of energy pulsed through the soles of his feet, and he glanced down. He was standing on a patch of wildflowers and grass. He could see each individual blade of grass; he could see the veins within the flowers; he could see the dirt shifting between their roots; he could see worms tunneling through the dirt.

He could feel the pure energy of it all; and for the first time, he understood what Jury meant by charging. Doc knelt and reached out his hand, tracing the petals of a delicate orange flower. The flower turned towards him, and Doc felt a shimmer of power whisper up his fingers. For just a moment, the flower looked even brighter, but then it slowly folded in on itself and faded to a brownish-grey.

With a sharp inhale, he jerked back his hand. He had taken the flower's life force; he'd stolen it for himself and left it with nothing. He hadn't meant to, but that was exactly what he'd done.

He'd never seen anything Jury touch die, but Jury had been at this for a long time; maybe there was a trick to it. He would ask him, but in the meantime, Doc was going to keep his hands to himself.

Except in the case of Elmina Comey, he thought as he walked up the long driveway.

A frisson of excitement shot down his spine because this

time he knew what to expect, and he could adjust accordingly.

Elmina's house was surrounded by growth and trees. Even in the dark of night, Doc could see the various flowers vibrating with color. It was lovely, especially with the splash of silvery light from the sliver of moon up above.

He stopped at the edge of the overgrown lawn, senses suddenly alert to something out of place. He studied the yard, eyes casually trailing after some colorful paths of magic, and then his eyes reached the knot at the end. It was a trap. What kind of trap, he couldn't say, but it was made of fire. He wasn't sure how he could tell it was fire; he just sensed that it was. The entire yard was laced with it.

It was possible that Elmina was expecting him.

He moved along the yard until he'd located the stone walkway, but it was also covered in magic traps. Beyond the yard, he could see magic glowing all over the walls of the house. He walked around the entire mansion, eyes scanning everything, looking for cracks in the wards; but he quickly found that Elmina was very thorough because there was not a single trap-free pathway to the house. He'd just have to play it a bit differently.

"Ms. Elmina Comey!" he yelled. "Won't you please come out to play?"

He was directly across from the second floor balcony; and if he was lucky, that was where Elmina would step out of the house to reply to him.

He grinned when the door swung open, and a tall handsome woman strode out onto the balcony and gazed down at him.

"Is there a particular reason you don't want to come inside, Mr. Holliday?" she replied, grinning cruelly.

"Now that you mention it," Doc replied.

It took him less than a second to visualize the balcony, and then he was there, hand wrapped around her throat while flames sizzled over his skin.

Her expression made it clear that she was shocked, but she didn't let the shock paralyze her. She immediately dropped backwards into the house, taking him with her. She hit the floor, and in the mere moment of space before Doc fell on top of her, she managed to yank a dagger from her waistband and shove it between them.

The dagger punctured the center of Doc's stomach and went out his back, but it missed his spine by a hairsbreadth. He knew this because he could suddenly sense every portion of his body; and in his mind, he could see every piece of tissue that had been torn apart by the dagger's blade.

He ignored the dagger, he ignored the brief moment of pain it had caused, he ignored the desire to watch his body heal around the blade, and he kept his full attention on Elmina.

He'd lost his hold of her throat when they'd fallen so he rolled off of her and jumped to his feet. He tore the dagger from his stomach and tossed it to the side. Then he waited for her to stand.

There was magic gathering around her. A mix of fire, water, and air; and he couldn't quite predict what it would do.

"You're playing cat and mouse," she snarled as she slowly stood. "I didn't think you did that."

"I usually don't," Doc replied. "Especially with witches."

"To what do I owe the pleasure then?" she asked.

She was playing for time. The magic strands around her were growing thicker and more intricate by the second. It was fascinating, and he allowed himself to get drawn into watching them.

"You're quite powerful," he stated.

"You can see it?" she demanded, tone revealing her disbelief.

"Why did you side with Phillip Jury?" he asked, knowing if Jervis had put her on the list that he wouldn't be able to spare her life, but curious why.

"Have you any idea how demoralizing it is to walk amongst powerless mortals day in and day out, but you're not allowed to do a damn thing? Your hands are tied by rules and laws, and why?" she spat. "We are gods; we should be treated like gods, not hiding in the corners, plying our trade for taliesins in the marketplace!"

"That's the problem with witches," Doc sighed. "You simply don't understand the nature of a god. A god is supposed to use their power to protect people, not to amass fortunes or take control."

The air above Doc began to weep, but it wasn't water. It was alcohol. He could feel the heat gathering, and he watched her face, waiting for the sign that she was about to ignite it.

"Out of curiosity," he said easily. "Are fire witches immune to fire?"

"Fire witches?" Elmina spat. "Peasants have better manners than you!"

"So no?"

The air around Doc suddenly burst into flames, and he allowed the fire to fully form before he shifted right behind her. He wrapped his arms around her, holding her in place while the fire that had tried to consume him blazed down her body instead.

"See, I'm immune," Doc said matter-of-factly, although he rather doubted she could hear him over her screams of pain and fear. "Because I thought to myself I can't see a fae burning to death, so I must be immune. I'm just getting used to things, but apparently it worked because you're burning and I'm not."

The air was steeped with the smell of melting hair, and Elmina was no longer fighting against his hold. She was simply writhing, and he could feel her suffering. It was starting to permeate his core, and he didn't like it, so he pulled his knife and killed her.

Her body continued to burn, but she was dead because heat finally touched him, and it was so much hotter than the flames consuming her. He dropped her body and stumbled backwards, pure power pouring into him with a force he'd never experienced.

Elmina's aura, the expression of her life force, the expression of her being, rushed into him through his tattoo, filling him with so much power that he felt himself pull away from it. He had to force himself to stay in the moment, to watch as he consumed her, to feel every moment of it.

When the heat of it had finally faded, leaving nothing but the heat of the burning room, Doc sat in her chair, mind still muddled from the experience, and stared at his tattoo. He could see Elmina's spirit in the depths of it. It was the brightest light, and it moved with frantic motion, something the other spirits lacked.

The soldier he'd killed suddenly sprang to mind. Was he still whole? After all, Doc had consumed him days ago. What happened as the souls were consumed? Which parts were lost?

"Are you in there, Jeremy Spice?" Doc whispered.

Inside the chasm of Doc's tattoo, the spirits shifted.

"Jeremy Spice," Doc repeated.

The multitude of spirits seemed to disappear deeper within

the depths of Doc's tattoo, leaving behind a lone spirit with a faded light-blue tint.

"Jeremy Spice," Doc said again, but this time nothing happened. The spirit of the soldier didn't move or suddenly appear before him. How could it? It was locked inside a prison; Doc had to open the door.

"Jeremy Spice, please come out so I can question you," Doc said.

Nothing.

All around Doc, the fire was blazing. He could feel the heat, he could hear the crackling as the fire consumed everything it touched, but the flames didn't touch him. And since he didn't want to lose this moment, he ignored the fire and focused on the spirit of Jeremy Spice.

There had to be a way to bring out the spirit. Tucker, with Apollo's help, had pulled forth Edgar Achaean from the tattoo; but Doc hadn't been able to understand Tucker's atrocious Greek pronunciation.

"I don't need a spell," Doc muttered. "It's part of me."

He was the prison, the gate, and the gatekeeper. Nothing was outside of his purview.

"Jeremy Spice," Doc said firmly, imagining the soldier's face. "Come forth."

Again nothing happened; so in his mind, Doc reached inside himself, wrapped his finger around the spirit, and pulled it out.

He'd forgotten that he couldn't see ghosts, but apparently fae could see ghosts because the spirit expanded once it was free of Doc and took on the distinct shape of a man.

"Jeremy Spice," Doc said softly.

"Who are you?" Jeremy whispered, eyes darting wildly from side to side. "Am I dead? Is this hell?"

"Yes, you are dead," Doc replied. "And no. In spite of the fire, this isn't hell. Hell doesn't exist," he added with a careless shrug. Unless, of course, one counted being consumed by Doc's tattoo as hell.

"If it's not hell, why is it burning?" Jeremy demanded.

That was hardly important, but Jeremy seemed rather fixated on it, so Doc said succinctly, "The house is burning; but you're already dead, so it's not a problem."

Jeremy didn't seem to understand this, but Doc wasn't inclined to spend all night explaining the situation to him so he said, "I just have a few questions for you."

At a quick glance, Jeremy didn't have any obvious signs of cruelty, but Doc needed to be sure before he released him. He knew Jeremy wasn't actually free yet because a strand of blue light was still connecting him to Doc's chest.

"Tell me about yourself, Jeremy. When was the last time you raped someone?"

"What?!" Jeremy exclaimed. His horror and indignation was so real that Doc felt it like a blow to the face. "I've never... I would never... Why would you even ask me that?"

"Extortion? Blackmail? Murder of small creatures for fun?"

"I don't know who you are," Jeremy growled, "but you'd better watch it."

His spirit had moved towards Doc in a threatening manner, and Doc grinned. He liked Jeremy Spice.

"Do you have a family?" Doc asked softly.

The abrupt change in subject seemed to derail Jeremy. He paused in his approach, blinked a few times, and whispered, "Do they know I'm gone?"

"I'm sure they do," Doc replied. "I will find them and take care of them. They'll lack for nothing. Jeremy Spice, I'm terribly sorry I killed you. You are free to go." With his mind he sliced through the strand binding Jeremy to him.

"I'm free to go? Free to go where?"

"I don't know," Doc admitted. "It's something only the dead know."

"I don't want to go."

"I don't suppose you have to," Doc shrugged. "I really don't know."

"Maybe I'll... Oh..." The fear on Jeremy's face suddenly faded away, and he said softly, "I see now."

Doc wanted to ask him what he saw, but he realized this was a moment that shouldn't be interrupted. Jeremy was moving on. He wasn't dying or fading away or losing himself. He was just changing. Maybe he was returning to the mother. Maybe he was returning to the spirit. Maybe he was gathering with his ancestors. Whatever he was doing, he wasn't being slowly eaten up by the dragon, and that was good because Jeremy Spice was a good song, and Doc wanted his melody to continue forever.

18

Doc stayed in Elmina's house long after Jeremy had gone. He was too fascinated by the flowing dance of air and fire to leave. It was a glorious song, one that from the outside looked like a song of destruction; but when you were sitting inside it, it became obvious it was a song of creation. The fire was eating the house and everything in it, but the ash that it left behind was beautiful and pure.

Doc was staring at a crumbling wall, watching the lovely black sprinkle to the ground when his vision suddenly shifted. He was still watching the wall, but time was speeding forward. The fire was gone; the wall was nothing but ash; green plants were poking through the ash, ten times as vibrant as normal.

Earth was reclaiming what man had built; Doc could see it. He could see it all, and it was beautiful.

He felt certain he was seeing the future, but was that Ivas's power or the fae?

Doc felt the floor waver beneath him and forced himself to focus on the present moment. Most of the house had already fallen to the ground. Only the section surrounding him was still intact.

He stood. It was time to let the fire complete its work. He stepped from his platform and dropped to the ground far below, landing easily on his feet. He walked through the remnants of flame out onto the yard where his every footstep triggered a trap. Fire ignited all around him, and it washed over him in waves, but it didn't touch him.

He supposed he could get used to this. After all, it would be nice not to have to beg Jury to fix his hair and eyebrows.

Doc visited the Goodling family next. It only took him a moment to decide to kill all four of them, which he did quickly and with hardly any effort. In spite of the fact that there were four of them, they put up less of a fight than Elmina.

The heat of their lives was still pulsing through Doc when he left their house and headed back to Dulcis. About halfway home, he remembered to call the Worms.

He was no longer concerned that someone he killed would come back to life after he was gone. Someone might be able to reanimate their bodies, but the Goodling family's souls were locked safely inside Doc, and no one was bringing them back.

He entered his suite in a bit of a daze. He was still a little lost in the ocean of time. Part of him was still feasting on the vicious Goodling children. Part of him was watching Elmina's house be overtaken by trees and flowers. Part of him was driving home. Part of him was standing at the edge of the world, gazing down upon it.

Only that wasn't him.

Doc leaned against his door and closed his eyes, trying to

focus on that moment. He could feel the rocks beneath his bare feet. He could smell the salt air. He was watching a small boat being buffeted by the waves and feeling a strange sense of amazement that a boat had managed to make it this far.

He didn't typically concern himself with the ways of men, but his curiosity was roused, so he calmed the winds and sent a gentle wave to push the boat ashore.

He didn't bother to walk down the stony pathway to the beach, instead he just moved himself there and watched as a haggard man stumbled from the boat onto the shore.

"I wasn't sure I would make it," the man laughed. "I cannot see my own future, which is a bit ridiculous, I think. My name is Ivasattam. I seek the fae."

Shock coursed through Doc, but the part of him on the beach merely said, "Greetings, Ivasattam. I am Mattasavi."

Doc opened his eyes and stared across his suite. That hadn't been Ivas's memory; it had been Mattasavi's. But that didn't make any sense. Ivas was in the ring. Doc could understand having Ivas's memories zipping around his head, but not Mattasavi's.

"You're back," Thaddeus muttered, interrupting Doc's confusing thoughts.

"I am."

"Something is different about you."

"I'm fae now," Doc said, working to keep his face serious.

"Would you kindly repeat that? I think I misheard you."

"You didn't. I said I'm fae now."

"As in fairy?"

"Yes."

"I don't know why you go out of your way to torment me," Thaddeus grumbled. "It's not as if I deserve your disdain. Not really. I haven't hurt anyone for nearly two hundred years. What year is it again? I lose track. Why won't you get me a calendar?"

"I don't think it's healthy to keep track of every single day you spend as a plant," Doc replied. "You have to try to enjoy it. That's what I'm doing."

"What you're doing?"

"Fae now. Remember?" Doc said with a soft chuckle.

Thaddeus lived for these moments, and as soon as he realized Doc wasn't pulling his leg, he'd be bursting with questions.

Doc sat on the couch and waited.

"You're not drinking whiskey," Thaddeus pointed out.

"Not in the mood," Doc shrugged.

He refused to analyze every single decision he made and wonder if it was really him or if it was the fae inside of him. Whiskey was an indulgence he rather enjoyed; but right this moment, he wasn't feeling it. He was too full of other things.

"My god," Thaddeus whispered. "You aren't serious?"

"About what? The whiskey or the fae?"

"The fae."

"I am."

"I don't understand. How could you possibly be fae?"

"I really don't know," Doc said. "It has something to do with this ring."

He held out his hand towards Thaddeus's pot, intuitively knowing the best position for Thaddeus to see it.

"It looks like it's part of your finger."

"It is now."

"How?"

"I'm a little sketchy on how or why it's happening," Doc said. "But I can see auras now. I can see your aura. It's bigger than I expected. Ten times the size of your form. I probably walk through it all the time. Can you feel it when I do?"

"I have an aura?" Thaddeus said. "I've never been sure about auras."

"It's there," Doc assured him.

"What is an aura?" Thaddeus inquired, voice full of curiosity.

"I think it's the visual expression of a person's life and vitality," Doc replied.

"Interesting," Thaddeus murmured. "How did you come to that conclusion?"

"For one, when I eat people, the aura goes inside of me."

"Really?"

If Thaddeus was in man form, Doc imagined he'd be bouncing on his toes with excitement.

"What's it like?" Thaddeus demanded.

"Very strange. I saw all these people when I was walking whose auras looked sickly or half dead," Doc went on. "Your aura doesn't look like that. It's vibrant, pulsing with life. Jervis's and Jury's are almost overwhelming they're so vibrant and big. And don't even ask me about Pecos's and Aylen's. Just looking at Aylen made me feel like I was standing right next to the sun. I keep almost shying away from people so their aura doesn't touch me, but I can't actually feel it."

Doc reached out his hand and held it inside Thaddeus's aura.

"Can you feel that?" he asked.

"No," Thaddeus replied. "What are you doing?"

"Just holding my hand in your aura."

"Oh. I don't feel anything."

"I don't think they're real," Doc mused softly. "That's not the right word," he said, trying to think how to explain it.

"The aura is nothing. It's just a picture of something; it isn't the actual thing. Does that make sense?"

"I suppose," Thaddeus said thoughtfully. "The body contains everything, the soul, the life, the blood. So if there is an aura, it's just an expression of that life, not the actual life."

"Exactly," Doc agreed.

"What else can you do?"

"I can teleport," Doc said.

"You cannot!" Thaddeus snorted.

"Can too," Doc insisted. "Watch."

He visualized his bedroom and was there instantly. "Told you!" he yelled.

"Get back here!" Thaddeus demanded. "I have so many questions!"

Doc considered ignoring him, but there was no reason not to indulge him. Thaddeus didn't have legs, and he had to live vicariously through others. He couldn't do that if Doc ignored him.

He imagined himself on the couch again, and as soon as he was there, Thaddeus said, "How do you do it?"

"I just think myself there."

"Could you go anywhere?"

"I don't know," Doc replied. "I've only tried going places I know."

"Interesting," Thaddeus murmured. "This is so incredible. Can you take others with you?"

"I haven't tried that yet," Doc admitted.

"What have you done?" Thaddeus demanded. "If I suddenly had the power of a fae, I would be doing everything I could." He cleared his throat awkwardly and added softly, "Which is probably why I'll never be given the power of a fae."

"You never know," Doc said consolingly. "I can see the elements now."

He spent the next several hours fielding questions from Thaddeus, and by the time Doc managed to escape, Thaddeus's many inquiries were bouncing so wildly around his head that he could hardly think of anything else.

And because he could hardly think of anything else, Doc realized that he'd only scratched the surface of his new power. If he was doing this, he was going to have to start thinking differently. Otherwise, he was just going to be the same old Doc, just a Doc who could teleport. And he wasn't sure that was enough to shift whatever it was he was supposed to shift.

Which left him with just one option.

"You want me to what?" Jury said sometime later.

He was staring across his pool table at Doc, eyes crinkled with absolute disbelief.

"You heard me the first time," Doc sighed.

He aimed absent-mindedly and broke apart the balls.

"I couldn't have heard you," Jury spat. "There is no way I heard you because I thought you said you wanted me to teach you how to wield magic."

"That is what I said."

"What? No! You can't just suddenly wield magic!"

"Why not?"

"I don't know!" Jury exclaimed.

"I can see the elements now, and I can see magic when it's formed," Doc explained slowly. "So it follows that I should be able to wield it as well."

"No!"

"I feel like you're making this more difficult than it has to be," Doc drawled. He hit another ball into a pocket and aimed once more.

"I'm not! You're making it simpler than it really is! People are either born with the ability to wield magic or not. You don't just suddenly inherit it someday. I was casting spells as a toddler. I didn't get to go to bed at night unless I could successfully do the magical task set before me. It was a slow, laborious process," Jury insisted. "You'd have to start with something ridiculous like making a spoon stir, and what good would that do you?"

"I could apply the basic principle to something larger," Doc pointed out. "If I could make a spoon stir, I could probably make a car stir."

Jury stared at him in shock. "I hope this isn't permanent," he said softly.

"Why's that?"

"No reason," Jury muttered. "Look, I don't know how to teach you magic. I really don't. No one ever explained to me the difference between the elements or the sub-elements and so on and so forth. I just knew. All they did was provide a structure for me to work within."

"Like sheet music," Doc said.

"I don't like this," Jury stated, gesturing towards Doc.

"I'm sorry," Doc replied.

He could see Jury's agitation, and it was a great deal more than the agitation Jury was allowing to be obvious.

"I just had a horrible realization," Doc said.

"What?"

"I'm too all-knowing."

"What?"

"I can see your feelings; I can feel them. If we were to play poker right now, there's nothing you could hide from me."

"I don't hide anything anyway," Jury snorted.

"You hide more than you think you do," Doc murmured as he watched Jury's emotions shift from agitation to worry.

He took another shot, dismay filling him as he watched the ball drop easily into the pocket. It wasn't just that he was all-knowing. It was something else. Something he hadn't noticed before, not with all the overwhelming sensations he'd been struggling to deal with; but it was glaringly obvious now.

It was a deep dark void, and now that he'd seen it, he couldn't unsee it. He couldn't look away from it. The knowledge of it made him lightheaded and queasy, but he couldn't change it. There was nothing he could do to bring it back because he wasn't on the beach anymore. He was on the top of the mountain.

"There's something a god doesn't need," Doc whispered, feeling completely bereft.

"What's that?" Jury asked.

"Luck," Doc said. "A god doesn't need luck."

Jury stared at Doc, then glanced down at the pool table. "You won," he said in disbelief.

"I absolutely hate this," Doc muttered.

He dropped the pool cue and headed for the door. He was trying to work with it, really he was, but it was just too much. He wasn't supposed to win at pool. And he hadn't won because of skill or luck, but because he'd simply been able to see how to hit the balls so they'd go where he wanted them to go.

If he played poker right now, everything would be visible to him and there would be no risk, no question, no surprise.

If he made love to a woman, he'd likely kill her. He couldn't see any particular difference between the life energy of a flower and the life energy of a person, and he was terrified to touch either one right now.

And that was the upside. The downside was that Lady Luck had abandoned him completely. The tide wasn't just out; she was gone because he didn't need her. There was no room for her to ply her trade.

He was outside Jury's apartment now, and he climbed into his car before asking, "Ring, when is the event happening?"

Before his eyes a different scene opened, and Ivas sighed heavily. "The question is inaccurate."

"Yes, I know!" Doc snapped. "But you understand what I mean. How much longer?"

"Not long. It is nearly to the point," Ivas said.

"How will I know?" Doc asked.

"I will alert you."

"Fine," Doc muttered, forcing his vision back out onto the road.

He'd continue onward until he had fulfilled Ivas's task, but once it was done, he was going back to the fae and shoving their "gift" down their god-like throats.

He was absolutely furious, but he knew there was nothing he could do to change things so he ruthlessly and expediently hunted down the three remaining witches on Jervis's list and killed them with an efficiency and ease that frightened him.

He hadn't realized how much he liked it when things required some skill or luck or a bit of both. Better yet, a lot of both. Working without either was too easy, and he didn't like it.

He sighed as he parked his car in Dulcis's parking garage. He was tired, and that made no sense. He'd feasted on more than enough witches to fuel him for months if he wasn't too careless, but he felt worn.

He didn't want to go to his suite because Thaddeus would surely pepper him with more questions than he could bear right now, and he didn't want to go to the sub-subbasement because Jervis would eventually come down to question him.

Furthermore, he was beginning to feel Dulcis. Not the building exactly, but the entity, the spirit within the building. It wasn't a bad feeling; in fact, if he wasn't feeling so completely overwhelmed by everything else, he would've enjoyed just lying on his bed and basking in its calming and steady presence. It was very much as if Jervis's spirit had somehow imprinted itself on Dulcis, and Doc wondered if like the ring that shared Doc's song, Jervis had been drawn to Dulcis because it shared his own song of stability and guidance.

Doc shook his head in frustration. He didn't want to think about Dulcis as a person or the city of Denver as a person. He didn't want to walk down the street and know if someone was going to die soon. He didn't want to hear the mice discussing the increase of alley cats. He wanted silence.

He considered one of his safe houses, but that wouldn't get him out of the city, and he needed to be out of the city. He could feel Denver's heartbeat; he could feel its fear and its anxiety, and he didn't want to. He'd always loved the pace of Denver, the speed at which everything moved. He loved the energy of the people and their ingenuity. But he'd never been able to sense the underbelly of it all; he'd never felt the quiet despair, the endless toil, the sadness; and he felt certain any other city would be the same.

Being fae was stripping him of his love of cities, his love of crowds and people, and that was just one more item on his very long list of grievances.

Doc closed his eyes and tried to visualize the quietest

place he knew besides Andrew's ranch. There was too much history at Andrew's ranch, and he was a little worried that if he went there again he'd get sucked into watching the past.

He considered going to Ahanu's cabin again. It had been quiet, but it was also so removed that Doc had begun to notice the lack Jury had once complained about.

Doc needed someplace that was both alive and quiet, and there was only one other place he could think of that fulfilled both requirements.

"Doc," August Naese said evenly.

His tone conveyed very little surprise even though Doc had very suddenly appeared in his study, but he was vibrating with confusion and wariness.

"August," Doc said as he sat in one of August's large chairs. "I'm sorry to drop by unannounced."

August struggled with his words for a moment before saying carefully, "The dropping by is very unexpected."

"It's a confusing story, one that I don't think I ought to share," Doc said apologetically. "I needed someplace quiet to think, and I came here."

"You are always welcome here," August said. "My wife has expressed her great desire to meet you."

Doc had been too busy trying to get everyone out of Blackwater to introduce himself to Elvira Naese when she had been released. He'd seen her joyful reunion with her family, and that was all. He was curious to talk to her though. After all, she'd been one of just a handful of people who had stood up to Mitcham, and that meant he already liked her.

"August?" a woman's voice called out. "I'm home. Are you in here?"

"Elvira, my love," August said as he stood to greet her. "Doc Holliday is here."

"Oh," she murmured, brows knitting in surprise.

Doc stood as she turned to acknowledge him. She smiled widely, and Doc knew his initial judgement of her had been correct.

"I'm so pleased to finally meet you," Elvira said as she moved towards him. "August told me about everything you did and all the changes you made; I'm just so sorry I missed your entire term as tetrarch. I would have loved to see you work!"

He had been so focused on her vibrant face that he hadn't realized she had taken his hand until she gasped and dropped it.

"I'm sorry," Doc said, stepping quickly away from her. "I didn't hurt you, did I?" He sounded like a child, and he hated it, but he couldn't stand the thought of hurting someone as lovely as Elvira Naese.

"I'm fine," she said. "Are you?"

Doc laughed, not entirely managing to hide the bitterness he felt. "I just need some quiet."

"You'll find plenty of it here," she said.

Her gaze was worried, but not nearly as worried as August's. He'd moved to stand beside her like a guard the second she had gasped, but he didn't understand what was happening.

"Would you like me to saddle you a horse?" August offered.

"No!" Doc and Elvira said at the same moment.

She grinned at Doc, and he returned her smile.

"What is going on?" August demanded. "First, you simply appear in my office, and now neither my wife nor my horses are allowed to touch you. I'd like an explanation."

"Doc doesn't owe us an explanation," Elvira said firmly.

"He is welcome here, no matter what. And I know the perfect place for him to rest. Come, Doc, I'll take you there."

August was none too happy about Doc going off into the woods with his wife, but Elvira was not a woman who needed a man to protect her. She was small in stature, but Doc could feel her iron will, and he felt quite certain that if Mitcham hadn't been protected by so much magic, he would have never stood a chance against her.

Doc followed her out of the house, but paused when she reached the edge of the woods.

"Perhaps this is a bad idea," he said, regret filling him.

"Why?" she asked.

He gestured behind him at the trail of footprints he'd left in the grass. Everything he'd touched had lost some of its vibrancy.

"Of course," she said. "I'm sorry; I should have thought. Just tell your body that you are full of life and you've no need for more."

Doc stared at her, and she laughed cheerfully before saying, "Please just try it."

"Aloud?" he asked.

"However you like," she shrugged.

He closed his eyes and murmured, "Body, I am full of life, and I have no need of more." He waited for a second, then repeated the line.

"Now come to me," she said, holding out her hands.

He didn't want to touch her; he didn't want to reduce her vibrancy one bit, but she smiled at him confidently and said once more, "Come to me."

He stepped towards her; and before he could stop her, she took his hand in hers.

"Isn't that better?" she said, smiling widely.

"Is it?" Doc asked worriedly.

"Yes, look behind you."

He glanced behind him, relief filling him when he saw that his footsteps were no more evident than hers now.

"You may have to remind your body quite often that you are full," she advised. "It is man's way to take whether or not they need it, and it's a hard habit to break."

"Thank you," Doc said.

"Of course."

She pressed her hand against his cheek and smiled at him with such an expression of tenderness that Doc felt a sudden rush of homesickness. It wasn't often he thought of his mother anymore or missed her tender care, but in this moment, he could barely think of anything else.

"I want to thank you," Elvira said as she removed her hand and headed into the woods once more. "August told me that you guaranteed my pardon before he even agreed to help you. He would have helped you either way. August is a good man. The way in which we differ is that he prefers to focus on his own and build his fortress accordingly, while I would prefer to change the fabric of the world."

"I favor your style," Doc said with a chuckle.

"Of course you do!" she laughed. "You stole Blackwater right out from under Phillip Jury's nose. I've heard that he's dead. Is it true? Is he really dead?"

"That truth belongs to the Jury family," Doc replied.

If they hadn't seen fit to bandy about the news of Phillip Jury's death, he wasn't going to either. No matter how much he liked Elvira.

"I do like you," she said with a grin. "I can't imagine the look on August's face when you just materialized in his study!"

She began to giggle, and Doc couldn't help but join her.

"He's so very particular," she laughed. "He'll be gnawing at this for months. How did Doc do that? It'll drive him batty!"

"If you like, you can tell him I'm a teeny bit fae now."

She laughed even harder at that. "What a fib!" she exclaimed. "A teeny bit fae! I've met actual fae who are less fae than you are right now."

"That does very little to relieve my distress," Doc grumbled.

"Oh, I'm so sorry," she said, sobering immediately. "Of course you're unhappy about it. I didn't even know it was possible. I'm sure it's never been done, and I can't imagine why it's been done, but I'm sure you'd rather it hadn't."

"You have no idea," Doc said.

"Is it permanent?" she asked.

"I wish I knew," he replied.

"I'm very sorry."

She had paused underneath a large tree, and she was looking up at him with such sorrowful eyes that he nearly laughed.

"You shouldn't need to be sorry," Doc said. "It shouldn't be a curse, and I think I must be the only person who would see it as one."

"That's probably why you have it," she said. "Would you like to speak with Rachelle?"

"No," Doc said.

He had no interest in dealing with another fae right now.

She nodded, turned from him, and stepped through an archway of vines. Doc followed her, feeling an immediate sense of relief once he was on the other side.

"This is my favorite spot," she whispered. "Isn't it beautiful?"

"It is," Doc agreed, eyes drinking in the scene.

There was a cheerful waterfall tripping down a smooth rock wall, and the rock wall encircled a little green meadow full of luscious patches of grass and colorful flowers. A tall weeping willow stood near the brook, and its long branches kissed the surface of the water as it rushed past.

Even pre-fae Doc would have thought it was beautiful, but fae him felt its beauty with such intensity that it nearly brought tears to his eyes.

"I'll leave you alone," she murmured.

"Elvira," he said. "Thank you."

She smiled at him, and he felt the pure joy of it.

"No," she said. "Thank you. Life is so precious and beautiful, and sometimes it's easy to forget that. Spending thirty-some years inside a completely empty space truly reminds one how wonderful life is. I didn't get to watch my daughter mature into a woman. I didn't get to see my granddaughter's birth. I missed so much, but because of you, I don't have to miss another second. And I assure you I will make every moment count."

She said it with such intensity that Doc knew it wasn't just a statement but a vow. Elvira Naese was making a vow to fully enjoy every moment of her life.

"Stay as long as you need," she said. "You are always welcome here," she added, gesturing towards the beautiful scene behind him. "And you are always welcome in my home."

She smiled once more before turning and leaving him alone.

Doc inhaled deeply as he walked slowly towards the weeping willow. He'd never been one to bask in the glory of nature. He'd always left that to Janey and Andrew. Janey had once basked in the glory of a flower for such a long time that Doc and Andrew had ridden into town, killed a group of vicious murderers, and ridden back out to camp before she was finished. She'd yelled at them for leaving her behind, but not as much as she would have yelled at them if they had interrupted her.

Janey would have loved this place, Doc thought as he settled himself beneath the tree and closed his eyes. She would have liked Elvira too. It was a shame they'd never met.

There was something so calming and familiar about Elvira that when he'd been with her, he'd felt quite at home. She didn't resemble his mother in any way. She was much too strong and vibrant, but the expressions he'd seen in her eyes were so much like his mother's expressions that it had filled him with a mix of happiness and sorrow.

He was glad she'd left him alone though. He was sick of trying to explain himself, and he was sick of people trying to convince him it was a gift. It wasn't. Not to him. Elvira hadn't actually done any of those things. She'd been sympathetic, and that had almost been worse.

He stretched out under the tree, enjoying the play of dappled sunlight on his face, and let the subtle sounds of nature lull him to sleep.

It was a memory dream, but once again it wasn't his memory.

Fiona was sitting across from him, grasping his hands with so much force that he could feel her fear.

"Please do not do this," she begged. "We do not interfere; you know we do not interfere!"

"We have," Doc replied, although it was with Mattasavi's voice. "We used to quite often."

"That was when we thought there was a point!" she cried.

"There is no point! Man refuses to be better, to be helped! It is not worth your life."

"Listen to me, my heart," he said as he pulled her into his arms. "There is no question in my mind that I must do this. If I someday lose my life because of it, I will know I have done what I must."

"Please don't," she sobbed.

"I am here with you now; do not mourn me yet."

Fiona straightened her back at his words and dried her tears. "As you wish," she said, voice firm. Her eyes were so full of sorrow that Doc wanted to promise her that everything would be all right, but he didn't know if it would.

They walked hand in hand to the council, and not a moment too soon. Ivas was sitting by the fountain, and if Doc hadn't been able to see the beat of his heart, he would have thought him already dead.

"I am ready," Doc said.

"I thought I might be dead before you made up your mind," Ivas chuckled.

Ivas was so weak now that he could barely open his eyes, and sorrow filled Doc at the sight of him. How he wished it didn't have to be this way. How he wished there was a way to preserve Ivas's life.

"You agree to the terms?" the head of the council asked.

"I do," Doc said.

"Very well then. We shall begin."

Doc drew Ivas to his feet and supported his weight while the council encircled them. Their voices filled the air, echoing off the stones around them, but Doc wasn't listening to them. His entire focus was on Ivas.

"I will miss you, my friend," Doc said.

"And I you," Ivas said, smiling widely. "Although I do

think we will meet again. I cannot see into my future, but I peeked at yours."

"What did you see?" Doc asked eagerly.

"I saw the end," Ivas replied "Only it's never really the end, just an end. You and I were there together though, and it was nice. There was an old woman who lived in the woods beyond my home, and she once told me that death was only an idea; that in truth it was just a different part of life. Like day and night, she said. If you skip the night, you never see the dawn. And if you skip the day, you never see the sunset. You had to live through both to appreciate it all, she said. I find myself hoping she was right."

Ivas grinned once more, but before he could say anything else, his eyes widened and Doc saw Ivas's spirit move from his body into the whirling ring of onyx in front of them.

Grief overtook Doc, and he collapsed to the stones with Ivas's body and wept over it. Beyond him, outside of his grief, he could hear the council members speaking, but his sorrow was too great for him to care.

"It is done."

"I cannot imagine what Mattasavi is thinking, and I believe he will regret it deeply if the time ever comes."

"There is no going back now, and it was the only way. The idea of a mortal, especially a human, with the power of the fae is unthinkable. We must have a way to end it if we need to."

"At the cost of Mattasavi?" Fiona demanded.

"Yes."

The dream swirled into grey before refocusing once more on Fiona's worried face.

"Does it hurt?" she whispered.

"No, my heart."

"You're so pale."

"I am merely human," Doc laughed. "It is not a sickness."

"It is for us," she replied.

"I find it interesting. I really had no idea how different we are. It is no wonder they are so careless; they have practically no feeling at all."

"This isn't funny," she grumbled.

"No, it is not," he agreed. "And I am sorry it is difficult on you."

"It's not me," she retorted. "It's you."

"I have had a long time to prepare, Fiona. I do not mind."

"I do not trust the council to decide if it needs undone," she insisted. "It's been so long since they've watched the world; their vision is faded."

"I have no fear," Doc said. "Everything will come to pass just as Ivas predicted."

Doc opened his eyes and stared at the swirls of lacy leaves above him. He loathed dealing with the fae. Absolutely loathed it.

"Mattasavi," he muttered. "You and I need to have a talk."

The words had barely left his mouth when Doc found himself standing across from a reclining Mattasavi.

"You are a very quick learner," Mattasavi praised.

"I do believe you left out a few details when you said 'here, have this ring, blah, blah, blah'."

"Did I?" Mattasavi replied, lips curving upward.

"The only consolation I find from this is that if I'm walking around with your powers, at least it's not permanent."

"You do not want to keep them?" Mattasavi asked, unable to completely contain his surprise.

"Why would I want to keep them?" Doc spat. "They're awful!"

"Awful?"

"Disgusting, repulsive, unfun, unlucky, unskillful, just un, un, un!"

He sounded ridiculous, but he was past caring. Not only had the ring put him on without his permission, but Mattasavi had also left out some very pertinent bits of information. Such as the ring's failsafe. If Doc didn't act in accordance with the fae's expectations, they would kill Mattasavi, which would also kill Doc.

"Fiona's right, you know," Doc said irritably. "A bunch of head-in-the-sand fae have absolutely no right to judge my actions."

"It is already in place," Mattasavi replied with a shrug.

"I see. Well, that's the difference between you and me. You sit back and let others fight for you; I fight for myself."

With that he reached out, grabbed Mattasavi, and imagined Rachelle's office.

"Mattasavi?" Rachelle Nesbit exclaimed.

She looked between them both, cringed, and said, "Surely not. Ivas's ring went to Doc?"

"Yes," Doc said, tone seething with irritation.

"I can't say I don't find that fascinating," she murmured, "but why are you here?"

"The council," Doc said.

"Yes, of course. You're afraid that they are so out of touch with reality they will take the sword to Mattasavi and kill you both."

"Precisely," Doc replied.

Mattasavi hadn't spoken yet, but now he did. "What can you hope to gain by this ploy?"

"I have no intention whatsoever of hurting you, and not just because hurting you would also hurt me," Doc said.

"Unfortunately, Ivas is fairly attached to you which means that I am fairly attached to you. Furthermore, I do not trust the council to know good from bad, but I do trust Rachelle, and since she is also a fae, that should satisfy things nicely. She can protect you and make a decision on the council's behalf if it is needed."

"I don't suppose I have any say at all in this," Rachelle sighed.

"You get as much as I had," Doc drawled.

"I see. In that case, welcome to the Cryptid Witch Academy, Mattasavi."

Mattasavi's eyes grew wide, and he sputtered, "Cryptid Witch Academy?"

"Yes," Rachelle said, tone a tad weary. "If our family would ever come out of their self-imposed exile, they might discover something worth knowing about."

She looked at Doc, and her eyes roamed his figure for a whole minute before she murmured, "Perhaps several things."

Doc could feel her desire, and it pulled at him, but strangely enough, even though he knew he could touch her without hurting her now, he held himself back.

Mattasavi was part of him, and Mattasavi loved Fiona. More than loved, he was completely devoted to Fiona. He had always been completely devoted to Fiona.

"You should have looked for her," Doc chastised.

Mattasavi turned to meet Doc's eyes, and Doc knew Mattasavi understood his words. He could see it in the pure devastation that filled them.

"If I loved someone as much as you love her, I would have torn apart the world until I found her. I would have never stopped. You have all the powers of a god, and you're worthless."

Doc shook his head in disgust and left the room. He wasn't going to continue on like this. There was an end in sight; he just had to find it.

19

"How strange," Ahanu said when Doc arrived on his doorstep once more. "Twice in one..." He frowned and said, "Is it still the same week?"

"Yes."

"Ah, twice in one week. Business or pleasure?"

Doc shrugged and said, "Although I find I do enjoy your company, business."

"I wish you would stop saying that," Ahanu murmured. "It is... unsettling."

"Sorry," Doc said. "But I think it's good for you. Ahanu, I don't not like you."

"You stole that from Andrew," Ahanu accused.

"I know," Doc grinned.

"Stop annoying me, and tell me what you want," Ahanu demanded.

"Not as much fun when someone zaps up on you and wants stuff, is it?" Doc laughed.

"I will admit that it is giving me a different perspective," Ahanu said earnestly.

Doc sat beside him and said, "You said to think myself back to the same time."

"Yes. Did you?"

"Yes," Doc said. "But I was wondering how you think yourself forward."

"In time?"

"Yes."

"Taking up your hand at meddling?" Ahanu asked.

"No," Doc snorted. "Not really. I mean, I suppose I do meddle, but that's not the point."

"It never is."

"Hush," Doc growled.

"You came to me. Again."

"Yes, I know. Put it on my tab."

"I'm not sure I'm keeping track," Ahanu said softly.

Doc cast him a sideways glance and grinned widely.

"We're a pair, aren't we? Two immortal beings, hiding out in a nowhere place, trying to figure out how to meddle better."

Ahanu chuckled and said, "I have always thought that if you are going to take up a craft, you should at least take the time to perfect it."

"Exactly," Doc said. "So how do I think myself forward?"

"It is a rather tricky business," Ahanu admitted. "You will need a clear moment to focus on, to pinpoint your movement. It would help if you were a scryer."

"But if I have a scryer's memories, I can just use those."

"Yes," Ahanu said. He studied Doc openly before adding, "Your quick wit is somewhat disquieting."

"Thank you," Doc drawled.

"I'm not sure," Ahanu replied.

Doc winked at him, then said, "But then what? Can I think

myself back or do I have to stay there? If I've done the task and I return, does it stay done?"

"Time travel is rather a mystery," Ahanu said. He lit his pipe and puffed on it for a moment, sending large rings into the air.

"The trick is to anchor yourself absolutely to the moment you wish to return to."

"How do you do that?"

"You leave part of yourself behind."

"Explain," Doc said.

"It is up to you to decide what."

Doc knew that was all the answer he was going to get so he changed direction and said, "Time is like an ocean, so if I go forward, change an event, and leave, what's to keep it from shifting back?"

"That really is not how things work," Ahanu shrugged.

"Why not?"

"You do not see me asking you how your special tattoo works, do you?"

"What does that have to do with anything?" Doc asked.

"Time is my thing; special tattoo is your thing."

"I see," Doc said. It was more of an answer than he'd hoped for, but less of an answer than he'd wanted. "To recap, use a clear moment to move forward and leave part of myself behind as an anchor to move backward."

"Yes."

"I don't suppose you'll come save me if I muddle the hell out of this?" Doc said hopefully.

"It is often difficult to know what time has in store for us," Ahanu replied, grinning slightly.

"Vague."

"Purposely so," Ahanu agreed.

"Do you want to play a hand before I leave?" Doc offered.

After a moment of long silence, Ahanu said softly, "I would like that."

Doc grinned and followed Ahanu inside. There had been times when he had hated Ahanu, times when he would have happily killed him, and times when he'd absolutely abhorred the sight of him.

But today he felt a strange kinship with Ahanu that he'd never noticed before. Perhaps it was the fae in him. Or maybe it was simply the realization that they were more similar than he'd ever imagined.

After a few hands of poker, Doc thought himself back to Elvira Naese's special place. If he was doing this, he didn't want to be interrupted.

He paced the green grass for a moment, trying to decide what Ahanu had meant by leaving part of himself behind. After several turns, he paused and looked at the ground, sighing in frustration when he saw the dead grass he'd left in his wake.

"Body, I am full of life, and I have no need of more," he said softly.

He couldn't feel the shift within himself, but it must have occurred because he reached out and touched a leaf and nothing happened. He knelt down and studied one of his footprints, sadness filling him. He didn't mind killing people, but he always did it with intention. He never did it by accident or with carelessness. Not like this.

"I'm sorry," he whispered, feathering his hand over the dead grass.

He felt the energy leave his hand, and he saw it rain down on the grass beneath it. Then the brown grass shuddered slightly, and the color slowly shifted until each blade of grass was a vibrant green again.

Doc stared in shock at the patch of newly green grass. He'd drained it, but he'd also brought it back to life. This power that he held inside of him was spectacular. It was so much more than he'd imagined, but he still didn't want it. It was simply too much. But at least he could correct the mistakes he'd already made.

He visited every dead footprint and visualized the grass within alive once more. Before long, he couldn't even tell he'd been pacing.

There was no denying that there was something incredible about this power, but he was beginning to see why the fae had hidden away. There was simply too much possibility for destruction. Even the right decision had the potential to bring about catastrophic results.

He sat by the tree and pulled his thinking back to the problem at hand. He had to leave part of himself behind. Ahanu still had all his visible body parts so Doc had a suspicion it wasn't a physical part. On the other hand, he'd never seen Ahanu's feet. He could be missing a toe or even several toes and Doc would never know.

"That's not it," Doc muttered. "It's not a damn toe."

He absently traced his finger over one of his bracelets, and the feel of it reminded him of how naked he'd felt when he'd removed them to face Gac.

He never took off his bracelets, and he always carried around his cards, button, and coin. They were his tokens, the gifts of his loved ones; and they were as much a part of him as anything else.

He carefully took everything out of his pockets and mounded them on the ground in front of him. Andrew's button, Charlie's cards, Tozi's coin. He added his bracelets, but it didn't seem to be enough. He didn't feel split enough to trust that it would bring him home.

He didn't bother with Amos's amulet because he had no particular attachment to it outside of its function, and all that left him was the necklace the Bakers had given him.

He'd tried to remove it once before, and it had staunchly refused. But he hadn't been fae then, and he hadn't needed it to anchor him to a spot.

"I need you," he whispered as he tugged on it. It resisted for just a second before it came loose in his hand, and he gazed at it in wonder. It was still whole. There was no clasp, and there was no break in the chain of hair. He held it up to the sunlight, imagining the children's cheerful faces.

The air around him began to shift.

"Stop," he said, forcing his eyes to focus on the forest. "I am here." Everything pulled back into place, and he was underneath the tree just where he needed to be.

He placed the necklace around his other tokens and leaned back against the tree. It was time. Maybe it wasn't the actual time, but it was time for him. He wasn't going to sit around any longer waiting for it to come to him. He was going to it.

He closed his eyes and said, "Ring, show me the moment."

Once more, he was Ivas in the cave, holding the plate of obsidian. There was a vast forest inside the stone, beautiful and green, full of life. But then men came. Men Doc had never seen; but having been hunted before, he recognized their type. These men weren't hunting for meat or to eat. They were hunting for greed.

He wanted to snarl in rage, but he couldn't. Ivas was merely watching the scene play out.

There was a village up ahead, and the hunters attacked it, using numbers and brutal weapons to completely annihilate the tribe of people living there.

Fury pulsed through Doc as he watched them reign down terror and destruction. But then the moment passed, and all was quiet except for the crackling of the forest as it burned.

"That's the moment," Doc said, pulling back. "I'll simply meet them at the edge of the forest and kill them."

"No," Ivas stated.

"What do you mean, no?" Doc spat.

"That is not the moment," Ivas insisted. "You cannot touch that moment. It is this moment."

The burning forest flared before Doc's eyes once more.

"That makes no sense," Doc argued. "I should stop them before this moment."

"That is not the right moment."

"I don't care about the right moment!" Doc exclaimed. "I care about protecting people, about saving an entire tribe!"

Without warning, he was inside the ring, and Ivas was standing before him.

"I know that you do not know me," Ivas said. "I know that you have no reason to trust me, but I am telling you the truth. The moment is after. Please believe me."

"Based on what?" Doc ground out.

"I spent my entire life watching this moment play out. Time after time after time. In one version you arrive beforehand. In one version you arrive after."

"You've seen me?" Doc questioned, fury suddenly directed at Ivas.

"To be completely honest, the figure I saw had no form. The ring had not yet made its choice. It would have been more accurate to say that in one version a champion arrives beforehand, and in another version the champion arrives after. Beforehand is not the right moment."

Doc was so tired of dealing with people who wouldn't just say what needed said.

"Here's what we'll do," Doc said. "I'll go to the moment after, just like you want me to; but if I decide you're wrong, I'll go to the moment before."

"You are wise," Ivas said, grinning slightly. "Do as you will."

Ivas faded away, and Doc snorted angrily at the empty air. "You are wise," he mocked. "Do as you will. I will do as I will, goddamn it!"

He opened his eyes to the woods and stared at nothing while his mind recreated the scene he'd just seen. The pines had been tall, but thin; and he hated that he knew they were pine trees. He also knew they were different than the pines surrounding him now. Everything about that forest had been different.

It didn't matter what type of trees they were though, just so long as he imagined them accurately. And it was more to the point to say the trees were burning. The fire was raging. It was hotter than the fire Elmina had brought into existence; it was so hot that it had burned the sheet of stone in Ivas's hand.

In all the heat, in all the destruction, there was one small circle of grass that wasn't burned. One piece of land that was untouched, and Doc pinpointed his focus there.

He felt the air shimmer around him, and he held his breath and kept his focus completely on that little ring of grass. Wherever it was, he was there. He was there. He was there.

Smoke suddenly burned the inside of his nose, and he was surrounded by air so hot that it curled the edges of his clothes. He blinked to clear his eyes and looked around in awe. He'd done it. He'd moved through time. At least he thought he had.

The soft sound of a pained whimper pulled at him, and he looked down. Right at his feet there was a small lump of fur, curled in on itself, weeping. The very last Takaheni of the tribe.

Doc knelt beside the sobbing child and said softly, "I'm sorry, little one."

The child's head swung up, and he glared at Doc with furious eyes. "You're one of them!" he spat.

The force of his anger was so intense that it nearly pushed Doc backwards. The anger pulsed through Doc, so full that the sorrow and grief the child was weeping from was just a note in the background.

Doc hadn't managed yet to refocus past the boy's rage when fire sprang from the boy's hands and wrapped itself around Doc.

"You'll die like them!" the boy screamed, face a mask of hatred.

"I am not one of them," Doc said softly.

"You are!" the boy howled. "You are!"

The boy was speaking a language Doc didn't know, but he understood it, and he knew he was responding in kind. The boy couldn't hear him though. He was lost in his hatred, lost in his despair. All he could see was a human. And all he knew was that humans had slaughtered his people.

Doc didn't move, just stood still while the fire tried to consume him. He still could not reason why Ivas had insisted that this moment was the moment. The damage had already been done. The Takaheni were dead, and the child was alone.

He stared into the boy's angry eyes and suddenly

recognized the expression he saw there. He'd seen it before. He'd seen it in a moment much like this one, and he'd also seen it older, harder, and fiercer. Meli. The Black Shaman.

And that was why Ivas had chosen this moment. This boy was so powerful that he'd burned the hunters to a crisp in a mere second, and he'd set the entire forest ablaze. He was teetering on the edge of the moment. Just like Meli.

When Meli had been teetering on the edge, she had chosen the path of cruelty and hatred. She'd twisted her considerable power for evil. She'd chosen to inflict pain and suffering; she had become the attackers. And this boy, he was standing here, consumed with rage, consumed with grief, consumed with hatred. One step one way and he would become the hunters, the very thing he hated, the very thing that had caused him pain. One step the other way and he would use his power to help others, to protect others, to stand in the way of future hunters.

The fire surrounding Doc intensified, and he felt his clothes burn away. He glanced down, sighing in irritation as he watched the Amos the Betrayer amulet curl and shift into ash. The replicating knife harness wasn't far behind, and as the leather blackened and crumbled away, the knife within the harness began to melt. Within a few seconds, Doc was standing in a pillar of fire, completely naked.

"That's really hot," he murmured, resisting the urge to check his eyebrows. He'd known he was fireproof, but this wasn't normal fire, and he hadn't been certain. He was sweating from the pure heat of it, but his body remained completely untouched.

The boy whimpered, and Doc looked down at him. He was still angry, but Doc could feel the fear pulsing from him now. He was frightened because he knew there was a difference between Doc and the hunters. The hunters had died instantly, but Doc couldn't be burned.

"I'm part fae," Doc said as he stepped out of the fire.

"Fae?" the boy whispered, absolute terror replacing his fear. "Forgive me! I didn't know!" He fell forward and started sobbing once more. "I didn't know!" he wailed.

"Hush," Doc soothed. "Hush."

He sat beside him and placed his hand on the boy's trembling shoulder.

"How could you have known?" Doc murmured. "Besides, I'm only half fae. The rest of me is human, but I'm not like the men who murdered your family. I kill men like them, and I would never hurt you or your family."

"My family is dead!" the boy wailed. "They're all dead!"

"I know," Doc replied. "I'm sorry."

He didn't know what else to say. Could he go back in time and stop it from happening? Yes. But he was afraid that if he did that, this child would simply be confronted with this moment time and time again. It had to be this moment, right now, because this child had to choose. He had to choose which song he was going to be.

Doc waited for a while, hoping he would suddenly just know what to do next. He'd never been good at this moment. The moment of grief.

He finally said softly, "My name is Doc."

"I'm Pazach," the boy managed to whimper.

"I don't suppose you can turn off the fire?"

Pazach shook his head violently.

"I didn't think that was a thing," Doc mused, "but I thought I'd check."

He surveyed the forest around them, quickly realizing that they were sitting within the only bit of forest that wasn't on fire.

"We should go," Doc said. "Are you fireproof?"

The boy shrugged, but Doc had a suspicion he was. Otherwise this wouldn't be a moment of merit; it would be a moment of death.

"I'm going to pick you up," Doc said. "And carry you out."

"I should have died with them," Pazach moaned. "Why didn't I die with them?"

"I don't know," Doc said. "I've never known."

There would be time later to tell Pazach that his family was still with him, that his family would always be with him. But this wasn't that moment. He could see it wasn't that moment, and he forced himself to focus on the child beside him.

Doc stood, then knelt and lifted the crying boy into his arms. He was heavy for a ball of fur and not overly cooperative, but Doc held him tightly and began walking through the flames. The flames passed around them like water. Doc could feel the heat of them, but neither he nor Pazach were burned.

Little bursts of power jetted through Doc's feet with every step, and somehow he knew he was stealing the vitality of the fire beneath him.

He was too overwhelmed with Pazach's grief to remind himself that he was full, but there was another emotion beneath Pazach's grief, and it wasn't one of Pazach's. It was an all-consuming desire, and when Doc examined it, he was filled with such appetite that he could barely control himself.

"I am full," he whispered, suddenly terrified that he was hurting Pazach. "I have no need of more."

The desire for more pushed at him, but he turned away from it and repeated his words over and over again until he finally broke out of the flames into the green forest beyond. He laid the now sleeping child onto the ground, and turned to study the forest behind him.

He could see the strands of fire elements dashing to and fro from plant to plant and branch to branch. The fire's hunger was insatiable; Doc could feel it. The fire burned hotter and hotter, and it wanted more and more. Doc knew if he didn't find a way to stop it, it would consume the entire forest.

He stepped forward and reached out his hand; the fire receded from him.

"I won't hurt you," Doc said. "I am full, and I have no need of more."

He could feel the fire watching him. It was alive. It was as alive as the grass and the birds and the trees, and it didn't trust him. It recognized him as a fellow predator.

"I won't hurt you," Doc said once more. "Look behind you. You have eaten well. You are full. You and I are both full. You have no need of more."

The fire pulsed, and Doc felt its absolute greed.

"No," he said. "You do not need more. You are not a man; you do not have man's greed. You have eaten, and you are full."

The fire leaped forward slightly, licking at the green grass by Doc's feet.

"No," Doc commanded once more. "It is time."

The flames reared up and surged forward, waving around Doc and devouring everything it touched.

"If you are not full, neither am I," Doc murmured.

He held out his hands, but he knew the fire wouldn't touch him. It couldn't. But Doc could touch it. He closed his eyes, watching its movements, then imagined his hand reaching forward and grasping hold of a flame. The fire writhed in his hand, trying to escape, but it couldn't hurt Doc. Doc was stronger than it was.

"You belong to me now," Doc whispered as his body siphoned power from the fire. The fire was now the prey, and Doc was its predator.

Try as it might, the fire could not escape Doc's grasp, and more and more power poured into Doc, filling him with heat, filling him with a vitality so intense that he could barely contain it. His insides felt as if they were on fire, his skin felt as if it was boiling apart, his eyes were exploding outward with flame, but he knew it wasn't from the fire. It was from the power.

He could see the fire diminishing with every second he was connected to it, and before long it was just a tiny flame beyond Doc's feet.

He released his grip on the fire and said firmly, "You have eaten, and you are full."

The fire flared, but then it bowed slightly and fluttered away on the breeze, leaving behind a quiet forest filled with ash.

"You stopped it," Pazach whispered in awe.

"Yes."

"How?"

"I don't really know," Doc replied. "I think I might have eaten it."

Pazach's feelings of guilt, grief, and anger were pounding into Doc; and between that and the vibration of power still coursing through his body, Doc was struggling to stay focused.

"You don't look well," Pazach said.

"I'm fine," Doc replied.

"Are you sure?"

"Yes."

He didn't feel fine, not really. Eating an entire forest fire was an entirely different experience than eating a person. He felt raw and overstimulated. He felt like he'd been turned inside out. He felt scorched.

He sat beside Pazach and said softly, "To be honest, I'm new to this fae business, and I'm a little overwhelmed by everything."

"You have to think of a quiet place," Pazach said. "That's what I do when I'm feeling overwhelmed."

"I can't do that," Doc said. "If I think of somewhere, I'll go there."

"Are you really part human?"

"Yes."

"I hate humans."

"You shouldn't."

"They killed my family."

"No, a group of hunters killed your family. They were human, but not all humans are hunters."

"I don't see the difference," Pazach said stubbornly.

"All pines are trees," Doc said. "But not all trees are pines."

Pazach didn't respond, but Doc could feel his confusion. He could also feel the boy's exhaustion and his ravenous hunger.

"Are you hungry?" Doc asked.

"No," Pazach muttered.

"I am," Doc lied. "What's to eat around here?"

"Don't you know?"

"No."

"There's some..." Pazach trailed off as his eyes surveyed

the burnt forest in front of him. "There's nothing," he whispered. "I destroyed everything."

"You didn't destroy everything," Doc said. "There's an entire forest still behind you."

Pazach glanced over his shoulder, and Doc felt the burst of happiness that filled Pazach at the sight of the unharmed forest.

"I shouldn't have hurt it," Pazach whispered. "I'm supposed to protect it. It's my job to protect it. I'm all it has left. There are others..."

A wave of guilt hit Doc, and he could hear Pazach struggling to breathe.

"There are others," he cried. "I killed them! I killed them all."

Doc couldn't say whether or not the other species and animals within the forest had survived. He didn't know. He could feel life in the green forest beyond them, but that was all.

Pazach was weeping again, so much shame and guilt pouring from him that it was hard for Doc to think outside of it.

He focused on Francisco's box and tried to shove Pazach's emotions inside of it, but that apparently wasn't how things worked. He couldn't rid himself of others' emotions, only his own.

He searched his mind for something he could say, something that would alleviate Pazach's pain, but there was nothing. The boy had lashed out in his anger and pain, and he had hurt other innocents. He hadn't hurt them intentionally, but that did nothing to undo the damage he had done.

The sun set and rose while Doc watched over the weeping child. Soon after dawn though, Pazach let out one last long whimper and fell into a troubled sleep.

Pazach's wild emotions went to sleep with him, and Doc heaved a sigh of relief when the intensity faded away. He was glad he was a man and not a god. He could read people well enough without feeling their emotions as well.

Now that Pazach was asleep though, Doc could feel other emotions. He could feel a different kind of fear. He could feel concern and worry.

"He's alright," he called out softly. "You can come see for yourselves."

For a while nothing changed, and the lush green of the untouched forest hid whoever was watching although Doc could have pointed at each of them and listed their species if he'd wanted to.

Finally one lone sprite stepped lightly out of the trees. She stood just at the edge of the little clearing Doc and Pazach were sitting in and stared at Doc for several minutes.

Doc didn't say a word. She was frightened of him, and she was worried for Pazach. She wanted to help Pazach, and she knew she couldn't do that unless she dealt with Doc.

He also knew there were trolls behind him. Several of them. And there were wood devils in the trees above him. And if he wasn't mistaken, which he wasn't, there was a unicorn out there somewhere too.

He had one of their own, and they were trying to determine if he was a friend or an enemy.

"You can't hope to kill me in my current state," Doc said easily. "But I can assure you that I'm not your enemy."

"You are human," the sprite said, tone derisive.

"Mostly," Doc admitted.

"Mostly?" she retorted. "Species don't mix."

"Some do," Doc said. "But that's hardly the point. I'm not going to hurt anyone."

The trolls and wood devils had closed the distance; they were just an arm's length away now, but Doc didn't take his eyes from the sprite.

"You stopped the fire," she said.

"Yes."

"We would be dead now if you hadn't."

It wasn't a thank you. It was simply an acknowledgment of a fact.

"What do you want with Pazach?" she asked.

They'd come to the heart of the matter.

"I want to help him," Doc said.

"He does not need the help of a human."

"I think perhaps he does," Doc replied.

"Why?"

"Because hate blinds. He would have killed you without my interference, and then the guilt would have driven him insane. Even now he wonders how many lives his careless actions have cost."

"None," she hissed. "Wake him, and you will see."

"Pazach, wake up," Doc said softly, knowing very well that the boy wouldn't welcome Doc touching him. Last night Pazach had been too exhausted to mount a fight, but today he would certainly protest. "Your friends have come to see you," Doc added.

Pazach didn't stir, so Doc focused on him in his mind, took part of his own energy and life force, he had plenty, after all, and sent it into Pazach.

The boy woke with a sudden jerk, eyes immediately finding Doc and glaring at him.

"Your friends," Doc said, gesturing all around them.

Pazach's eyes moved past Doc and widened when he saw the sprite. "Yuvum," he whispered.

The relief that swept through the boy was so powerful that Doc nearly cried from its intensity.

Pazach stumbled to his feet and ran to the sprite, hugging her tightly. "I thought you were dead. I thought you were all dead," he cried.

"Pazach," she chastised. "You should not have let your grief rule you. You did nearly kill us. If it hadn't been for this naked half-human, we would all be dead, and the sin on your head would be greater than the sin of the hunters you sought to kill."

"Volume down," Doc whispered, struggling not to be swept away by all the different emotions battering at his senses.

"What is wrong with him?" Yuvum asked.

"He is part fae," Pazach replied. "It's hurting him though. He can't control it."

"That explains much," Yuvum said. "Come."

Yuvum turned and flittered back into the burned out forest. The wood devils skittered down from the trees and climbed onto the back of the trolls, and then the trolls walked after her.

Pazach didn't move, however; he just stood still and looked after them with an expression of horror.

"What's wrong?" Doc asked, trying once more to shield himself from Pazach's turmoil.

"I forgot. My anger overtook me, and I forgot."

"Forgot what?"

"We know when the hunters come into the forest. They have never found our village before though. I don't know how they found the village. I was out fishing. I wasn't there. I came back to find them skinning my grandmother, and I forgot."

Tears were rolling down Pazach's furry cheeks, and Doc had to fight back the urge to hug him tightly. He hated to see the boy in so much pain. He hated feeling the pain. He hated the loss. There was so much loss, so much pain, so much hatred, both outward and inward.

"Forgot what?" Doc prodded once more.

Pazach didn't answer. Instead he started running after Yuvum. His little feet padded so swiftly through the black ash that he soon passed her, but he just kept running.

Doc ran after him, finding it difficult to distinguish between his own emotions and Pazach's. He didn't know where this hopeful joy had come from. He didn't understand it, but he knew he was running towards it.

There was a tight stand of burnt trees up ahead, and Doc imagined that when they were alive, they'd been so tight and thick that no one who didn't know the way would have ever gotten through them. But he didn't have to imagine it. He could actually see it. He could see the forest as it had been before the fire, and he could see the purpose of the trees. They were a wall.

A burst of pure joy filled him, and he struggled to contain it. He didn't know why he was joyful, but then he saw her and he understood.

"Pazach!" a small Takaheni shrieked as she rushed from a cave made of earth.

The fire had nearly overtaken the cave in its greed to eat more and more and more. There was just the smallest sliver of green along the mouth of it, and the top was completely burned. Doc could see that the forest creatures had used what magic they could to hold the fire at bay, but they had been losing. They had nearly lost the battle; and if they had, Pazach would have been lost as well.

"Kamŭk!" Pazach cried. "Oh, Kamŭk! I am so sorry. I'm so sorry."

The two small Takaheni were indistinguishable from each other now, so tightly were they hugging, but Doc could feel their mingled grief and happiness. It was pounding at him like a raging river.

More Takaheni children suddenly burst from the cave mouth, and there were other creatures not far behind them.

It was too much. Doc was drowning in their joy, drowning in their sorrow, drowning in their desolation. He stumbled backwards as he tried desperately to contain it or put it in the box or turn down the volume.

The onslaught of emotions was so strong that he barely felt the hand that touched his shoulder.

"Peace," Yuvum whispered. "Peace."

Her voice flowed through him like warm sunlight, pushing back everything else.

"Peace," she whispered once more.

Doc closed his eyes and focused on her voice. Only her voice. He held onto that word; he made it his anchor, and he drifted for a moment in the calm.

When he felt contained once more, he opened his eyes, and Yuvum's silvery purple eyes stared back at him.

"Thank you," Doc said.

"A human is not meant to be fae. It was unkind of them to put this on you. I am surprised you are still..." She trailed off, shrugged one thin shoulder, and said, "Alive."

"He forgot about the cave," Doc said, turning the subject away from himself.

"It would appear so," she murmured, eyes narrowing as she studied him. "The animals are swift enough to flee the forest if need be," she added. "The trolls and small ones are not. We have always had this place, and if the fire had been natural, we would have been protected, but it was not."

"Pazach summoned it," Doc stated.

"Yes. He is a very powerful child. More powerful than he understands. I cannot imagine what would have happened if he had destroyed us."

Doc could. He could see it quite clearly. He could see it because Ivas had seen it. Blinded by grief and anger, Pazach would have become a destructive god. One powerful enough to rival Meli.

"You saved him," Yuvum said. "You saved him from himself."

"Actually," Doc murmured. "Ivas saved him."

Why Ivas had chosen this moment or this boy, Doc didn't know. There were others out there capable of such destruction. There were others whose abilities could tear the world to shreds. But Ivas hadn't seen them. He'd seen Pazach. And he'd given his life to save him.

The moment Ivas had predicted had passed, and Doc felt sure that Pazach had made his choice. He would remain the protector and keeper of the forest. He would watch over his people.

But as Doc stood at the edge of happiness, watching the Takaheni children weep and laugh, he knew he couldn't just leave them. Pazach was only a boy. He wasn't yet a man, and he had an entire tribe to lead and no one to guide him.

The boy was strong, but his mind and his will needed to match his strength. Otherwise, there would always be the risk that Pazach would lose control of himself.

"Are you leaving now?" Yuvum asked.

"No," Doc said. "It seems to me that Pazach could use some guidance."

Yuvum was quiet for a long while, but she finally said, "I am glad to hear it. I am afraid that our isolation has made us weak."

"Hardly," Doc replied. "Your isolation has made you kind."

"So our kindness has made us weak?"

"Kindness is never a weakness," Doc said firmly. "But it should and must be tempered with steel."

This lesson was long in the teaching because the forest needed to be cared for before anything else. A section of burned timber was left standing, both for the birds and for the reminder, but the rest of the burned forest was cleared to make room for new growth.

The sprites and wood devils worked together to bring back the abundance that had overflowed before the fire, and Doc and the trolls helped the Takaheni children rebuild their homes.

Throughout it all, Doc showed them a different way to live, and the lessons he taught them were many and varied. He taught them patience. He taught them focus. He taught them how to fight, but most importantly, he taught them when to fight. A cryptid hunter only had to step foot within the forest to sign his death warrant. There was no waiting until the deed was done; the intent to murder was enough.

Humans without ill-intent were left alone and often wandered freely through the forest, but Doc warned the creatures of the forest to never reveal themselves. Not because humans were inherently evil, but because they could never keep their mouths shut, and there were far more evil humans than Takaheni warriors.

Pazach and the others learned their lessons well, but they

gave as good as they got. Pazach showed Doc how to seek out a calm place within, and Yuvum taught Doc how to shift the elements one way or another.

It wasn't magic. Sprites didn't practice magic. They were part of nature, and it would never have occurred to most of them to try to harness the elements to their will. They only knew how to tickle the elements about, and that was enough for them. It was enough for Doc as well.

Days and months passed. Years passed, until one day Doc found himself looking up into Pazach's open face.

"You've grown," Doc said in surprise.

"You haven't," Pazach replied, grin revealing his shiny white teeth.

"How long have I been here?" Doc mused, wondering where he'd been before and how he suddenly knew he didn't belong here. He couldn't remember a time before this, but there was a niggle at the back of his mind, a thought that this was only a moment to him, not his life.

"A while, I'd guess," Pazach chuckled.

It had been a while, Doc thought as he watched a Takaheni cub roll around in a flower patch.

Doc could feel something pulling at him, an anchor he'd almost forgotten was there. He'd placed it there though because he distinctly remembered someone telling him he needed an anchor.

"I didn't mean to stay so long," he murmured. "At least I don't think I did."

"I'm glad you did. If you leave, will I see you again?" Pazach asked, tone full of sadness.

"I don't know," Doc said.

"I hope I do."

"I don't know..." Doc paused, trying to remember where

he was even supposed to go. This wasn't his time, but he didn't know why it wasn't. There had been a time when he hadn't been here, when he hadn't been fae, but he couldn't remember it. He simply couldn't remember anything beyond this forest, beyond his home, and try as he might he couldn't remember where he truly belonged. He wanted to panic at the thought, but he couldn't. He was too fae to panic.

"It's time for me to go," he said, knowing it was true.

"I will miss you," Pazach said. "We will all miss you. I'm sorry about all the times I put snakes on your head and pushed you into the water."

Doc laughed and said, "It was a small price to pay. I'm not good at goodbyes," he added, not sure how he knew such a thing about himself. He couldn't remember a time when he'd ever had to say goodbye, but his sorrow at the thought was deep.

"I don't think I am either," Pazach said. "In fact, I'm going to go play with the cubs." His open face was full of sorrow, but he tried to smile widely. "Thank you for everything," he added.

"Thank you," Doc said. "Goodbye, Pazach. It is an honor to be your friend."

"It is an honor to be yours," Pazach replied before he turned and walked away.

"Pazach," Doc called out.

"Yes?" Pazach asked, pausing, but not turning around.

"Tell the others... Tell them..."

"I will," Pazach promised. "I will."

Sorrow filled Doc as he watched Pazach join the cubs. He didn't want to leave them, but he knew it was time; he just couldn't remember why. He felt as if there was something else he was supposed to be doing. Something important.

He struggled to remember the anchor, tried to focus on it, but he couldn't see it, he couldn't remember it, not fully.

Ideas were coming to him, thoughts he'd never had.

He'd lived in a different moment. He'd been a different person. He'd been human, not fae. He hadn't been able to see the beat of someone's life inside them; he hadn't been able to see the current of every living thing. But he could hardly remember that. All he remembered was that he'd come here long ago and that he'd saved Pazach and his people. What more was there for him to do?

A child's face flashed in front of his eyes, but it wasn't a Takaheni child. It was a human child, with red hair. He knew her. He knew her name. Addison.

Visuals tumbled around in his head so fast he could barely see them, but with them came a sense of clarity. He loved Addison. She was his unicorn witch. He loved her, and he needed her, and she needed him. Jules and Johnny needed him. Frankie needed him. He couldn't remember them precisely, but he felt his love for them, and he could feel them pulling at him.

The forest around him wavered. He could see different grasses and different trees. There was a weeping willow and a brook. There was a small stand of aspens, and the pine trees were thicker and shorter.

That was the forest he belonged in, not this forest. He didn't belong here.

"Hans," a voice said sternly. "Where are you?"

It wasn't Doc's voice; it wasn't Pazach's voice; it was a voice Doc hadn't heard in a long time. He knew it. He loved it. He'd certainly missed it, even if he hadn't remembered missing it.

"Come home!" another voice demanded. "Now!"

Doc loved that voice just as much. If only he could remember why.

"Goddamn it, Doc!" it snarled. "If I have to hunt down Ahanu to find you, I will, but if you make me do that, goddamn it, you'll pay!"

Doc smiled. Jury. Jervis. Addison. Jules. Johnny. Frankie. They were waiting for him. They were his anchor, dragging him home.

He closed his eyes and visualized Jury's angry face and Jervis's tightly contained one. He knew they were in the forest with the weeping willow. He could feel them there. And just like that, he was back in Elvira Naese's special forest grove.

20

"For fuck's sake, Doc!" Jury exclaimed. "What the hell have you done?"

The shields Doc had worked so carefully to construct over the years cracked under Jury's worried tone, and Doc felt a wave of fear and concern wash over him. He turned inward and carefully mended the shield, blocking himself off to further assault, before opening his eyes and gazing at the two men staring at him.

Jervis, Doc thought. Jury.

He knew them. He just didn't know them. He knew their names, and he remembered their faces, but he wasn't quite sure who they were that they were so concerned about him.

"What?" Doc asked.

"What the fuck happened to you?" Jury demanded.

"This is the right moment, is it not?" Doc asked carefully. He was certain that he'd meant to return to the moment he'd left. His mind was still a little muddled, but he couldn't for the life of him understand why Jury and Jervis were so upset if he'd only been gone a short while.

"What's wrong?" he added since they hadn't yet spoken.

"You disappeared without a word," Jury snarled. "It's been over a month, and now you just suddenly reappear, naked as the day you were born, dark as a child of the desert, with braided fucking hair, and glowing fucking eyes, and you want to know what the fuck is wrong?!"

Jury's fury bashed against Doc's shields, but it wasn't nearly as difficult to handle as Jervis's quiet concern.

"I'm sorry," Doc said. He cringed because even he had heard the question mark at the end, not that he was sure why it mattered. "I'm sorry," he tried again.

"I'm not talking to you," Jury spat. "Jervis, you deal with him."

Jury turned on his heels, stomped across the clearing, and sat with his back to Doc.

"Hans," Jervis said softly.

Doc stared at him, trying to remember why Jervis was calling him Hans.

"Are you... You don't smell very much like Hans anymore," Jervis said, tone tight.

"I'm sorry," Doc said. "I'm having a little trouble remembering... who I am. I forgot completely, I think. But then I remembered you and Jury, but I'm still a little muddled."

"Is this you now?" Jervis asked carefully.

"I don't know."

Jervis's worry radiated out, and Doc frowned, not sure what was so wrong with him. This was who he was. This was who he had always been. Wasn't it?

It wasn't. He knew it wasn't. He could remember flashes of Jervis and Jury, flashes of laughter. He saw himself holding a small pale child while she cried. He saw a laughing woman with grey eyes. And he saw a man with twinkling brown eyes, a man he knew he knew, but he couldn't remember his name. Why couldn't he remember the man's name?

Something was wrong. Jervis was looking at him like he didn't know him, but Jervis did know him. He knew Jervis. Confusion spiraled through Doc's mind.

The forest he'd just come from was still imprinted on his soul. He missed it. He missed the cadence of it, the song of it. And he couldn't understand why he didn't remember this forest and its song.

"It seems you have forgotten yourself," a voice said from behind him.

Doc turned. There was a short old man standing there, gentle smile on his face. Doc stared at him, senses reeling. He didn't know this man's species, and he couldn't feel his emotions. He couldn't feel him at all.

"You will remember me in a moment," the man said with a wink.

He reached out his hand and touched Doc's face. Time seemed to slow, and Doc watched as his naked body fell slowly towards the ground. He watched as Jervis rushed forward to catch him. He watched as Jury sprang to his feet and dashed across the grass, yelling his name.

"They cannot see me," the man's voice said. "But you won't be gone long."

Doc suddenly found himself inside a prism of light, and all around him there were images flashing past his eyes. Images of him.

The images crashed into him, and he lived every moment of his life all over again. His mother was dying, and he wept for her. Francisco was stitching his wounds, cautioning him to be more careful.

He steadied his hand as he drilled out a tooth. He killed a man with his scalpel. He shed private silent tears for Francisco.

He was dying, and he didn't want to. He donned a pair of six-shooters and became a wild gambler. He fell drunk onto Kate's bed, ignoring her yells.

He coughed to death, but he didn't because Tozi was there. She was a goddess of light, and he loved her. He had always loved her. She was lying to him, and he wanted to shake the truth from her. Tozi was always lying, but not about the pleasure she felt from his touch. Never about that.

He was immortal. He'd never die now. Not unless someone took great pains to kill him.

Booming laughter. The man with the twinkling brown eyes. Andrew. Andrew Rufus.

Memories pelted him. Janey, Bill, Charlie, Doyle, Joe. Pino and his mother. Carmina. Enrica. Pin-up girl playing cards. Ravens. Brings the Rain. A glowing scythe.

They were only mortal though, and he wasn't. Not anymore. He ran away from them. Ran until he found someone immortal. Someone who would never leave him, not like they were going to.

Jervis. The immortal vampire. Brokenhearted and lost. The hunt. Triumph and despair. They killed the Sons of Solomon, but made no changes. So they went home.

Denver. Dulcis. The throne room.

Lena. Lena's beautiful voice and sweet kisses. Her cold dead face.

Despair. A vampire draining him dry. Fierce, loyal Ana and Ina.

Jury. Petulant, angry Jury. Blue magic.

Magic was real. The Hidden.

Andrew's death. Absolute grief. Cult Desolare. The dead would rise, and they did. The Acolytes rained down hell, and Doc returned in kind.

And then his heart felt warmth again. It began to beat again. Because she looked up at him with giant green eyes. Bree. His daughter.

Dublin, Aine, Darius.

Sofia. Naughty Sofia, lying Tozi.

The Bakers. How he loved the Baker children and their wayward babysitter.

Tucker. Loud-mouthed, crazy Tucker. His brother. His little brother.

Witches died at his hand. He woke Meli from the dead. He ruled the Hidden. He freed the Akashii. He lived. Goddamn it, he lived!

And he wasn't fae! He was Doctor John Henry Holliday. Human child, born to Alice and Henry Holliday. Immortal being, stronger than most men, cleverer than most men, downright lucky as hell, but not a goddamn god!

"Chosen champion," the voice of the memory whispered. "Knight protector, soul eater, witch slayer, Níðhöggr, destroyer of souls, protector of the earth, boogeyman, breaker of prisons, protector of the innocents."

"You forget feckless gambler," Doc drawled.

"I forget nothing," she replied. "You have remembered yourself."

"Yes. Thank you."

"The pleasure is mine."

Doc's eyes exploded with light, and he sat up with a gasp.

"I am so goddamn mad at you right now," Jury growled.

"You're only mad because you love," Doc said, batting his eyelashes rapidly.

"I hate you," Jury ground out. "Loathe, really. The only reason I'm here is because Jervis insisted that you might need us both, and all because Ahanu said your anchor wasn't strong enough."

"He kept an eye on me," Doc grinned. "He must really like me."

"That's a terrible endorsement!" Jury snapped. "What the hell happened to you?"

"I think I'll feel more me if I have a shower and a shave," Doc said casually.

"Like I care about you!" Jury spat.

"I think that you do."

"I'll allow it, but only because I'm already sick of looking at your naked ass. And besides that, your braids look ridiculous."

"I think they're stylish," Doc murmured.

"Check him for head injuries," Jury ordered.

Jervis grinned slightly, offered Doc his hand, and pulled Doc to his feet.

"Thank you for coming to get me," Doc said.

"I wouldn't have needed to come if you'd just invited me in the first place," Jervis chastised.

"That wouldn't have worked at all," Doc said. "Because then we'd all have braids."

"I don't think Sami would like that," Jervis stated.

"I needed you here," Doc said firmly. "Thank you."

Jervis nodded and said, "Let's get you cleaned up."

Doc could have easily thought himself home, showered, and returned, but he didn't want to be fae right now. He was a little worried that reaching out to touch that power would make him forget himself all over again. And he couldn't risk that; he just wanted to be Doc.

They walked silently back towards the Naese's house, and Doc was grateful for the quiet. He'd just left his home of undeterminable years, returned to the past, and relived his entire life in just a matter of minutes. He felt a little exhausted, and his walls weren't holding up. He could feel Jury's impatience. He could feel Jervis's acute relief. And he could feel Isabel Naese's shock at his appearance.

"Mr. Holliday," she stuttered. "You're... You... I mean..."

"Yes, he's naked and looks like a woodland creature," Jury growled. "Is there a cabin we can use so he can clean up?"

"I'm sorry, yes," Isabel managed to say. "That one."

She pointed at the cabin Doc had used previously, mumbled something about calling if they needed anything, and rushed off.

"She likes the braids," Doc drawled.

"There's simply no accounting for taste," Jury retorted.

Once they were inside, Doc took a long hot shower. He couldn't remember the last shower he'd taken. At a guess it had been over fifty years ago. He'd swam in the lake, and he'd let the waterfall cascade over his skin, but he had not taken a shower.

While he showered, he made up his mind that it was time to rid himself of his fae half. There was a part of him that knew it would be easier to defeat Eli Gac and Alex Baudelaire and any other villain who might arise if he kept the power, but that wasn't him. That wasn't how he operated. It was much too easy to lose himself to the power, and being Doc Holliday was what made him such a difficult opponent.

Doc Holliday had luck and skill and cleverness, and he didn't view the world through quite the same lens as everyone else. But right now, Doc wasn't that man. He was a fae, and fae saw things in so many layers that one could easily lose themselves trying to evaluate each and every layer, kind of like Doc was doing right now.

He was fae, but he didn't want to be. So he wouldn't be fae anymore.

He stepped from the shower, satisfied with his decision. As soon as he was dressed, he was going to hunt down Mattasavi and force the ring onto his finger instead.

Doc dried himself, smiling slightly when he saw that Jervis had had the foresight to bring a change of clothes and Doc's razor. Jervis knew him so well, and it filled Doc with a sharp sorrow to know that he'd forgotten Jervis and Jury both. That he'd forgotten everyone.

The thought of forgetting them made him so sick that he had to force it away and focus on the motions of getting dressed. There was something strange to his movements, something stilted. He hadn't dressed in so long. He hadn't needed to.

He pulled on his pants before cleaning the mist off the mirror and gazing at himself in the glass. Jury was right. He did look like a woodland creature.

A wave of grief crashed over him. Pazach was lost to him. Yuvum was gone. Kamŭk was gone. They were all gone. And once he wasn't fae, he'd have no way to reach them. Not ever. Even as a fae, Doc had loved them. He had loved them fiercely, and he would miss them just as much. He bowed his head, allowing the grief to flow through him; then he shook himself free of it and quickly shaved.

When he was finished, he opened the door and called Jervis.

Jervis appeared instantly and said, "Are you alright?"

"I'm fine," Doc assured him. "I've just had my fill of magic for today. Would you mind cutting my hair?"

"Certainly," Jervis replied, voice full of relief. "Just like Bolivia."

"Except for the braids," Doc pointed out.

"Except for the braids."

"I know I owe you and Jury a full accounting," Doc said, "but there's something I have to do first."

"I understand."

"Jury won't."

"He'll certainly gripe, but he will understand."

"Thank you," Doc said.

"What happened earlier?" Jervis asked. "When you collapsed?"

"Yiska sent me into the memory, and she helped me remember."

Jervis didn't respond, but he finally said, "You really forgot?"

"I really forgot."

"If Ahanu hadn't come to me..."

"I would have never remembered to come home," Doc finished.

"I suppose we owe him one."

"I suppose we do," Doc chuckled. "Although I hope I'm getting the friends and family rate now."

"One can hope," Jervis said dryly.

Jervis made one last cut and said, "There. All finished."

Doc stood and looked at himself in the mirror. He still looked different, but at least he didn't have braids. He could have worked with them, but he was glad he didn't have to.

"Burn the hair, please," he said.

And then he imagined himself in Rachelle's office.

"I've decided I find that unsettling," Rachelle said from behind her desk.

"It is," Doc agreed. "Where is Mattasavi?"

"Teaching philosophy. I see that you have developed a new form," she purred.

"Not for long," Doc said. "Take me to him."

"So commanding. I like it."

Doc leveled his gaze on her and said, "I can't. Not in this form. Some other time, when I am me again."

She shrugged and said, "That's only mildly disappointing. After all, man-you is quite satisfying enough."

"I'm glad to hear it," Doc drawled.

He followed her through the school and into an open classroom. Mattasavi was just finishing, and when he saw Doc, his expression twisted slightly. Doc read his emotions instantly. He was surprised, confused, and conflicted.

"You completed the task?" Mattasavi asked once they were alone.

"Yes," Doc said.

"I didn't expect it to be done so soon," Mattasavi murmured. "Is it really done?"

"Yes," Doc insisted. He held out his hand so the onyx ring was in front of Mattasavi. "Now take it back," he ordered.

Mattasavi took a step backward and said, "I can't."

"What the hell do you mean, you can't?" Doc growled.

"The ring is yours. It chose you."

"I don't want it."

"If you can find a way to break it, you may. But if you break it, Ivas is lost."

"He's not just free to move on?" Doc demanded.

"No. It will kill his essence to destroy the ring."

"You're beginning to irritate me," Doc said. "What about your power?"

"What about it?"

"Can you take it back?" Doc ground out.

"I never really expected to live to see the end of it," Mattasavi murmured. "In human form, I am old already. Another few years would have seen me in my grave."

A strange sense of regret was flowing from him; a sense of regret that Doc couldn't understand.

"You want to die?" he asked incredulously.

"Death is not the end," Mattasavi said.

"But it is an end," Doc argued.

"Perhaps. Do you not want to keep the power?"

"No!"

"Why not?"

"Because I am human," Doc said. "I am meant to be human. I do not want to sense emotions; I do not want to see death; I do not want to move the elements."

"You have the power of a god, and you would give it back?" Mattasavi questioned.

"Yes!"

"I begin to understand why Ivas chose you."

"Why didn't you just become the champion?" Doc demanded.

Mattasavi's face grew grave, and he said, "Because Ivas did not choose me. I offered, and he said my intention was not strong enough. He did not explain what he meant, but he also would not change his mind. He only came to the fae because we would live to see the moment, but he did not choose of us for his champion. He said he could see that none of us would make the right choice when the time came."

Mattasavi shrugged and said, "It was his way. He was never quite in the present. Always a little bit ahead. Thank you for taking on his task. I am happy the moment is past."

Doc didn't bother to correct him. The less Mattasavi knew, the better.

"If you ever see Ivas, please give him my highest regards," Mattasavi said as he reached out his hand towards Doc.

Excitement rushed up Doc's spine as he felt Mattasavi's intention. Mattasavi was doing it. He was going to take back his power. Doc was ready to be himself again; he was ready to be lucky again.

Except...

"Wait!" Doc exclaimed, jerking backwards.

Ivas had seen something besides Pazach. He'd seen himself with Mattasavi, but they couldn't have that moment together if Ivas was stuck inside the ring forever.

"What did you mean that Ivas would die if I broke the ring?"

"His essence is fused to the ring," Mattasavi said.

"That's it?"

"Yes."

"Can't you unfuse it?"

"No," Mattasavi said, confusion making him frown. "I cannot unfuse it."

"Maybe not," Doc muttered. "But I bet I can."

His memories were still fresh in his mind, and he clearly remembered reaching inside his tattoo to release Jeremy Spice. If the ring was part of him, and Ivas was part of the ring, he could release Ivas as well.

He stared at the ring intently, trying to see it, trying to see the sliver of life that was Ivas.

"Ivasattam," he said. "Come to me."

His mind suddenly shifted, and he was inside the ring, facing Ivas.

"No," Doc said. "You come to me."

He forced his mind free of the ring, but as he went, he reached out and caught Ivas's hand. He opened his eyes to the empty classroom and Mattasavi's shocked face. Ivas's hand was still clutched in Doc's, and Doc released him with a grin.

"You are free to go," Doc said.

Ivas stared at him, and Doc could feel the joy he felt.

"Thank you," Ivas whispered. "I didn't see that. I couldn't see that. I didn't know. Thank you."

"Thank you," Doc said. "Pazach's beautiful song is preserved because of you. You saved him."

"I did not save him," Ivas murmured. "You did that. I merely pointed the way. Tell Mattasavi that I will see him soon."

With that, Ivas disappeared.

"What... What just happened?" Mattasavi demanded.

"I released Ivas. He said to tell you he'd see you soon."

"You released him?" Mattasavi gasped.

"I did."

"How?"

"I just did," Doc replied with a grin.

"He's not bound to the ring anymore?"

Doc stopped himself from rolling his eyes, but he was glad he had to. He was certain it had been years since he'd rolled his eyes.

"We covered this," Doc said. "Ivas was in the ring. Now he is not."

"But... I don't understand."

Doc smiled slowly and said, "It is not for you to understand."

"You take to being fae very well," Mattasavi said with a soft chuckle.

"A little too well," Doc said. "Take it back."

"I'm not sure I should," Mattasavi muttered. "You are so much more powerful than I am, and you use it better than I ever dreamed of."

"I don't need it," Doc said firmly. "Take it. If you don't, I'll woo Fiona in your stead."

He was lying, but Mattasavi didn't know that, and his eyes flashed with anger. The threat was enough to move him because he reached out his hand and grabbed Doc's arm.

Doc could feel Mattasavi trying to take back what was his, but it didn't want to go. The power was Doc's now, and it had no desire to leave him.

Over the years Doc had learned to see all forms of life as beings. The fae power inside of him was an entity all on its own. It was an entity apart from Mattasavi and apart from Doc. It couldn't exist without one of them, but it was not fully either of them.

Doc focused on the strange swirl of power that had been with him for so long, and he said softly, "Go. It is time for you to go." The power resisted his outward push, and Doc sighed. "I do not need you," he said firmly. "Mattasavi does. He'll die without you. I will not."

"I cannot take it," Mattasavi hissed, face tight with strain. "I am sorry."

"It's alright," Doc said, keeping most of his focus on the fae power and not on the helplessness radiating from Mattasavi. Mattasavi was weak because he thought he was weak. Even with the fae power, he was weak. He hadn't found Fiona, he hadn't saved Ivas, and he hadn't changed the future. He wasn't capable of doing any of those things because he believed he was incapable of those things.

Doc knew better. And Doc also knew that he'd changed

the fae power inside him. It was no longer the same as it had been when Mattasavi gave it to him. It was altered. Perhaps, just perhaps, it could alter Mattasavi, perhaps it would show him that he wasn't weak, that he didn't have to hide away on a hidden world doing nothing with his power, that he could, in fact, change the world.

"Go," Doc insisted. "He needs you."

The power still resisted, but Doc was stronger. He knew what needed done, and this was it.

"Go," he ordered.

The fae power finally listened. It finally released its hold on Doc and swooped into Mattasavi. Doc had lived with it for so long that it was truly part of him now, and losing it was like losing an arm. He felt it tearing free of him. He felt its loss, and it filled him with sorrow.

But as soon as it was gone, he also felt silence. He felt contained. He felt himself. He couldn't feel Mattasavi anymore. He couldn't feel the presence of the others outside of the room. He couldn't feel the trees. And he couldn't see the strands of elements that covered everything. He was human once more. Just plain old human, give or take a soul-devouring tattoo and a few other enhancements.

He grinned widely. Now all he needed was to play a couple hands of poker and lure Lady Luck back to his side.

It took Doc several hours to assuage Jury's and Jervis's many questions, and when he was finished all Jury had to say was, "I'm just glad you're not fae anymore. That was really freaking me out. Although it would have been convenient if you had bothered to get me my stones and water before you gave it back. You're going to have to work harder for them now. Not my problem though." Then he yawned, stretched out sideways on the couch, and said, "I'll see you in the morning."

Doc swallowed a yawn of his own and realized that he was exhausted.

"I haven't slept in years," he murmured. "Not in all the time I was away."

"Are you really alright?" Jervis asked.

Doc didn't answer right away. "Everything feels a little off," he finally admitted. "I remember everything now. My mortal life, my immortal life, and my fae life. It's a lot," he said softly. "I miss the ones I left behind, or left in front of me, however you want to look at it; but I know it was time to leave. I couldn't stay there forever. And if I had remembered myself, I never would have tried. I'm sorry I forgot you. I didn't think... It doesn't seem possible that I could have."

"The fact that you were able to contain the power of a fae without burning out entirely shows how strong you are," Jervis said firmly. "It doesn't surprise me a bit that you lost yourself along the way. And we both know that you kept what was important."

Doc couldn't argue with that. He'd stayed to protect the forest denizens, and protect them he had. He hadn't just protected them in the way one did when he stood guard at the window but when he walked away the window was left vulnerable. Doc had taught them to guard the window themselves. He had taught them to be both kind and strong. He'd taught them to be both protectors and destroyers.

"Perhaps," Doc finally said. "Do I smell like myself again?"

"Mostly."

"Mostly?"

"I'm sure you'll always be a little altered," Jervis shrugged.

"How could you not be? There's something I didn't tell you earlier," he added softly. "I didn't know if it would influence your decision."

"It wouldn't have," Doc said firmly. "I've had my time on the mountain; and tide in or tide out, I'm glad to be back on the beach."

"In that case, I may have found Gac."

Doc felt only a moment's regret. How easy it would have been to face Gac in fae form. He could have finished it once and for all in the quickest way possible. He could have just reached out and grabbed Gac; there would have been no escaping him. But the risk had been far too great.

He was Tozi's champion because he was who he was. He'd killed a multitude of evil people, and he'd saved as many more. He was the witch slayer. He was the dragon. He was the knight protector of the Hidden. He was all those things. And fae Doc was none of those things. Fae Doc had forgotten his friends and his life. He had forgotten his daughter. He had forgotten the children he'd promised to protect. Fae Doc was powerful beyond reason, but he wasn't lucky and he wasn't loyal, and those were two things Doc valued the most.

"I'm glad to hear it," Doc finally said.

"Are you?"

"Yes. I'll be glad to get rid of Gac once and for all."

"Do you know how to kill him?"

"Absolutely," Doc said as he yawned and stretched. He was all Doc again, ready for a fluffy bed with silk sheets, and if he was really lucky the company of a lovely woman.

"Explain," Jervis demanded, interrupting Doc's sleepy daydream.

"It's easy," Doc replied, grinning widely. "All I have to do is eat him."

Don't Miss Out on a Single Book in the Amazing **Doc Holliday** Series...

Visit Amazon.com to read all the wonderful Doc Holliday novels. Just search for **M.M. Crumley** OR *The Immortal Doc Holliday.* Also visit **www.mmcrumley.com** and sign up for the VIP newsletter to receive your **FREE eBook** *Regnum* and always be the first to know when a new M.M. Crumley book releases!

Don't Forget to Read *The Legend of Andrew Rufus*...

If you're willing to follow a boy down the bloody road to manhood, fighting shoulder to shoulder with legends, then start reading Andrew Rufus today. You won't regret it. The entire seven-book series is available on Amazon.com; just search for **M.M. Crumley** OR *The Legend of Andrew Rufus*.

Grab Your **Free eBook** Today @ **www.mmcrumley.com**

If you don't have an eReader, you can download it to your computer to read, just choose the "My Computer" option as shown below.

And While You're Downloading *Regnum*...

Give our **TRY BEFORE YOU BUY** option a whirl. You'll find the first few chapters of ***Andrew Rufus***, as well as, the first few chapters of ***The House of Graves Book 1: Three Little Graves & the Big Bad Wolf,*** featuring Tessa Graves from *The Immortal Doc Holliday Book 1*. You'll also be able to read a sample of M.M. Crumley's bestselling psych thriller ***My Better Half***.

The House of Graves Series

Psychological Thriller Collection
writing as **M.M. Boulder**

And now a special message from
Thaddeus Whythe

Fellow literary critics, I'm sure you are asking yourself why you should bother leaving a 5 star review for the Doc books. I ask myself that same question, but **if you don't... who will?** I certainly can't. I don't have hands anymore, not that anyone ever remembers. I point this out because people who don't like something ALWAYS make time to leave a critical review, which confounds me, but I digress.

Your 5 star review helps my dear friend M.M. Crumley keep selling books so she can do mundane things like buy groceries and keep the lights on. And more importantly, it means you'll get to see more of me. After all, I am the hero of the series.

I have it on good authority that leaving a review only takes a second, and it encourages other readers to give these wonderful books the chance they deserve. You wouldn't want to deprive them of my company, would you?

So please, click the little 5 star icon in the review section for all the great M.M. Crumley books.

Thank you so much. I look forward to seeing you in the next Doc adventure. He's quite the reprobate, but when you're just a plant... you take what you can get.

Please leave your amazing review at **Amazon.com** by going to your orders and selecting the book.
Thank you! You're the best!

M.M. Crumley grew up in the woods of Colorado. She spent most of her time outside weaving stories in her mind while she explored.

About her writing, she has this to say:

"My characters are real to me, and on the page they become three dimensional. They are not stagnant. They change; they screw up; they conquer their fears. Sometimes they're unlikable. Sometimes they're broken. Sometimes they're on top of it all. Sometimes trouble finds them, sometimes they go looking for it, and sometimes that trouble defies explanation."

She also writes psychological thrillers under the name M.M. Boulder.

Sign up for M.M. Crumley's VIP newsletter at www.mmcrumley.com to receive notifications of new releases and other fun stuff!

To connect on **Facebook**, just search for **M.M. Crumley**

Made in the USA
Las Vegas, NV
15 September 2023

77617392R00196